ALSO BY **JANET McNALLY**:

The Looking Glass

JANET McNALLY

An Imprint of HarperCollinsPublishers

HarperTeen is an imprint of HarperCollins Publishers.

Girls in the Moon

Copyright © 2016 by Janet McNally

All rights reserved. Printed in the United States of America.

No part of this book may be used or reproduced in any manner whatsoever without written

permission except in the case of brief quotations embodied in critical articles and reviews.

For information address HarperCollins Children's Books, a division of HarperCollins

Publishers, 195 Broadway, New York, NY 10007.

www.epicreads.com

Library of Congress Control Number: 2016949903

ISBN 978-0-06-243625-2

Typography by Jenna Stempel

18 19 20 21 22 PC/LSCH 10 9 8 7 6 5 4 3 2 1

❖

First paperback edition, 2018

To my own girls in the moon,

and to Jesse, who has made so many mixtapes for me.

Sing me a lullaby. Sing me the alphabet. Sing me a story I haven't heard yet.

—The Weakerthans, "My Favourite Chords"

one

SECRETS, MY MOTHER TOLD ME ONCE, are just stories turned inside out.

We were sitting in the backyard on a clear dark night, and because I could see Cassiopeia's lazy zigzag in the sky above me, I pictured a star folding in on itself until it collapsed. It would leave a blinking black space above the atmosphere, I knew, yawning and hungry and full of words. It would be insatiable.

But I didn't tell my mother this. Instead, I told her that she sounded suspiciously like a lyric from one of my father's songs. I knew she'd know the one: *Inside this secret are all the stories you used to tell, years and months and days ago, when I knew you so well.*

My mother smiled and shrugged.

"Yeah, because I wrote that line." She turned her face up toward the jet-black, star-dusted sky and, true to form, wouldn't say anything else about it. This story stayed front to back and right side in, always.

So I looked for proof on my own that night, like I had so many times before, sneaking back down the stairs after my mother went to bed. I went to her CD cabinet and stood in the circle of amber streetlight shining in through the window. I ran my finger over the ridged plastic of their spines until I saw his name, *Kieran Ferris*, and the title of his first solo record, *Haven*, which came out when I was three. I slipped the glossy liner notes from the case and I found the space for the song called "Secret Story." Their names—K. Ferris, M. Ferris—huddled close in parentheses after the title, a year after they broke up. In a few dozen songs, in a sprinkling of small places like this, they'd be together forever.

In three hours I'll be on a plane to New York to see my sister, Luna, but right now I'm in the kitchen, trying to get my suitcase to close. It's August and the room feels like a fever. I lie down flat on top of the case and pull the zipper as hard as I can, but its edges still won't meet. I rest my cheek on the nylon and take a deep breath. It's so hot I could almost believe all the water in my body is slowly evaporating into the air. My hair slides damply across my forehead and pools on the hardwood floor.

Lying there, I take out my phone and type a text, a lyric that just floated into my head. *Sunbeam headed in the wrong direction, mixed-up gleam in the sky.* I look at the words on the screen for a second, and then I press send.

Just then, my mother's face pops up in the window closest to me and I jump.

"Almost ready?" she asks. Through the screen her face is blurry, a pale oval with a mass of dark hair piled on top. She's been a little jittery since I bought my plane ticket, though I know she won't admit it. Instead, she's cleaned every inch of our house and just this morning declared war on the weeds. She's been in the backyard for hours, yanking out crabgrass and decapitating dandelions. Over her shoulder I can see the enemy combatants wilting in a sad pile at the edge of the driveway. Of course, with my mother, it's never enough for her just to *do* it, either. She also has to narrate it through the window while I'm eating my breakfast. The gist of it is *I am woman, hear me weed*, et cetera, et cetera, through my whole bowl of oatmeal.

"Um, yeah, I'm almost there." I sit up and bounce lightly on top of the suitcase, finally managing to yank the zipper shut. It's Luna's old one: small and dark green, a little dirty at the corners. It's stuffed to bursting. I had a hard time making decisions about what to bring because I can't be certain which Luna I'll find when I arrive. Will it be Sweet Syrupy Luna, exhaling love and kindness with every breath, or Dormant Volcano Luna, all her energy and leftover anger channeled somewhere beneath the surface? She's always changing, shifting, and I want to be prepared.

My sister last came home in April for her spring break, and that's when she told my mother she wasn't going back to Columbia for her sophomore year. Not now, she said, but she'd go back eventually. This fall, she'd tour the West Coast with her band beginning in September.

"They're letting me take a leave," she said. "I went to the registrar and everything." She was looking out the window instead of at my mother. The magnolia tree bloomed furiously just past the pane, pressing its long creamy petals against the glass. "I'm keeping the scholarship," Luna said.

My mother didn't say anything. Her brow was furrowed and her lips were pulled thin.

Luna took a deep breath. "I thought *you'd* understand," she said to our mother. "You left school before you finished too. And you went back. Eventually."

From my spot on the couch across from her, I didn't see how Luna could expect her to understand. Our mother wouldn't even talk about her time in Shelter. How could anyone think she'd be fine if Luna left school to follow more or less the same path?

"I have to do this now," my sister said. "I won't get another chance."

I waited for my mother to tell her no, but she just took a breath and let it out.

"Okay," she said. Then she went out to the garage and started working on a ten-foot-tall, spiky sculpture she sold a month or so later to one of the Buffalo Sabres. He had it installed in front of his McMansion way out in Spaulding Lake, where it glittered hazardously in all that wealthy-neighborhood sunlight. I joked to Ben later that the sculpture was basically forged out of anger. He nodded.

"Hockey players need that energy," he said. "They're always bashing heads."

"So what you're telling me," I said, "is that I should be happy my mother makes art from her rage, rather than the alternative—whatever it might be."

He nodded.

"Just checking," I said.

My mother is still at the window, staring at me. Her forearms rest on the windowsill, and I can see that she is displaying her "concerned mom" face.

"Nothing to see here," I say. "Just having some technical difficulties. It's under control."

She ducks down again, no doubt looking for rogue ragweed tucked under the hydrangeas. She could go all day. For one thing, the woman doesn't feel the heat. She's an artist who sculpts with metal, and she's happiest with a blowtorch in her hand, its arc of blue flame as focused as a shooting star. Her art department pal Jake calls her Goddess of the Forge, and it has as much to do with her temper—like Luna's, a slow burn that leads to an eruption somewhere further down the line—as the metalwork itself. She works in a studio she built in our garage, and I try to stay out of the whole thing lest I be smited (smote?) by her.

My dog, Dusty (Springfield, obviously), slurps water out of her silver bowl and I walk over to refill it. When I put the bowl back on the floor, I look out the window, stuck open just more than halfway in the humidity. The inside tracks are lined with a hundred years of paint and it never goes any farther in the summer, which is one of the many charms of a Victorian house. Luna and I were born in New York, where my parents lived in a loft in the West Village, cluttered with records and amps and guitars. I was almost two when they broke up and my mother took us back to Buffalo, where my grandparents lived—where she herself had grown up. She bought our house, which was crumbling. She fixed it up. My grandparents helped as much as she'd let them, but she did practically all the work herself. Which explains this window.

Looking at her in the yard right now—weeding her garden in a purple sundress, her hair in a messy bun, her feet bare and a little dirty—you'd never know her secret, the person she used to be. You'd never know that twenty years ago, my mother was the first girl on the moon.

It sounds crazy, I know. But it's not what you think. There was no puffy white space suit, no sky filling with stars until it looked like a geode split open in the dark. She didn't get to stand at the edge of an empty lunar sea, ankle-deep in dust, and look back at the jewel of our planet, spinning. It was simpler than that, more earthbound and symbolic. In any case, as I've said before, she won't talk about it: the moon, the music, and all the other things that happened before my sister was born.

Now, I lug my suitcase over the threshold, trying to hold the door open with my foot at the same time. Dusty rushes to leave too, and we have a minor traffic jam until she frees herself by hopping over my shin. Outside I consider pitching my suitcase off the edge of the porch so I won't have to bump it down the stairs, but I think better of it. My mother is eyeing me.

"Looks pretty heavy," she says. She's leaning back against the car, her hot pink gardening gloves tossed aside into the grass.

"Um, not so much." I continue tugging, trying not to grunt audibly. I keep my eyes on her as I bump the suitcase down each stair, a small (fake) smile frozen on my face. At the bottom, I take a deep breath and pull out the handle to use the wheels.

"On the plus side," I say, heaving the bag up into her open trunk, "I'm totally working on my muscles." I flex one bicep as a demonstration.

"I can really tell," she says dryly. Dusty dances around her feet making quiet snuffling sounds, trying to convince my mother to take her somewhere in the car.

"Soon, Dusty," she says, and at her words Dusty lies down in the grass, her chin on her paws.

I can smell the knockout roses, sweet and heavy as vintage perfume, releasing their scent under the window as if they're animals frightened by my mother's onslaught. I bend my head toward them.

"Don't worry," I say in a stage whisper, "she's not coming for *you*." My mother smiles.

"Hey," she says. "I'm an efficient weeder. It looks great out here."

"Queen of the Garden," I say. She nods.

"Well, I have one more thing to add to your suitcase," she says, raising her pointer finger. "It's in the studio. Why don't you take Dusty out front and I'll be ready when you come back?"

This is a strategy my mother has employed since I was a toddler: distract and occupy. I open my mouth, ready to protest, but she's already disappearing into the garage. So I follow Dusty out toward the street and hum a song I tried to forget a long time ago.

The sun is a gleaming white hoop in the sky and the sidewalk is hot under my bare feet. Down the street, a lawn mower whirs like a sleepy bee. I'll be gone from this spot in a few minutes, from this city in a few hours. My summer ends for real in a week. So of course this is the moment—when I'm so close to leaving, to finally being gone—that Tessa finally shows up.

two

MY BEST FRIEND APPEARS OUT of nowhere, sailing up her driveway on her old blue bike. Her hair glows gold in the sun. Dusty turns and looks across the street, her silky ears swiveling like satellite dishes. She stretches out her nose and sniffs the air, searching for Tessa's scent on the wind. She wags her tail.

"Traitor," I whisper, and Dusty looks back at me, still wagging. I wonder why I didn't hear the squeaky back wheel of Tessa's bike—*screeeee, screeeee*—like a warning, but the breeze is making a racket in the leaves overhead. Or maybe I just wasn't listening. I didn't expect to see her. I've been out here every day this summer, and she hasn't appeared once.

But I can see her bedroom window from mine, just above the honeysuckle trellis we'd use to sneak out of her bedroom late at night. It's been months, but I'm sure I could still do it blindfolded and barefoot if necessary, and I'd know just where to drop my shoes so they wouldn't end up in the rosebushes. When we were twelve we'd sneak out to talk and twirl on the swings down the block, happy just to cast shadows in the streetlights. Later we'd go to parties, and once, to a dark bar on Allen Street where they didn't ask for ID. On the rare nights she snuck out alone, Tessa would send me a text once she got home and then signal a Morse code *OK* with her flashlight: three long flashes, then long, short, long. I still look at her window every night out of habit, but I never see her looking back.

Even now, she tosses her straw-colored hair like a pony but doesn't turn her head in my direction. The garage is already open, a catalogue of items from Whiting summers past and present: faded plastic wading pools stacked like seashells over a turtle-shaped sandbox, a net bag of soccer balls underneath three tennis rackets fixed to the wall. Near the door there's a beat-up Radio Flyer wagon that we would use to pull our dolls around the block.

Two months ago, or for years before that, I would have been across the street by the time Tessa reached the garage. I might have even known she was coming before she came, but things are different now. So I'm not sure whether to run into my backyard or to turn slowly, revolving around the tree until I'm facing my own house and I can pretend I haven't seen her.

Something makes me stay.

Tessa hops off her bike and slides it to a stop just inside the garage. I expect her to use the secret door to the backyard and disappear again, for another few months, a year, forever. But then she turns and looks at me.

My breath catches when I try to inhale, and I can feel my heart butterflying around behind my rib cage. Tessa walks halfway down her driveway in my direction. She looks thin, flushed, and her hair blows around her head like streamers in the wind. She pokes a marigold gently with her sandaled foot. She waits. Dusty pulls on the leash, then looks back at me.

Before I can stop myself, I start walking over to Tessa's side of Ashland, the asphalt warm under my feet. At the edge of the sidewalk I stop and look at Tessa, standing halfway between the garage and me.

"Hey," I say. I drop the leash and Dusty pads over. She sniffs Tessa's knees.

Tessa is wearing sunglasses, so I can't see her eyes. It doesn't matter, though, because she bends down anyway. She puts her hands on Dusty's head.

"Hey," she says, but it's not clear whether she's talking to me or my dog.

I met Tessa the summer I was five. Luna was seven, and annoyed that the girl who moved in across the street was my age, not hers. Still, the three of us played all summer in our yards, and when Luna started second grade and found her own best friend, Pilar, our group became four.

I liked Tessa right away because she was funny and brave, even when bravery meant nothing more than standing still while a bee buzzed around her head, or jumping between two park benches that were almost too far apart to make it. Her parents fought a lot, and sometimes, sitting with our backs against Tessa's house and listening to their furious whispers, I thought it was just as well that my parents had been divorced for as long as I could remember.

I take a few steps onto the driveway toward Tessa, my first foray onto Whiting property all summer. Then I open my mouth. I'm so used to telling her what's going on that I can't help myself, even after two whole months of radio silence.

"I'm going to New York today," I say. "Luna and my mom are barely speaking. I think I'm being sent as an emissary or some-thing." I make an arc on the sidewalk with my pointed toe. "An ambassador." Synonyms pop SAT-style into my head: a *diplomat*, *envoy*, *messenger*. My brain has become a deranged vocabulary pro-gram.

Tessa is quiet, still crouched down on the pavement, and I stand there, willing her to speak. Finally, she does.

"Luna was on Pitchfork," she says, still talking to Dusty or possibly the driveway below her. "In July."

"I know," I say. The music site ran a photograph on the homepage about a month ago, along with a small story about the Moons' fall tour. *Luna and the Moons Rise Across America*, the cap-tion said, and below, a subtitle: *Meg Ferris's Daughter Follows Her Mother's Orbit*. In the picture Luna sits on a bench with the guys standing behind her. She's laughing, her hands flat on the reddish wood on either side. A slant of sunlight falls perfectly through the window into her lap. It's been four months since I've seen my sister in person, and sometimes I have trouble believing she's real. Pic-tures like that one, where she's luminous and looking somewhere past the camera, don't help.

Tessa stands up, and I'm suddenly afraid she'll leave before I can say anything that matters.

"I'm going to go see my dad," I say. "I've decided. Even if Luna doesn't want to."

"Good luck," Tessa says, her voice neutral. She doesn't ask me what my plan is, or why I finally decided to do it after thinking about it for so long. Then she shakes her head. "They played 'Summerlong' at least three times while I was at work yesterday."

This is another one of my father's songs, and it doesn't surprise me that they'd play it where Tessa works, at a store for skaters and snowboarders. The music in there is relentlessly peppy and energetic, trying to push people to buy gloves and hats and two ski jackets when they need only one. Or, when it's warm out, two skateboards, or two plastic pairs of kneepads. "Summerlong" would fit right in since it sounds happy—most people don't realize the message is sad.

The song came out on that same first solo record as "Secret Story" the year after Shelter broke up, but they still play it on 92.9 FM Hot Mixx Radio ("Heat up your day with a mix of your favorites!") from May to September. Last month I heard it at the grocery store. I was in the cereal aisle, and my mother was in the frozen section, and as a result we have more Rice Krispies and raspberry Popsicles than a household of two can use in a year. We both had the same strategy: keep picking up items, slowly and deliberately. Read the ingredients, make a show of trying to make the right choice, then choose both. It was fine grocery shopping theater, but nobody was watching. The main point was to avoid each other until the song was over so we wouldn't have to talk about it. She had the cart, so I was the weirdo carrying a half dozen General Mills boxes. My arms so full that I could barely see around them. By the time I found her, Bananarama's "Cruel Summer" was playing and my mother just looked at my box tower and nodded, like *It's totally normal that you have selected six boxes of cereal.* I dumped them into the cart.

I think about telling Tessa this story, but I don't.

"I'm sorry," I say, in a mock-serious voice, "on behalf of my whole family." For a moment, I see a shadow of a smile pass over Tessa's face and I think maybe things are going to be okay. Then she shakes her head.

"I've learned to tune it out at this point," she says. She crosses her arms, her posture a kind of fence, a border protecting her from me. One of the things I've always liked best about Tessa is that she's willing to be uncertain. She's not always so sure of everything like my mother and my sister are. Or at least, she wasn't before. She looks pretty sure now.

It isn't supposed to be like this. Tessa is supposed to understand. She's the one who came up with the Horizon Theory in the first place.

My father dropped out of my life three years ago the way the evening sun slides behind the horizon line: you know it still exists, but you're not sure exactly where. It floats back into view from time to time; in his case, in the pages of *Rolling Stone* or performing a song on a late-night talk show. And Tessa's the one who Google Mapped my father's studio in Williamsburg and helped me find the magazine—the magazine I'm bringing to show Luna—on eBay. She let me use her credit card. I don't think I ever paid her back.

Now Tessa glances over her shoulder at her house, but there's no one there that I can see.

"The magazine came," I say, "um, a while ago. Do you want

to see it? I could get it."

"That's okay," she says.

"I think I still owe you eight bucks."

"I'll add it to your tab," she says, taking a step backward, but she doesn't walk away. She keeps standing there, though now she's looking up toward the top of the oak tree above us so intently I almost turn and look too.

A sudden desperate feeling runs through me like a shudder. I've wanted all summer to have the chance to talk to Tessa, but now I'm here and she's sort of listening and I can't remember what I wanted to say. This whole mess happened because of a secret—a secret I kept in hopes of protecting her, but now I know you can't keep a secret safe. You can try to treat it carefully, like an eggshell or a tiny cocoon. But secrets aren't hollow. They have heft and weight. They orbit us like little moons, held close by our gravity, all the while pulling us with their own.

I want to tell her this, but I can't get my mouth to form the words.

"Tessa, I'm sorry." I can feel my voice start to shake. "I—I thought I was doing the right thing."

She's looking somewhere to my left, so I end up saying this to the side of her face.

"I know," she says. Her voice is soft. "But you weren't. I really liked him, Phoebe," she says.

"I know," I say, and then some kind of Honesty Demon gets inside my mouth. "So did I."

Her eyes narrow a little then, and she bites down on her bottom lip. She nods, not as if she's answering a question, but as if she's made up her mind.

"Good luck in New York," she says. "Have fun with your famous family."

This last part comes out not as mean but almost sincere. Is it possible to say something like that and not be sarcastic?

She turns around and walks up the driveway, her flip-flops making a thwacking sound on the concrete. She disappears into the dark cave of her garage and I stand there, still watching, as the automatic door lowers slowly until it kisses the concrete.

Dusty looks up at me, her head tilted like she's listening to something very carefully, as if to ask me, *What the hell is up with her?* I drop my fingers to her head and she presses her ear to my thigh. I'll go inside in a second, but I can't seem to move my feet yet. And just then, when I've let my guard down, the words to "Summerlong" come marching back into my head. *The light will trap you, the light will catch you, but summer's not long. Summerlong.*

I've never understood what that means. Is he saying it's long or it isn't? Maybe it's a special kind of long. As in, not long— Summerlong!

Whatever.

I'm sure my father meant for it to be a metaphor for the end of his band or his marriage or some other thing he screwed up, but right now, it's hard for me not to take it literally. In a few weeks, this white-hot sunlight will fade into amber and summer will slip into fall. I'll have to go back to school and face everything I've been avoiding since June. But there's a week between now and then, and some questions I plan on getting answered. Good thing I have plenty of audio-visual aids, and I'm willing to start here and work backward.

three

MEG

JUNE 2001

THE KEY WAS STUCK IN the lock. I was trying not to see it as a sign.

"Everything all right?" my sister asked from behind me, and I answered without turning around.

"Perfect," I said. I took a deep breath, closed my eyes, and wiggled the key to the left. When I turned it back, it clicked. The door unlocked.

I left it closed, though, and hopped back down the stairs to the lawn. Kit was there with the girls, standing next to the little garden that lined one side of the yard. Phoebe was picking dandelions and Luna was talking to the rosebushes, I thought. Above us, a silver maple arched toward the sky. This was one of the things I liked best about the house the first time I saw it: the tall tree on the front lawn, the big bushes next to the sidewalk. It was an old farmhouse in the middle of the city, but it was like a fairy-tale cottage. You could barely see it from the street.

Luna had taken off her shoes in the soft grass, and she was counting her steps between two rosebushes: *one-two-three-four*. She'd taken half a year of ballet classes and was a natural, leaping across her mirrored dance studio and across our loft's living room floor. Not *our* loft anymore: the loft we sold a week before to a banker and his pregnant blond wife. I thought about it—that place that was until very recently *home*—and my breath caught in my lungs. Then Phoebe crashed into my legs with a handful of dandelions, laughing, and I could breathe again. She looked up at me, smiling and squinting into the sun, and I was almost certain about this decision I'd made. Almost.

"All right, girlies," I said, taking Phoebe's hand and twirling her once over the grass. She laughed and sat down hard in a patch of clover. I picked up a cardboard box from the driveway, the only thing I'd brought in the car besides our suitcases. The movers wouldn't bring the rest until tomorrow, and I'd have to remember then what things I'd taken and what I'd left behind. "Let's go inside and see our new house," I said.

"New house!" Phoebe repeated. She'd be two in a couple of months and she was just starting to put sentences together, though I knew she understood almost everything.

Luna stopped counting, turned back my way. "Can I see my room?" she asked.

I nodded. "Of course you can."

She reached out to take my hand, and Kit swung Phoebe onto her hip. We stepped up five stairs to the narrow porch, and I stood again in front of the heavy wood door.

"What if there are squatters in there?" Kit said, shooting me a lopsided smile. She'd given herself a pixie cut a month earlier in a hotel room in Chicago, during the last week of our last tour. It made her eyes look enormous, but it suited her.

"There aren't any *squatters*," I said. I opened the door and kicked the box over the threshold.

"Raccoons, then." Kit touched the weathered wood of the door frame. A long scratch ran the length of the trim, and I wondered when in the last hundred years it had happened.

"What's a squatter?" Luna asked. She looked up at me, blinking her long eyelashes.

"It's hard to explain, sweetie," I said, "but our house doesn't have any."

It was dim inside, with the curtains pulled closed on all the front windows, but a shaft of sunlight fell straight from the dining room window to the floor. It made a perfect gold square on the hardwood, and right then all I wanted was to sit in that spot, forever if I had to, or as long as it took to figure out what I was supposed to do next.

But instead I pulled Luna inside, and Kit and Phoebe followed. We stood for a moment in the cool, dark quiet. The windows were closed, but I could still hear birdsong.

"It's not exactly the Ritz, is it?" Kit said.

"It's not," I said. Luna let go of my hand and walked toward the kitchen. "But the Ritz was never really that great anyway."

Kit laughed. "I thought it was fantastic." She shrugged as she said this, but she was smiling and I was grateful because my sister didn't think I was crazy. Or if she did, she hadn't told me yet.

"Tell me again," Kit said, setting Phoebe down on the floor. "Why are we not telling Mom and Dad we're here?" She crossed the living room and unlocked a window to my left.

I ran my hand over the banister. The wood was dusty but smooth and glossy underneath. "Because Dad is just going to start trying to fix stuff," I said. Our parents lived maybe fifteen minutes away, still in the house where we grew up. They were kind and quiet, and I loved them, but I needed a day in this house before I invited them into it.

Kit strained to open the window, but it stayed closed.

"Um, I don't think that would be a bad thing," she said. "Plus Mom has every cleaning supply ever invented."

"We have a can of Comet," I said, "somewhere in that box."

Kit dragged her toe across the wood floor. It left a trail in the dust. "I think we're going to need more than that."

"We'll call them in the morning," I said. "The phone should already be connected, if we can find the jack." I leaned down to dig through my box. I was looking for an olive green rotary phone from the sixties, which I'd had my whole life, or at least since I'd pulled it out of my grandmother's attic before I left for New York years ago.

"I should probably call Kieran anyway," I said.

Kit looked at me. "Really?"

"Yeah," I said, nodding, even though I wasn't sure at all. I hadn't figured out the new rules. "He'll want to know we got to Buffalo okay. I mean, that the girls did."

The last time I saw him was two days before, when the movers were packing the last of our things from the loft. Kit had already taken the girls to her apartment in Brooklyn, where we planned to spend the night. Kieran and I walked around the loft awkwardly, supposedly supervising the splitting of our things. I finally sat on the living room windowsill just to get out of the way. Kieran came over and leaned his hip against the sill. I hopped down, bare feet on the floor.

"Are you sure?" Kieran said, his voice low. "We could still fix this."

Fix what? I wanted to say. *Our family? The band?* I looked past him and accidentally caught the eye of one of the movers across the room, a dark-haired guy in a bandanna and white T-shirt, carrying a bookshelf. He smiled at me and I wondered what we looked like to him, here in our apartment, breaking up. I looked back at Kieran.

"How?" I asked.

"We'd figure it out," he said, and looking at me without blinking. He rested his fingers on my cheekbone and traced my lips with his thumb. "You could stay."

For a second I felt frozen, my feet locked to that space on the floor. I wanted to believe him. I can admit that. I felt myself lean toward him just a tiny bit. Millimeters, maybe. Then I heard the scrape of furniture on the floor behind me. I leaned back onto my heels.

"I can't," I said. "This isn't the life I want for the girls. Or me."

Kieran shook his head, and I didn't know what that meant, that he disagreed or that he wasn't going to start this conversation again. He smiled then, and before he could say anything else, I turned and walked out into the hallway. Down the stairs, to the street, to the subway.

Now I found a phone jack in the kitchen, mounted in the wall above the counter. I plugged in the cord of my grandmother's phone and lifted the heavy handle off the receiver. Nothing. There was no dial tone, and I felt the hot rush of tears come to my eyes. I shut my eyes tight without turning toward my sister, but I knew she could see.

"There are pay phones up on Elmwood," Kit said, her voice soft. "Or we'll meet some neighbors after dinner. I'll call Mom when we wake up tomorrow, and later tonight, I'll call Kieran and tell him we made it. Okay?"

"Okay," I said. Once again, my sister saved me.

"Now," Kit said, walking to the window next to the staircase, "let's keep looking for those squatters." She pulled the curtain aside and leaned against the bannister. "They might be holed up on the second floor."

Phoebe stood in front of me, reaching toward the ceiling.

"Up," she said. "Up." I leaned down and scooped her into my arms.

Luna walked over to Kit and put her hands on Kit's knees. Her hair was coming loose from her ponytail, wisps falling down her neck. She looked so serious, and so grown-up.

"Can we go see my room?" she asked. Kit glanced at me, asking for permission.

"Sure," I said. "It's the one right at the top of the stairs. It's blue now, but we can paint it any color you want."

"Purple," Luna said, without thinking about it.

"Okay," I said. "Purple it is." I turned to Phoebe. "What about you, girlie?"

"Purple," Phoebe said.

"No!" Luna said. She twisted toward her sister. "You can't paint your room purple." Then, more kindly: "Okay?"

Phoebe frowned and looked up at Luna, her eyebrows drawn together.

Kit ruffled Luna's hair. "Phoebe can choose whatever color she likes, little bossy," she said. "Let's go."

They walked up the stairs, holding hands, and I looked down again at my cardboard box. That night, we'd sleep on this air mattress, all four of us, and I'd watch my daughters breathe in the light from the street lamps. Then, tomorrow, my mother would come with her caddy filled with Pine-Sol and bleach, and my father would bring his green metal toolbox, the one with his name on the top, spelled out on label-maker tape. They'd try to fix my life in their quiet Foster way, without admitting it's broken. And then, in the fall, Kit would go to law school in DC and this whole rock-star life would start to feel like a dream.

"Do you want to see your room, Phoebe?" I asked. "You can see the backyard from there. All the trees and flowers."

Phoebe nodded, her face serious, and I picked her up. She felt so light, this tiny person, and once again I was amazed that Kieran and I had made her from scratch. And so glad I had her, even if I hadn't expected to have two kids—and no Kieran—by the time I was twenty-seven.

At the bottom of the stairs I stopped and turned so we could both see out the window. Phoebe pressed her palm to the glass. I could see our reflection dimly, so I knew Phoebe was smiling.

"Do you like the house?" I asked. Phoebe nodded.

"New-house-our-house," she said, as if it was all one word. As soon as I heard it, I felt a song taking shape in my mind, building its particular architecture, filling its rooms. And then I shut it down. Stopped the construction before it really began.

I didn't have to write songs anymore, but someday I was going to have to explain all of this—everything that had happened—to the girls. I could save the words for that moment. Maybe I'd start it at the ending, and tell it like a fairy tale: *Once upon a time,* we were four girls in a nearly empty house, and I wasn't afraid.

Or maybe only a little.

four

WHEN DUSTY AND I GET back into the yard, my mother is still missing. I'd left my shoulder bag on the back porch earlier, and I pick it up. It feels light now, compared with my suitcase, but when I slide my hand into the pocket inside, I can feel the magazine in there, hidden away. I take out my phone and text another lyric: *Secrets heavy as glass paperweights in our pockets.* The answer buzzes back right away: *Are you writing about us? (Ha.)*

My mother comes out then carrying a small sculpture that looks a little like a flower, if flowers were spiky and futuristic and made of steel. She hands it to me.

"A robot flower," I say. "How thoughtful. Maybe I can store my toothpaste in it." I turn it over to look at the underside.

"Hush, you. Flowers and sculpture. I'm trying to meld my interests." She makes a gesture that I'm assuming is supposed to mean *meld*, but it looks like particularly enthusiastic taffy pulling.

"Besides, it's for Luna," she says, "not you."

Right. Luna, who abandoned me all summer on tour with her band after telling our mother she wasn't going back to school. She conveniently skipped Buffalo, went right from Pittsburgh to Cleveland without stopping. I figure this was because it was easier for her to say no to my mother if she didn't have to be in the same room with her.

"So you're not going to *talk* to her," I say, "but you'll send metalwork her way?"

"I talk to her." My mother is looking at her raspberry bushes instead of me, and stops to straighten some bird-shield netting that flopped to the side. She yanks it a little harder than she has to, and I watch some unripe berries ping off toward the fence.

"When?" I'm still holding the sculpture in both my hands. There's nowhere to put it down, and I don't know what to do with it.

"I sent her a text message a few days ago." She kneels down and pulls a weed with pointy leaves from the loose dirt under the berries.

"I'm just saying, I can't fix this between you. You are sending me, but I am not that girl."

My mother looks over and smiles at me in a way that says she's pretty certain I am, in fact, that girl. So I shake my head in what I hope is a clearly vehement fashion. Side. To. Side. I'm determined to get the message across.

"I'm not 'sending' you," she says. Her voice makes the quotation marks practically visible in the air. She stands and brushes the grass off her knees. "You're going to visit."

"Right." I sweep one foot through the grass and snag a toe on some clover.

"And if the opportunity to talk presents itself, nothing's stopping you from giving it a shot." My mother opens her car door and starts rummaging in the backseat. "She'll listen to you." Her voice is muffled with her head in the car, so I lean forward. "Just ask her to consider going back to school in the fall."

I take a breath, and suddenly things feel a little off kilter. All I've wanted this whole summer is to leave, and now I'm not sure I want to go.

"I've got enough to worry about without taking on Luna," I say.

My mother turns around, then reaches forward and tucks a piece of hair behind my ear. I feel unexpected tears prick my eyelids.

"I know it's been a rough summer," she says. "But things will get better when you go back to school."

"Unlikely," I say. "I ran into Tessa out front. It didn't go well."

My mother knows only some of the story, that I was keeping a secret I thought would hurt Tessa, something I thought I could make go away on its own. She doesn't know what really happened. She doesn't know about Ben, or the fact that my friends Evie and Willa haven't called me all summer either.

I hold the sculpture out to my mother. It feels leaden, literally. "Will you just take this?"

She reaches into her backseat again and pulls out two squares of bubble wrap. She hands the first to me.

"Stress relief," she says. I lean back against the car and start popping the bubbles, hard and fast enough that Dusty wanders over to see what I'm doing, and if she can eat it.

My mother pulls a long piece of black electrical tape off a roll.

"You carry that tape in your car?" I say. "I'm pretty sure that's a kidnapper trait. Like, if you were a suspect on *Law & Order* they'd totally be bringing you in on the evidence of the tape alone."

She shrugs, zigzagging the tape over the wrap. "You never know when you'll need it."

I can feel the heat of the car through my dress. I shift my weight. "Fine. I'll try. But no promises."

"That's my girlie." She hands me the package, fluffy-feeling from the bubble wrap but heavy, as if it has a dense core. Like a comet.

"This is going to get me kicked off the plane, Mom." I poke it in her direction. "They'll X-ray it and think it's a weapon—a weapon wrapped really carefully. An heirloom weapon."

She smiles her wide smile, which looks exactly like Luna's. "You're going to have to check your bag, seeing as it weighs one thousand pounds. And anyway, in the right circumstance, almost anything can be used as a weapon."

"Says the woman who spends her days making pointy things out of metal." I shake my head. "You would totally be *Law & Order* suspect number one."

I unzip my suitcase just a little and try to cram the package inside. When I look up again, my mother is staring at me with what Luna calls her "sad mom" look. I guess it's time for the Big Goodbye. Better here than at the airport, I guess.

"I don't know what I'll do without you," my mother says. She smooths back a flyaway piece of hair and the sun glints off her ring, a silver band speckled with holes.

"It's only a week," I say. A glorious week when I won't have to come home from my job at Queen City Coffee smelling like South American Blend and muffin grease. When I won't have to listen at the cash register to another forty-year-old guy with a lawyer-ish suit and a wedding ring tell me that I have pretty eyes. A week when I won't have to look over at Tessa's window and see an empty square of glass. And besides, in spite of my mother's sad eyes, it shouldn't be that hard for her to let me go. Unlike Luna, she knows I'll come back.

"I know. Oh, I almost forgot," my mother says. "I made this one for you."

She pulls a thin silver bangle off her wrist and slips it over mine. It's warm from her skin, and I can see that she's hammered it to give it a wavy finish. It looks like the surface of a pond on a windy day.

Luna and I used to joke that it was only a matter of time before our mother forged us a matching pair of dog tags so we'd never forget who we belonged to. For years, we've been weighed down by necklaces and earrings, bracelets pulled over our wrists and wound around our ankles. Somehow it's still easy for Luna to leave, even with all that hardware pulling her down. Maybe she just takes it off. What I'm wondering is this: Why can't I do the same?

My mother shuts the trunk and pulls herself up to sit on its edge. She looks like she means business.

"We should talk about the rules," she says.

"Rules?"

"Just a few."

"Can't wait to hear them." I lean against the side of the car.

"Good," she says. "Number one: be careful."

"Check."

"No drinking," she says. "Or . . . not much drinking."

"No problem." Alcohol and I haven't mixed well so far, and I'm not in a big hurry to try that whole thing again.

"No musicians."

She says this and I see it lit up in my mind like a sign: NO MUSICIANS, NO DOGS, NO SHOES, NO SERVICE.

"I'm pretty sure there will be musicians there," I say. "Like, um, your daughter. For example."

She shakes her head. "That's not what I mean."

"Okay," I say. "What *do* you mean?" I have a pretty good idea, but I want to hear her say it.

"I mean that you need to watch out for yourself."

"Not everyone's like Dad," I say. "At least, I'm assuming. James is great. Oh, that's right, *Luna* is dating a musician, isn't she?" Once again, Luna has a different set of rules. Or is it just that Luna doesn't follow anyone's rules but her own?

My mother nods begrudgingly. "I like James, even if I don't like that he's encouraging Luna to leave school."

"You know that Luna only does what Luna wants to do," I say. "You can *encourage* her until the cows come home, but it won't matter."

"Cows?" My mother raises her eyebrows.

"Whatever. You know what I mean." I look up at the puffy white clouds drifting above me like balloons escaped from a parade. "Anyway, I'm pretty much done with boys for a while. I've had enough trouble."

"That's smart," my mother says, "because boys *are* trouble."

She's smiling when she says it, white teeth flashing like pearls, but I know she's serious. This is one of her basic philosophies. *Girls Are Best, and Boys Are Trouble.* Someday she'll print it on a T-shirt, the first part on the front and the second on the back. The real question is, when things flamed out with my father, why didn't she start a band like the Bangles or Sleater-Kinney, or go out on her own like Liz Phair? She could have been done with men altogether. She could have had it all.

And honestly, after the last few months I've had, I'd be first in line to buy that stupid shirt. I'd buy it in every color and wear it all week long.

My mother bends down and picks up my shoulder bag, which I left lying on the grass next to the steps. She peeks inside.

"Do you have any snacks in here?"

I practically leap across the grass to snatch the bag back from her. Thank god for ten years of halfhearted ballet lessons. I land near the edge of the driveway and scoop the bag up in one fluid motion.

"Yes!" And then, because I feel my leap needs some context, I say, "And you can't have them." I hug the bag to my chest.

She gives me a look like she's pretty certain I'm deranged, but she's willing to let it go because I'm leaving soon.

And I smile innocently, no teeth, because I don't want her to see what I'm hiding: a copy of *SPIN* magazine from February 1994—the one Tessa and I bought using Tessa's MasterCard.

The magazine is a little beat-up, but in pretty good condition for a pile of paper two decades old. The girl on the cover is wearing a black dress with long sleeves, her lips painted plum purple and her eyes outlined in charcoal. She's wearing torn gray tights and boots laced up close to her knees. She's not quite smiling, not really, but she looks as if she'd be willing to smile if you told her the right joke. So, if you'll forgive me for speaking in Madonna lyrics: *Who's that girl?*

Bing! You guessed it.

The girl on the cover is my mother, and printed across her knees in purple ink are the words *Meg Ferris, First Girl on the Moon.* Behind her is a pale silver moon, just like the one that was on Shelter's album cover for *Sea of Tranquility* when the magazine came out. And off to her left is the rest of the band: the bassist and the drummer, Carter and Dan, who still visit my mother sometimes when they come through Buffalo. They're like kind uncles: they bring records and concert posters for Luna and me and take us all out for pizza.

Last on the cover is the guitarist, handsome and lanky in a black T-shirt and jeans: my father, Kieran Ferris. Recent deadbeat dad, man of mystery, and writer of ambiguous and baffling songs about summer.

In the yard, dark pink daylilies bloom in verdant clumps and yellow-eyed daisies gleam, sharp as stars. I'll leave and my mother will still be out here, deadheading roses and pulling slugs off the dahlias. She'll make three or four small sculptures in the week I'm gone, each destined to end up in some rich person's living room. And she'll wait to hear what Luna does when I see her, when I drop off this message my mother wants me to deliver.

I turn toward the car. My mother has climbed into the driver's seat and the Smiths are blasting from the speakers. Dusty is in the back, nose pressed to the window on my side, her tail a windmill blur behind her.

"You have to take care of Mom," I say to her through the glass, as if she were that nanny dog in *Peter Pan* or something. But I know Dusty can't manage much more than barking at the motorcycles that drive down our one-way street, or keeping the garden free of bunnies. There's no way she can keep Meg Ferris under control. I walk up to my mother's window.

"Let's jet," she says. She pulls her sunglasses down over her eyes. "Make like a tree, etcetera, etcetera."

"When we drive away? Let's leave the bad puns behind," I say. I walk around the car and stand still for a moment to text another lyric before I forget it: *I'll stitch the words together, string them like pearls on thread, remember them out of order, and forget what it was you said.*

"Phoebe!" my mother calls. I press send.

I open my door, holding my purse close to my body, as if there were a kitten or a baby inside, something that needs to be treated tenderly or protected from both the world and itself. This magazine is a sign of why I exist, but it's also a sign of Tessa and how I screwed everything up with her. Finding this magazine might be the last nice thing Tessa will do for me, because the last nice thing I tried to do for her went so totally wrong.

five

LAST APRIL, WHEN WE WERE still friends, Tessa and I went to a party in a big old house off Parkside. It was one of the first nice spring days in Buffalo and we were still winter desperate and happy to be outdoors. Every green thing seemed like a miracle. The leaves on the trees looked lush and glossy and the smell of grass made me giddy, even though I didn't really want to go to this party. Still, I put on jeans and a sweater and pulled my bike out of the garage, then followed Tessa through the darkening streets to Delaware Park.

The house was a huge purple Victorian half a block away from the zoo, so we left our bikes locked to a fence by the giraffes at the edge of the park. We wanted to show up on foot. It's awkward bringing bikes to a party, because you can't just leave them out front, and Tessa always worried there wouldn't be a place for them in the back. When we passed the giraffes' enclosure, they were walking slowly around the yard looking stunned and ethereal. I saw one of them bring its head down to the ground as slowly and carefully as a construction crane, and even then it had to bend its legs to reach the grass.

I leaned against the fence for a moment, wanting to keep watching, but Tessa marched on. She was the one who wanted to go to this party, thrown by a kid we sort of knew from St. Clare's brother school, Alfred Delp Academy. I knew it would be a bunch of private-school kids drinking beer and wine coolers and trying to stay just quiet enough so that the neighbors wouldn't call the cops. It's safe to say this wasn't really my scene.

Still, an hour later I had a bottle of beer in my hand, already getting warm since I was mostly ignoring it. It was more of a prop, or a talisman, maybe, than something I planned to drink. Tessa would have said I was afraid, if she had noticed. But she had a different philosophy regarding alcohol. She was on her second beer, and that one was still cold.

The backyard was lit with fairy lights strung like bright beads along the fences. The lawn was a perfect emerald green, and tulip stems in the garden pushed their blooms straight up toward the sky. We were sitting around a metal fire pit with our friends Evie and Willa and a bunch of other St. Clare's girls. Or rather, I was sitting in a rusty metal chair with my feet on the rungs underneath and Tessa was standing, leaning with her hip against the fence. She liked to stand. She was like one of those birds with the long necks— a crane, maybe—balancing on one leg or two when it got a little windy. She always wanted to see what was coming.

"Where are the boys?" Tessa said. "Isn't this party hosted by someone from Delp Academy? Where are his friends?"

"The ratio of girls to boys can't be worse than Emerson's party in December," Evie said.

Willa stretched her legs out in front of her and crossed her ankles. "Whatever. If we can avoid visiting urgent care tonight, I'll call it a success."

The last party we'd gone to, over winter break, was at Emerson McGrath's huge old mansion on Lincoln Parkway. It was lit up with so many Christmas lights you'd think her parents were expecting visitors from outer space and wanted to make sure those aliens could find their way. Emerson told everyone it was a *Great Gatsby* party, but that seemed to be just an excuse for her to wear a silk nightgown as clothing and drink gin out of an old crystal glass. Tessa and Evie weren't wearing nightgowns, but they drank the gin, so they were both listing to the side like sailors by the end of the night. Willa and I tried to keep them in line on the way home, but when we walked across the lawn of the Albright-Knox Art Gallery, Evie hopped up on this sculpture that looks like a papier-mâché banana, then slipped off and twisted her ankle. She had to call her brother Daniel to pick her up. I was running for junior class secretary that week, and Evie was going for president. Somehow we both won, even though Evie had to give her pre-vote speech on crutches.

"The first step to safety is avoidance of modern art," I said, raising my eyebrows at Evie.

She held out her right foot, wearing a sparkly silver ballet flat, and rotated it in a circle. "All healed," she said.

"She's learned her lesson," said Willa, fastening her curly red hair on the top of her head. "Or at least she knows Daniel won't pick her up next time she falls off a banana sculpture."

"You wish he would!" Evie said, poking Willa in the shoulder. Willa blushed. Evie calls Willa's crush on Daniel a known entity, even though Willa has denied it since we were freshmen.

My phone buzzed in my purse then, so I pulled it out. *Happy Saturday*, it said. *What's going on?*

Backyard high school party, I typed. *Warm beer and fairy lights, a few bright stars in the sky.*

My screen lit up. *That's a lyric right there. Maybe the start of a whole song.*

I smiled. Across from me, Willa stood up and grabbed Evie's arm. "Come on," she said. "We have to find a bathroom. I've got to pee."

Evie rolled her eyes, but she let Willa drag her away. Just then, Tessa stood up on her tiptoes, looking out toward the street. Even from my seat, I could see a bunch of boys in sweaters and khakis, led by a blond with a lanky build. They came up the driveway in a cluster and then spread out through the yard.

"That's him," Tessa whispered, too loudly. She leaned down toward me so her hair touched my shoulder, and pointed toward the guys who had just entered.

I turned my head to look at the blond boy, in whose direction she was pointing. "Who?" I asked.

"Lacrosse Boy." She had been talking about this guy for months. Even in the middle of winter, she'd see him biking down Delaware with his lacrosse stick fastened to his back like an antenna. She once got so close to him while driving her dad's car around Gates Circle that she nearly hit him. She hung back after that, at my suggestion. "What's the point of a crush if he's dead?" I had said.

Now I craned my neck to see him over by the drinks. "Are you sure?" I asked. "He's not carrying a lacrosse stick."

"I'm sure!" Tessa said, stage-whispering.

The blond guy brought his beer over near where we were sitting, just beyond the ring of chairs. One of his friends followed, a dark-haired guy with almond-shaped eyes and nice shoulders in his pullover sweater.

"Hey," the blond one said to Tessa, seeing her looking his way. He came around the chairs to sit in front of us. "I'm Tyler." His hair was long and nearly fell into one of his eyes, so he kept his head perpetually at a slight angle. But he was cute.

"Tessa," she said. "And this is Phoebe." I lifted my hand in a wave. His dark-haired friend smiled.

"I'm Ben," he said. He was looking at me when he said it, but then he held his hand out to Tessa, who was closer. She shook it.

"You guys play lacrosse?" Tessa asked. *Very subtle, Nancy Drew,* I thought, but they didn't seem to think it was strange.

Ben nodded and Tessa widened her eyes at me. I smiled.

"We do," Tyler said. He pointed to Ben with the neck of his bottle of beer. "This kid's an ace."

Ben smiled. "My mom grew up on the reservation. I played a lot with my cousins growing up."

"Seriously, he's a star." Tyler made a motion with his hands that I figured was supposed to mimic a lacrosse throw (toss?), but really he looked like he was shoveling snow in a very weird way. "I practice all the time and he still kicks my ass."

"My eight-year-old cousin could kick your ass," Ben said, "so that doesn't mean much."

A peacock screamed then from somewhere inside the zoo, a shrill and sharp sound louder than anything in the yard. Fitting, I thought. Tyler and Ben were basically peacocks, sparring with each other in hopes of impressing a drab brown female. Shaking their bird booties and fanning out those iridescent tail feathers, and for what?

Someone across the yard turned the radio up a little louder, and I could hear the plaintive voice of a pop starlet over electronic-sounding riffs.

"Taylor Swift," Tyler said, wrinkling his nose.

"What?" said Tessa. "You're so sophisticated that Ms. Swift can't possibly satisfy you?"

"I wouldn't say that exactly. I've just been listening to a lot of nineties rock lately. It's a different sound: dirtier, fuzzier. Nirvana, you know? Early Weezer. Sometimes Shelter."

Tessa laughed, a soft, honking sort of laugh that managed to sound sweet and mean at the same time.

"What?" Tyler said. He leaned forward.

"Are you for real?" Tessa asked. She looked at me, then back at him. "If you want to impress us, you're going to have to try harder."

I tried to send Tessa a message with my eyes, like *Maybe you should wait a little bit before you start playing hard to get.*

Tyler looked so genuinely confused that I was sure he didn't know who I was. I decided to let him off the hook.

"My dad is Kieran Ferris," I said.

"What?" He looked floored. "And so your mom is—"

"Meg Ferris."

"Oh my god," he said, his eyes wide. "I knew she lived in Buf-falo, but I thought she was a hermit or something." He was shaking his head. "I never see her anywhere."

I thought about pointing out that just because he hadn't seen her—where? The grocery store? Gas station?—that didn't mean she was a hermit. But I decided to keep my mouth shut.

"She's a professor at UB," Tessa said. "Sculpture."

"So that means . . ." Tyler appeared to be doing some calcu-lating in his head, and then he looked at me. "Are *you* the one who broke up the band?"

"What?" Across the yard I could see our friend Evie standing on a chair, dancing to Ms. Swift.

"Meg had a baby, right?" Tyler said. "And that was it."

"The baby was her sister, dipshit," Tessa said, and then looked over at me.

"Could have been me," I said. "Maybe I was the tipping point." I leaned close to Tessa's ear. "You have a salty mouth tonight," I whispered. Tessa shrugged.

But Tyler wasn't paying attention to Tessa anyway. He leaned way back in the lawn chair and looked at me as if he was going to say something very serious.

"Is your mom dating anyone?" he asked.

My exhale came out as a laugh. "Why?" I said. "Do you want her number?"

Ben laughed. Tyler shrugged, smiling.

"Maybe." He set his bottle down on the ground, making a clinking sound on the slate tile. "I just meant, is she dating another musician?" He leaned forward. "I guess I was hoping for some stories."

"No," I said. "She's not dating anyone at all. And she doesn't really talk to many of the people from her old life anymore, so I don't have any stories."

He appeared to consider this. "Maybe she's a lesbian," he said.

"*Tyler,*" Ben said. His voice was calm, and there was both a smile and a warning in it.

"She's not a lesbian," I said, shaking my head. I thought about what my mother would say if she were here, or rather, what she wouldn't say. She'd probably just sit back and listen to the whole thing with an amused smile on her face.

"Hey," Tyler said, shrugging, "there's nothing wrong with being a lesbian."

"Phoebe's aunt Kit is a lesbian," Tessa said in a thoughtful voice, as if she was trying to be helpful. "So is my cousin Christy." I gave her a look that said *irrelevant* and turned back to Tyler.

"*Of course* there's nothing wrong with being a lesbian," I said. "But my mother isn't one. She just doesn't need to have a man around all the time." I tilted my head. "Right now, I can really see why."

He put both his hands up, palms toward us, as if to say *okay*. "Tell me something, though. Do you know the other rock-star kids? Like Frances Bean?"

"Oh, totally," I said. "We have a little club. We meet once a month and Frances Bean always brings the blow." Ben met my eyes then, shaking his head, and mouthed, *Sorry.*

I wasn't even sure which drug *blow* was, but Tyler didn't have to know that.

Just then I heard a peacock scream again, a chilling, human-like screeching.

"Is that the zoo, or is someone being gruesomely murdered?" I turned to Tessa. "Come on, let's get out of here before the killer birds show up."

Tessa set her beer bottle on a metal table and stood up, a little wobbly on her feet.

"Do you have to go?" Tyler said. He was still sitting, holding the arms of his chair like a king on a throne. I decided then that he wasn't obnoxious, exactly, just overconfident. He was even a little funny. I figured I could deal with him if Tessa wanted him.

"We should go," I said.

Ben punched Tyler in the arm. "You're the one who is scaring them away! Do something!"

"Phoebe's the boss," Tessa said, swaying a little. "Phoebe's always the boss."

Ben actually stood up when we were leaving, like I imagined a gentleman would. It seemed like he wanted to shake my hand or something, but we couldn't quite make it happen. There was some awkward gesturing. I could feel a smile move slowly across my lips.

Out on Parkside, cars whispered by, making shushing sounds on the pavement. It was late, and there was a slim eyelash of a moon in the corner of the sky, cracking open one small piece of the night. Sea lions barked through the cool night air. We walked quickly, quietly, until we came to the streetlight.

"So Lacrosse Boy's name is Tyler," I said, as the light changed. We stepped into the street.

"What?" Tessa said, snapping her eyes toward me. "No. Lacrosse Boy's name is Ben."

I could feel my heart sink as she said it, as clearly as if she had tied a metal fishing weight to it and dropped it in the middle of the sea. I saw it spinning through the water, saw the flash of metal catching moonlight as it fell. I looked away from Tessa then, toward the zoo. The giraffes' yard was empty now, just a square of green grass. It looked so small.

"Oh," I said to Tessa, but what I thought was, *Shit*.

When I think about it now, I'm pretty sure that I could feel what was happening.

I think I already knew things were going to fall apart.

six

MEG
AUGUST 1999

WHEN I CLOSED THE DOOR to the loft I was still shaking. I wondered if Phoebe could feel it, strapped to my chest in her baby sling. She was asleep—she'd been sleeping since the playground, and straight through the two blocks it took for us to walk back to our building. Though really I'd been doing something closer to running to keep up with Kieran's long strides, his right hand holding my left, pulling me along. He held Luna with his other arm, and I could see that she wasn't afraid. She was smiling at me, hanging on to Kieran's shoulder, her hair shining in the late-August sun. But that didn't make me feel better.

We didn't speak the whole time we walked back—we were moving too fast for that. But now, when Kieran set Luna down in the corner where we kept her toys, I walked to the other side of the loft and he followed.

"Where *were* you?" I asked. "You said you'd be there at three."

He raked his hand through his hair. "The interview ran over," he said. "I called but you had already left." He pointed to the blinking light on the answering machine as if that were explanation enough.

"Yes, because we said *three*. I left at two fifty."

"I'm sorry, Meg," he said. "I got distracted." He sat down on the couch. "Come here."

I sat down carefully, trying not to wake Phoebe in her sling. Moving like this—with a baby attached to my front—reminded me of being pregnant, that top-heavy feat-of-physics feeling that causes you to move like a modern dancer on muscle relaxers. And that big, bright, wide-open room felt like a stage, though even I didn't want to see the show playing there that day.

I'd loved the apartment as soon as I saw it, loved the water view and the open living room and kitchen, the bedrooms tucked away at the back. Now my memory flashed on a different version of this apartment: empty, the first time we saw it, following our Realtor in her black pumps and panty hose around the rooms. I was five months pregnant and wearing a short skirt and one of Kieran's flannel shirts. I can remember my reflection in the bathroom mirror, and the way my Doc Martens looked against the smooth wood floor. One of our favorite pizza places was just two blocks away, next to the hole-in-the-wall sushi place where we ate all the time before we had money.

"We could get to Sakura in less than five minutes if we walked fast," Kieran had said then, slipping his arms around me and burying his face in my neck. He laughed. "That pretty much makes our decision for us, doesn't it?"

"I guess it does," I said. That and the view of the river from the window, sapphire blue and sparkling like broken glass. Not to mention the playground I'd seen from the taxi, where the baby in my belly would play some day.

Where we had been earlier.

We went to the playground because I wanted Luna to be able to go down the slide. She was two and she'd never been to a playground in her own city. I wanted to put her on the swings. I wanted her to know what the last few days of summer felt like.

And it was fine . . . at first. Kieran was late, but that was nothing new. The only ones who noticed us were a few teenagers walking home from school. For a while they just sat on a bench and watched so they could decide if it was really me. I didn't mind signing their notebooks when they got up the guts to come over, or smiling while they told me their favorite tracks from our new record. But then two photographers showed up. Freelance, I figured, because they didn't tell me where they were from. One tried to put his camera right in Luna's face, and I heard her call for me, her voice small and scared. I couldn't see her, and for a moment I couldn't breathe at all, as if someone were squeezing my rib cage. As if there weren't any air left in the world. The other photographer stood five feet away from me, his face hidden behind his camera.

"Meg! Can we see the baby?"

I didn't say no. I didn't say anything. I just tried to get to Luna, but he wouldn't let me pass.

"Get out of my way," I said, and it came out like a growl. Luna was crying by now, and I managed to lurch past him and grab her hand.

"Come on, Meg," the photographer said, his camera still clicking. "Just let us get a few shots."

I pulled Luna into my hip, and then, out of nowhere, Kieran appeared and scooped her up. He stopped for a fraction of a second in front of the photographers while they flashed away, and then he took my hand.

Now, remembering, I felt that same anger well up inside me. "You *posed* for them," I said.

"That's ridiculous," Kieran said. "I didn't pose. I paused. I was trying to figure out where to go."

"You go *out*," I said. "You get away."

"I was trying," Kieran said, but I shook my head. Luna was pretending to read to herself on the floor, a book with a purple raccoon on the cover.

"Anything could have happened," I said. I could feel the tears at the edge of my voice. "I was scared."

"Meg," Kieran said. "they were photographers. Not random maniacs."

"They acted like maniacs," I said. Kieran put his hand on mine, but I pulled it away.

"What if this was a mistake?" I said.

"What?"

"All of it." I shook my head. "Thinking we could have Shelter and a family at the same time." I put my palm on Phoebe's warm, fuzzy head. She slept on. "I don't want the girls to grow up like this."

"Babe, it was one bad experience," he said. He took my chin between his fingers, looked right in my eyes.

"Right," I said. "And it's the first time she's been to a playground. Ever."

"She won't remember," he said. "We'll take her again, and it'll be better. That was just bad luck."

The week before we'd been in Chicago for a festival on the lake, our first show since Phoebe was born. We played into the washed-out sunshine of early evening, and I sang so hard my voice was scratchy and raw. When we got back to the hotel the girls were already asleep. Kit was too, stretched out on the king-sized bed next to Luna. I didn't wake her.

In the morning we all ate blueberry pancakes and melon in the hotel restaurant. I saw a couple of girls at a table in the back, early twenties, watching us and whispering to each other. A few minutes later, one of them came over with a flyer from the festival.

"Would you mind signing this?" she asked. I didn't say anything, but I tried to smile.

"Of course," Kieran said. She handed him a pen and he took it. He scrawled his name across the page. He handed me the pen, and I signed below.

Luna looked on, watching us.

"Would you like to sign it too?" the girl said. Luna's face broke out in a smile and she picked up the green crayon with which she'd been drawing earlier. She drew a loopy scribble near the bottom of the paper.

"Thanks, Luna," the girl said. Hearing this stranger say my daughter's name made me shiver, but no one noticed. The girl went back to her table and Kieran started eating again, but I didn't feel hungry anymore.

"Starting her young," Kit said, a smile in her voice. I looked at her, and she seemed surprised by my expression. She frowned.

Kieran shrugged. "It's part of the game," he said.

I looked at him. "Our lives are not a game."

"It's just an autograph," Kieran said. "Price of admission."

Admission to what? I wanted to ask. But I didn't.

Now, in our living room, I looked at him. "You love it," I said. He wouldn't meet my eyes. "You love that everyone knows us."

He snapped his head toward me. "And you don't. You never have."

In the light from the window, I could see the scar that ran along his jawline, fine as silk thread. He fell off his bike when he was six years old and his family was on vacation on Cape Cod. His mother told me that story the first time I met her at that same cottage, my feet in the sand.

I almost reached out to touch Kieran then, to trace the scar on his jaw or rest my fingers on his shoulder. I think I wanted to make sure he was still real. A person—not a rock star. Not an icon. Flesh and blood.

But then he bent down to take his guitar from the stand and turned away toward our bedroom. Phoebe kept sleeping, her head against my chest. I could feel her breath, soft as dandelion fluff. Luna leaned forward and chose a new book.

There was a photograph of us on the wall, blown up to fill the space over the sofa. Our friend Alex took it, and after Kieran passed it to *Rolling Stone*, Alex enlarged it and had it framed for us. We're onstage in Portland, way back when *Sea of Tranquility* was new. In some other time and place, my hair shines in amber lights. I'm looking across the stage toward Kieran, my mouth open in a delighted smile. And he's looking back, right at me, his left hand forming a G chord on the frets of his guitar. We look like we're having so much fun.

There on the couch, I couldn't even remember if that was true.

seven

THE SKY ABOVE THE CLOUDS is Windex blue, so bright it hurts my eyes. So I close them and listen to the whoosh and hum of the plane's engines, feeling their vibrations through my seat. I've only flown by myself twice before, most recently in February to see Luna in the city, but I like the anonymity of it. I could be anyone, sitting here next to the window with a plastic cup of orange juice and ice, an empty packet of pretzels and a paper napkin. No one needs to know anything more than my snack choice right now.

When we're halfway to New York and the virtual airplane on my seat-back monitor is turning south somewhere around Binghamton, I take out the magazine even though I told myself I wasn't going to do it. It's weird, I know, to carry around such an old magazine, as if I were some time traveler from 1994 who just scrubbed off her maroon lipstick in the airport bathroom.

Tessa and I first saw it on *SPIN*'s website in the cover gallery, in the middle of ones featuring Jane's Addiction and Weezer and Kurt Cobain, both while he was alive (October 1993) and after he was dead (June 1994). There was my mother, looking small and beautiful and foreign on the screen. It felt like proof to me that my parents had been together once, that they had existed, and they had made something out of it besides Luna and me. There was barely an internet when Shelter was together, so the information you can find on the web is limited. Plus I wanted to hold something solid in my hands, something that had existed at the same time as my parents' band. I was suddenly an anthropologist and I wanted an artifact of this civilization, long dead and gone. So we scoured the internet for an hour before we found a paper copy, then ordered it with the credit card Tessa's dad had given her for emergencies. If this wasn't an emergency, neither of us knew what was.

Now, on the tray table, I try to smooth the crumpled cover with my fingers. It had come that way, already a little damaged, taped inside a cardboard envelope with my name and address scrawled in Sharpie across the front. The band has headlines printed over their shoulders and above their heads. Everyone else's gaze is fixed on something just off in the distance, but my father is looking right at the camera. I haven't seen him in a while, obviously, but I know this face. Twenty years later, I bet he still looks like this: satisfied, in control, as if he knows something I don't. Like how to write a hit song. Or how to leave.

My mother couldn't see it because, well, sometimes she even goes so far as to pretend she isn't and never was Meg Ferris, rock star. We'll be at the farmers' market, for example, and some guy will come up to her by the organic carrots (greens still attached!) and he'll say, "Hey, aren't you Meg Ferris?"

That's when she puts the whole plan into action.

She's perfected a series of facial expressions for dealing with this situation. First there's *Who, me?* and then *Oh, not this again* and then, *Sure, but she's not me! Thanks for the compliment, friend!* The whole sequence takes about ten seconds. She'll say, "You know, everyone tells me I look like her. I wish!" She'll smile dazzlingly and the poor guy will look confused, holding a bag of tomatoes or artisanal cheddar. He'll say, "Oh, okay," and wander off slowly, or he'll say, "A case of mistaken identity!" with a peppy exclamation point you can actually hear and they'll both laugh weird fake laughs that belong in bad theater. Sometimes a wife or girlfriend will appear and pull him off in the direction of the lettuce. (My mom may be forty-two, but she's pretty hot.) And then Meg Ferris in Disguise will look at me, triumphant, as if she's waiting for applause.

Every time, I think about telling the random fan the truth, just to see what my mother would do. Which is why it's funny that I don't do it when I get the chance, right here on the plane, with my mom back on Earth.

The woman sitting next to me is in her late thirties, I think, wearing a turquoise sheath dress and high-heeled sandals. She offered me a piece of gum as the plane taxied down the runway before takeoff (I accepted), but that's been the extent of our interaction so far. But when she sees the copy of *SPIN* she lets out a little gasp, and I feel the lies start to bubble up from some secret Ferris spring.

"Shelter!" the woman says. "I loved that band. Is this a throwback cover?"

"It's vintage," I say. I consider the stories I might tell and choose one. "My dad has a lot of old magazines."

"Cool dad," she says. She's leaning forward a little, looking at me conspiratorially. I shrug and smile.

"I was so bummed when they broke up," she says, and I don't know if she means the band or my parents. "Meg Ferris was such a badass, and Kieran was adorable." She drops her voice to a theatrical whisper. "I was so jealous of her. Sort of hated her a little. Listen to me, I sound sixteen again." She shakes her plastic cup of ice like a maraca, looking wistful. She sets the cup down.

"I'm Jessica," she says. "May I?" She holds her hand out. It's perfectly manicured, each nail a narrow oval painted in coral pink. It makes me feel a little bad about my own chipped gold polish.

I give her the magazine and she begins flipping through, looking for the article.

"Page seventy-seven," I tell her. She nods, not seeming to think it's weird that I have it memorized.

"Oh my god." She flips back to check the date on the cover. "I can't believe it's been twenty years." She puts her hand to her lips, then touches her cheek as if she thinks she might find a different face there. "You've heard their music, right?"

"Yeah," I say. "I like *Sea of Tranquility*."

"That's the best! I loved that record. And the song." Jessica finds the article and spreads the magazine flat on her own tray table. There's a photo of the record cover, a navy blue background with a shadow-covered moon in the center. "Oh my god." She turns toward me. "My favorite song was 'Still.' Do you know that one?" She starts to hum.

I nod and glance at the old lady dozing across the aisle, half-worried Jessica is going to start full-on singing it. But she stops after a few bars.

"I bought Kieran's new record," she says. "He's still pretty amazing. *And* still cute." She touches the picture of my father's face. "But Meg, she's been gone for years."

I think for a moment about that statement. It depends what you mean by *gone*, I guess. It's true that I rarely even hear her sing, and when I do, it's always from another room. Like the call of some bird everyone thought was extinct, its song ricocheting around in the forest, getting caught in all the leaves. By the time you get close enough, she's already stopped.

"She's an artist now," I tell Jessica. "She works in metal. Sculptures and jewelry." I don't tell her that I'm wearing some right now: the thin silver bangle on my wrist, the sharply geometric studs in my ears. Nothing big enough to set off the airport's metal detector, but still here. A couple of years ago *Rolling Stone* wanted to do a tiny article about my mother's sculptures, a "Where Are They Now?" sort of thing, but she refused to be interviewed. They put in a blurb about it anyway, a photo from the installation outside the Albright-Knox under the headline *Shelter Singer Sculpts in Metal*. They ran a picture of her from the university website, standing in front of a stark white gallery wall. She looks official, somehow. Responsible, and still beautiful.

Now, Jessica looks at me. "You know a lot about them. And you're so young! Is your dad a fan?"

Good question, I think. *Is he?* I'm not sure. So I shrug my shoulders and give a safe answer.

"He used to be."

She nods knowingly. "But you *are*."

"Totally," I say. This is the truth, even though I've had to be a fan in secret. It's as if my mother can't stand to hear the sound of her own voice coming out of a speaker. But I've listened to Shelter for as long as I've had an iPod—earbuds only. I can catch the woman I know in those songs, but only sometimes. Only fleetingly.

Jessica leans back on the seat, holding the magazine in front of her, and for a moment, I consider telling her the truth. She might believe me, if she looked closely at my mother's photo: we have the same green-blue cat eyes, the same cheekbones, though Luna is the one who really resembles her. If I told her, it would give her a story to tell when she gets wherever she's going, and let me pretend to be famous for a few moments, if only by association. But then the flight attendant comes by and tells me I need to stow my purse away, and Jessica hands me back the magazine.

"Thanks," she says. "Nothing like reminiscing to make you feel young and old at the same time." She takes out a lipstick from a tiny pouch in her lap and starts to apply it without a mirror, tracing it over her lips quickly, as if she's done it a thousand times before. I feel the plane's nose ease downward toward the earth and I turn back to the window. Outside, the clouds whip away and I can see the water, the wide blue Atlantic, and the curving shore of Long Island.

As the plane falls slowly from the sky, I look at the front-cover picture of my mother's face. If I wanted to tell the story, where would I even start? "My mother named us both for the moon," I'd say. She tried to make a space for us in the life she already had, but then something made her change it all. Our father kept making music, stayed in New York, stayed famous. And eventually, close to three years ago, he just stopped calling.

The airport comes closer and so does Luna, somewhere down there in its big-windowed space. She's applying her lip gloss, she's reading a book, she's humming a song on her iPod.

She's waiting . . . for me.

eight

MEG
APRIL 1997

When we pulled up in the town car, Luna woke in her car seat and stretched, slipping her tiny fist out of the blankets. Our doorman Thomas opened my door for me and a spring breeze blew straight through the backseat.

"Mrs. Ferris," he said. He called me that no matter how many times I'd asked him to call me Meg. "Welcome home." He peeked in toward Luna. "And hello, little one."

"We named her Luna," I said, unsnapping the buckle of her seat.

"Beautiful," Thomas said.

He put out his hand and I took it. I slid out of the car, holding Luna in the crook of my other arm. She felt so light, and I realized I'd never held a baby like this, out in the real world. I'd never really held a baby at all, at least not since I was three and my sister was

57

born, and even then, it was supervised, sitting on the sofa with my arm propped by pillows. I didn't remember, but there were pictures to prove it.

Kieran had already gotten out of the other side of the car and was standing on the curb. He put his arms out and I transferred Luna to him awkwardly, holding on with both hands until I was sure he had her. He held Luna in her blankets up to face the building.

"This is where we live," Kieran said. We were in the shadow of the building, but still she blinked into the light. He looked at me, put his lips close to Luna's ear. "Your mama is going to write so many songs about you."

I saw someone out of the corner of my eye and I stiffened, thinking it was a fan or, worse, a photographer. But it was an elderly woman with a stick-straight spine and a Chanel suit, one of those New York ladies you were more likely to see on the Upper East Side than in the West Village, where we were. I was sure she had no idea who we were, but still, she stopped on the sidewalk in front of us.

"That's a beautiful baby," she said. She was wearing wraparound sunglasses, and she pulled them down for a moment. Her eyes were blue and watery.

"Thank you," I said. I felt as if I'd just passed a test.

"She is," Kieran said. "Isn't she?"

We all nodded, me, the woman, Thomas. We were all smiling.

The woman stood for a moment on the sidewalk, looking at us. It was like we were posing for a photograph, but no one was there to take our picture, because no one knew where we lived. Yet.

"You should love her just as much as she needs," she said. "And not too much." She raised her pointer finger. "That's the secret."

"I'll try my best," I said.

She nodded. "You're swaying and you're not even holding her," she said, and I realized she was right. Three days with this baby and I'd already changed the way I stood. I couldn't be still. It was like some kind of new music had found its way into my bones, and it was trying to get back out.

The woman smiled and said, "I think you're going to be just fine." She kept walking. Luna started to cry then, a thin, sharp peal. I thought of sirens cutting through the quiet night. Kieran held Luna out so I could take her.

I settled Luna into my arms and she stopped screaming for just a second. Then she closed her eyes tightly and opened her mouth to let out another ear-shattering shriek.

"She's got your lungs," Kieran said.

A bubble of panic floated up from somewhere below me, but Kieran grabbed my hand and I brushed the bubble away. I looked up at him, and then toward the building, the roof, the sky.

Scream to the rafters, baby, I thought. *Let the world know you're here.*

"Damn straight," I said, holding Luna a little tighter.

nine

LUNA'S STANDING OUTSIDE THE BAGGAGE claim with her hip resting against the metal rim of the carousel, and for a moment, I see
her before she sees me. Her hair has grown since May and hangs
dark and shiny past her shoulders. She's wearing a black sleeveless
dress and flat gold gladiator sandals, buckled around her ankles and
across her toes. Her left wrist is strung with thin ribbons woven into
bracelets and a few half-inch Lucite bangles. Nothing metal. Nothing "Mom." I study her face, looking for the ways it might have
changed in the months since I've seen her last, but she looks mostly
the same. If there's something different, I can't spot it.

It's always hard to figure Luna out when she's quiet. So much
of my sister is her voice. She's loud, for one, and her voice is like
homemade caramel in a saucepan: warm, golden, and sweet in a
deep, bubbly kind of way. We overlapped for two years at St. Clare's,

and I'd always hear her before I saw her, which is part of the reason I felt at home there immediately.

The first day of my freshman orientation, she was a junior-year leader and stood at the front of the banner-draped gym in skinny jeans and a St. Clare's T-shirt, calling out the names of the freshmen who had been assigned to her. She saved my name for last, and the whole time I worried that I wasn't going to be paired with her, but when she got to me, she said as loud as she could without actually yelling, "Phoebe Ferris—that's my sister!"

I was immediately famous by association, because all those new, anxious fourteen-year-olds could tell that Luna was someone they wanted to know. During the school year Luna's voice would echo in the hallways and I'd hear her from inside my classroom or from one flight down the marble stairs. She was always around.

She sang in the chorus and when I passed the music room on my way to lunch I could pick her voice out of the rest. I saw it in my head as one golden thread running through a perfectly ordinary carpet. It was the thing that made her different, the thing that would let her do anything she wanted to do. Later I joined the chorus too, because it was an easy arts credit, but my own voice is ordinary, softly scratchy, not gold or silver or even a dull bronze. I didn't get whatever it is that the rest of my family has.

Now, in the bright open space of the airport, Luna's eyes catch mine and she starts to walk toward me. She weaves around an Orthodox Jewish family with four children, all holding hands in a row. The last and smallest kid—maybe two years old—reaches out to touch Luna's jersey skirt as she passes. My sister smiles down at her, resting her fingers on the girl's brown curls for a second. Then she walks on.

"Fifi," she says, opening her arms for a hug. This is her childhood nickname for me, the name she called me when she was two and I was just born. She had it embroidered a couple of years ago as a joke, sewn in fancy script above my heart on a V-neck, navy blue preppy sweater from J.Crew. I still wear it sometimes.

She squeezes me tightly, and for few seconds I find it hard to breathe.

"There's a *B* in there," I say into her shoulder. She smells like citrus and sweet almond. "You're missing it."

"Bibi?" She steps back, smiling. "You've changed it?"

I roll my eyes. "Yeah. I'm starting over."

When I see my suitcase, I bend to hoist it off the carousel. It's heavier than I expect and makes a clattering sound when the wheels hit the floor. A few people turn to look at me.

"Let's take the AirTrain," Luna says. "I'd rather save the cab fare and go out for Indian tonight."

"Okay," I say.

"But I should warn you that it's not as glamorous as it sounds." She's already walking away. *"AirTrain,"* she says, making air quotes around the word. "We'll be traveling through the swamps of Queens, basically."

"Sounds lovely." I follow her as she follows the signs, and we end up on the platform in the AirTrain station listening to a calm electronic voice announce the imminent arrival of a train.

"Do you want a snack?" Luna asks. She pulls a bottle of hand sanitizer out of her purse and shakes some into her palm.

"Sure," I say, taking the bottle. "But you asking that makes me feel like I'm five years old."

"Adorable little Fifi," Luna says, patting me twice on the top of my head. She hands me a bag printed with Korean characters.

"What are these?" I ask.

"Freeze-dried green beans," she says. "I can't stop eating them. There's this great Asian market near our practice space. I go there practically every time."

I take a few of the beans and crunch them between my teeth. They're good—sweet and grassy—and I realize that I'm hungry underneath that frothy feeling of traveling, of being in a new place.

I lean back and take out my phone then, and send a text: *I'm here*. The answer buzzes back almost immediately. *In real life?* I smile.

Waiting for the AirTrain, I type back. *Feels pretty real to me*.

Luna is looking at her own phone, so I pull a pack of M&M's from my purse and toss them into her lap. Her face lights up.

"Yes," she says. "Perfect."

This is my first offering to Queen Luna, and I wish it were this easy to please her all the time.

The truth is, if she had an altar we'd all be out there burning bags of M&M's, scooping them up like sweet colorful beads and dropping them with decadent abandon into the flames.

ten

WHEN WE COME UP FROM the Borough Hall station in Brooklyn Heights, it's as if we've entered a different country. The city smells like hot asphalt and stale pretzels, and my stomach growls in spite of Luna's green bean snacks and the M&M's. The sun is dazzling, reflecting off the cars sliding through the streets and the flat white concrete of the plaza. Luna knows where she's going and I follow her, dragging my dead-weight-on-wheels suitcase behind. While we're waiting to cross Court Street, a bus stops at the light next to us and breathes on us like a giant animal. It's a relief when it pulls away, even though the air is hot and still. My skin already feels gritty with city dust, but I don't mind.

It's so warm I can feel the heat of the pavement through the soles of my sandals. My suitcase makes a rhythm of the sidewalk cracks, *brrrrrrrr bump brrrrrrrr bump brrrrrrrr bump.* A few blocks down Court Street from Borough Hall, Luna turns down a leafy side street. There's a chain bookstore on the corner and as we pass, I see a couple of kids, twelve or thirteen, sprawled and reading in the aisle close to the window.

I can also see our reflections, Luna's and mine, as we walk into the shade of her street, so I look at myself, wondering if I belong in this city, on this street with Luna. I think I do. Our hair is almost the same dark brown, and our skin is the same shade of ivory. If you looked quickly, especially at our reflections, you might not be able to tell us apart. In real life, you'd know the difference. She's a little glowier, sparklier than I am. She has perfect posture and she looks everyone right in the face.

I turn away from the windows. "Bookstore on the corner," I say. "Not bad."

Luna nods. "Yeah, it's great for the AC. I spent a whole day reading there last week when it was ninety-five degrees. My favorite bookstore is farther down Court Street, though. I'll take you there later on." She points behind us, back toward the traffic swishing slowly by.

Luna stops in front of a dark red brownstone halfway down the block, one in a series of similar buildings, all connected to each other. Some of the buildings have stoops with sets of stone stairs, but this one is fronted by a low stone wall bordering the sidewalk, topped with a foot-high wrought iron fence, and has stairs leading down to a wooden door just below sidewalk level. There are garbage cans down there, but still, it seems a little magical. I'm not sure why. Maybe because this is the door into Luna's new life.

"Fourteen Schermerhorn Street," Luna says, pronouncing it

Skimmerhorn. The word sounds Dutch, or charmed, or both. She hops down the stairs and pulls the heavy door open, gesturing like a game show hostess.

"Come on in," she says, and disappears inside.

It's cool and dark in there, though the glare of sunlight is still visible through a leaded glass window on the left side of the door. We stand for a moment in the small, square foyer, where there's a mess of mail spilled over a small wooden table. Luna rustles through the magazines and envelopes and pulls out a copy of *Rolling Stone.* She checks the label.

"Mine," she says, holding it up like a prize. It makes me think about the copy of *SPIN* tucked into my bag, the creased cover, and our parents, frozen forever, inches from each other. I want to show it to Luna, but not quite yet. First I want to figure out how she's feeling about them, both my mother and my father. I want to take her temperature.

The apartment is on the fourth and top floor, and Luna climbs the stairs quickly, cheerfully, like she's scaling a mountain in *The Sound of Music.* I expect her to start singing vaguely Swiss-sounding songs. I follow slowly, bumping my suitcase behind me. From time to time I look up and see her higher than I think I'll be able to manage to go. She told me it was only four floors, but there must be some kind of optical illusion, because it seems to me twice that.

Her voice floats down from somewhere above me. "Sorry about the stairs!"

My reply sounds something like "Umphhhh."

When I get up there, I'm practically panting. The door is open just past a doormat that says WELCOME, KITTY, with the silhouette of a small, whiskered cat. I pull my suitcase over the threshold and see that the apartment is mostly one big room furnished with a couple of couches and some chairs in the center, bookshelves lining the walls. Three guitars are hung on the wall over a small square table, and there are concert posters for Vampire Weekend and Florence + the Machine fastened to the wall with purple washi tape.

Luna is standing in the living room with her arms folded, looking at me expectantly.

"Welcome, Kitty," I say. I slip off my shoes and leave them by the door, still following my mother's rules from our house at home.

"Came with the apartment," she says. "And it also happens to be awesome."

"That's debatable. Aunt Kit would like it, though." I take a deep breath. My heart is still thudding in my chest. "On the plus side, you won't have to go to the gym," I say, "like, ever in your life again."

She smiles. "The stairs aren't so bad unless you're hauling a fifty-pound suitcase," she says.

"Which I was." I pull the case against the wall when Luna gestures in that direction.

"Right. Pack lighter next time." She smiles. "So, what do you think?"

The first time I visited Luna, she was living in the dorms at Columbia, a double on the fourth floor of a building on Amsterdam. I slept on the floor between her bed and her roommate's, listening to a muffled White Stripes album play on repeat through the wall. This feels different. It's her own space, no roommate, unless you count James. Which I suppose I have to, but he's a different kind of roommate.

"I like it," I say. "It looks like you."

"The bedroom is over there." She points to an open door off the living room. "And here's the bathroom."

I peek into Luna's bedroom, which I guess is James's bedroom too. Her room at home is pale purple with gauzy white curtains and a plum-colored silk bedspread from India. Luna got my grandmother's mahogany furniture when she moved into a retirement home and I'm still jealous, especially because it's still in Luna's room at home and she's barely ever there. Here, the mattress is on a low platform, and there's no headboard. There's not really space for a headboard. The room is still pretty, though, painted the deep and glossy blue of the ocean at night. It's small enough and dark enough that it seems like a cozy little cave. I see James's clothes sticking out of a tall wardrobe next to the dresser—a pair of black dress pants, a pearl-gray collared shirt—because there's only about two feet of space between those pieces of furniture and the bed.

Luna shows me the kitchen, which is not much more than an alcove off the living room.

"You actually have to step out of the way to open the oven." She demonstrates, opening the oven door while sweeping to the side with a curtsy.

"You can't cook anyway, right?" I open one of the narrow cabinets next to the sink and see that it's full of cereal.

"You'd be surprised!" she says, then shrugs. "We eat a lot of frozen veggie burgers. I think that counts." She straightens the bottles of spices on the back of the stove. "I'm learning." She frowns a little. "I'm trying to eat healthier."

I can tell she loves it here, even with the four flights of stairs and the miniature dollhouse kitchen.

"Are you keeping the place when you go on tour?"

"Yeah, we're going to sublet it. To a British tennis pro, if you can believe it." She smiles. "He's very cute. I must be sending off a signal that attracts British men. Some frequency only they can hear. I bet most of the neighbors won't even notice James is gone." She heads back into the living room. "Which is good because I'm not sure our sublet is legal."

I sit down on the sofa, which is wide and low and a little bit lumpy. "When are you leaving?" I ask. This is the temperature-taking. I'm sure she's still going on tour, and not going back to school, but I want to see how she's feeling about it.

"September sixteenth," she says. "Three weeks or so."

"What are you going to do in the meantime?"

"We have shows in Brooklyn and Hoboken. One in Manhattan, too. Tomorrow night." She looks at me with her head tilted at an angle. "I told you that, didn't I?"

"I think so." I drop my purse to the floor, and just then I hear my phone chime inside it. My mother. *Safe landing? How is it?*

I assume *it* means the apartment. I don't think their relationship has deteriorated to the point that my mother would refer to Luna with a genderless pronoun.

Super safe, I type. *Luna's place is great. No metal flowers, though. We'll fix that.*

Ha. Thanks for being my messenger.

Yeah, well . . .

It takes a minute for my mother to reply. Then my phone chimes again. *Just give it a try.*

"What's all the texting?" Luna asks.

"Nothing," I say. "Mom sent you a gift. She wants to know if I've given it to you yet."

I kneel down by my bag and unzip it, pulling the taped-up sculpture from my bag. It still feels heavier than you'd expect from looking at it, like an Easter egg, maybe, with coins inside. I hand it to Luna.

"Metal?" Luna asks as soon as she feels the weight in her hands.

I shrug. "I think it's a peace offering."

She pulls a pair of scissors from the desk drawer and begins to cut into the package. Some of the bubbles pop indignantly, but most go quietly.

"So she isn't mad anymore?" Luna asks.

"I wouldn't say that."

Luna smiles and peels the rest of the tape away.

I lean back on the couch. She pulls the sculpture out of the wrapping and there's the metallic vegetation she never knew she wanted. "Uh, wow."

I know what she's thinking. *Lots of spikes.*

I'm quiet for a minute, watching her look at the flower. I bite my lip. "I think Mom's just scared," I say.

"Could've fooled me." Luna looks up. "Scared of what?"

"I don't know." I can think of a thousand possibilities, but I can't settle on one. "That you won't go back to school? That you'll turn out like her? You know, angry about the whole thing?"

"I'm not going to turn out like her," Luna says, looking right at me. She pulls her mouth tight. "Anyway, she's happy, isn't she?"

Huh. That's a good question. Is she? I'm not really sure. She seems it, but sometimes she's sad and I don't know exactly why.

I pick up my phone again and type a text: *We try to figure out each other and make the pieces fit. But sometimes happy is an accident, and we forget not to give up on it.* I send it, and I put my phone back in my purse.

Luna turns the robot flower over in her hands, her fingers finding the smooth parts under the petals. She shakes her head.

"I'm surprised they let you bring this on the plane." She sets it down on the coffee table.

"That's exactly what I said." I poke the sculpture with my foot, and it slides across the wood with a squeak. "The good news, from what I gathered, is that you can always use it as a weapon if you need to."

Luna smiles, nodding. "I'll remember that if you get out of line."

Near the end of Luna's senior year, my mother donated a large sculpture to St. Clare's. Luna had been caught skipping school. She'd left early one day to drive to Toronto for a Weakerthans show ("It might be their last one!" she'd said), and so she had to serve detention for a half hour each morning in the little waiting room outside of Sister Rosamond's office. She was my ride, and I often sat in there with her because I didn't have anywhere else to go at that hour. We did our homework, so it wasn't much of a punishment. I liked it, truth be told, sitting there quietly with Luna, our pens scratching away at our notebooks on the table. Sister Rosamond would peek her head in from time to time, and Luna would smile widely at her, showing all her teeth. Honestly I don't think Sister Rosamond was even that angry, but my mother used it as an excuse to offer some major metal.

The sculpture looked like some far-off version of a solar system: a large silver sphere in the middle surrounded by smaller ones at various distances, all tethered to the center by thin strips of steel. It was large enough that drivers could see it from the street, but not in any detail. They would see only a delicate shiny thing floating over the lawn, unless they pulled into the curving driveway of the school and took a closer look. In the months after it was installed, some people did. They got out of their cars and stood for a while at the edge of the drive, watching the sculpture curve the sunlight it caught along its surface. Then they'd get back in their cars and drive away.

"It's like the mother ship, bringing the aliens in," Tessa said once, months after it first appeared. She was looking out the window of our math classroom at a guy in a Sonic Youth T-shirt staring at the sculpture. He reached his hand out and looked around, then seemed to figure he shouldn't touch it. I had to admit that my mother did something magical with metal, something that seemed to go beyond just bending or shaping it. Her pieces were made of materials besides steel, forces besides heat.

The St. Clare's sculpture was unveiled after school on a Friday, and a lot of Luna's and my friends stayed past their buses to be there. The nuns wore pantsuits and sensible shoes and generally looked a little confused but happy. Our friends had that rumpled, end-of-the day look: sweaters unbuttoned, skirts rolled up higher than we were actually allowed. But they were excited; this was what passed for big news at St. Clare's, and my mother was pretty much the most famous person any of our friends knew.

I was disappointed to find out that "unveiling" was an exaggeration—the sculpture was out in the open from the beginning. I had imagined my mother pulling a cover off it like a magician, a white sheet, maybe, or a big piece of parachute cloth like the ones we used in gym class when we were little. There might be music; the chamber orchestra could sit in chairs on the grass and play some suspenseful song. People would honk as they passed in their cars.

A few people did end up honking, though I think it was boys from Delp Academy on their way to the far-out suburbs. Even so, my mother seemed to enjoy the unveiling. Sister Rosamond gave a small speech ("We're so grateful to this talented artist and alumna, plus mother to two of our shining students," she said, and Luna elbowed me and whispered, "Did Rosie just make a metal pun?") Then my mother came up and stood with Sister Rosamond in front of the sculpture so Sister Monica could take their picture, and then they called Luna and me up there to be in another photo. Tessa and Evie made faces at me from the crowd. After that, there was a reception in the library and we all ate crudités and cake. I noticed halfway through that Luna was missing.

My mother was talking with Tessa and Sister Lisa, the only nun at our school under the age of forty and a mystery to all of us. No one saw me go. I walked through the hallways, so quiet now that my footsteps echoed, then out through the foyer with its delphinium-blue stained glass windows. There are two flights of stairs leading down from the front door at St. Clare's, and from up at the top I could see Luna on the front lawn leaning against a maple tree, facing the sculpture.

It took me a minute to walk down the stairs and across the grass, but when I got to my sister I sat down next to her, crossing my legs in the grass. She was quiet, so I watched the traffic swishing by on Main Street and the traffic light turn from yellow to red to green. Then she spoke.

"Didn't you ever want a normal mom?" Luna asked.

"No," I said. I didn't have to think about my answer. But I didn't know exactly what she meant, either.

"Like a mom who's a lawyer, or a doctor, or a librarian or something." She pulled a small handful of grass out and then dropped it. "A high school teacher."

"Mom *is* a teacher."

"It's not the same thing. Mom used to be famous, and now she's not, except she still is, a little. I mean, all this sculpture stuff. If you don't want to be famous, then just don't be, you know?" She looked toward the school as if she were talking to our mother, up in the library with her appetizer plate. "But I guess how else is she going to prove that she's the best?"

I was surprised to hear Luna say this, to admit that she worried about being able to live up to my mother's talent. But the way that Luna felt about my mother, that was the way I felt about Luna. She was always shinier. She would always be better at things than I was.

"Mom's going to wonder where we are," I said.

"More important, Sister Rosamond is going to wonder, and

I can't afford to piss her off again." She sat forward onto her knees and brushed grass off her lap.

Luna stood up and walked to the edge of the sculpture, just outside its orbit, then touched one of the smaller spheres. It was like a tiny planet in her hand.

When she pulled her hand away I expected for some reason to see the steel ball still in it, but her palm was empty.

Later, when the cake was gone and so were my friends and teachers, my mother pulled out of the parking lot in the Volvo with me in the passenger seat and Luna in the back. She stepped on the gas a little bit harder than she had to and squealed out onto Main Street.

"We may not be able to donate money like the families with lawyer daddies," she said, "but we donate art, bitches!" She punched the air emphatically.

"Are we the bitches, or is that the nuns?" I asked, leaning my head against the back of the seat.

My mother thought about it. "It's a rhetorical *bitches*, I think."

I looked back into my visor mirror and saw that Luna was smiling even though she was trying not to. She had turned her face toward the window but I could still see her.

We were a poorly drawn triangle that day in the car, the angles between us always shifting, but always adding up to the same thing. In the end, we were always trying to understand one another, even if we only made it halfway most days.

eleven

MEG
SEPTEMBER 1996

WE WAITED IN MATCHING BLACK leather chairs, hands in our laps. Through the hotel room window, I could see the gray drizzle of a Seattle sky. I had memorized the pattern of the wallpaper, the shape of the four tulips in the painting above the bed. On the table between us was a pregnancy test. I had already peed on it. Kit had bought it at the drugstore down the street from the club where we were doing sound check, brought it to me wrapped in a plastic bag.

Now I looked down just as a blue plus sign appeared, faint at first and then stronger, like a star that seems to brighten as the sky grows dark. I looked up at Kieran. His eyes were wide. He covered my hand with his own and squeezed, and that's when I realized that I was holding my breath. I let it out in one quick exhale, and then I closed my eyes and opened them again. Still a plus sign, still Kieran, looking shocked. Still those tulips, red and graceful, painted in a blue vase. I heard a voice and it took me moment to realize it was Kieran's.

"Shit."

twelve

THE FIRST TIME I MET JAMES, Luna took me to a diner near Columbia with sticky red vinyl booths and chrome-edged tables. We had eggs and toast, and he showed up when there were only crumbs and crusts left on our plates. Then he ate the crusts.

He was tall and almost pretty, with messy chestnut-colored hair and liquid dark eyes, slim jeans and a black T-shirt. He said he had come straight from a class called "Poetics of the Warrior."

I crinkled a sugar packet between my fingers. "Does the class make you feel like going to war?" I asked.

"No," James said. "It makes me feel like having a cheese omelet." When the waitress passed by again, he ordered one.

I found James charming immediately. He was sweet and funny and wicked smart. He had lived in London until he was twelve and his playwright parents moved him to Manhattan, so a posh British accent hid beneath the rounder American vowels of some of his words. Sometimes it depends where he learned the word, he told me once, so things like *geometry* and *Beyoncé* sound fully from the States. Sitting in a vinyl booth at the diner, it occurred to me that I could listen to James talk all day.

They were going to start a band, Luna told me, and James nodded enthusiastically. They'd met at a show on the Lower East Side, and she'd pressed her phone number into his hand at the end of the night. She'd written it on her ticket stub.

"Why didn't you just put it into his phone?" I asked.

"Romance!" Luna said. "You want me to say, 'Excuse me, James, may I program my number into your phone in case you need it later?'" She pantomimed typing numbers. "Are you kidding me?"

Clearly I had no understanding of love.

"But where did you get a pen?" I asked. She rolled her eyes and went up to the cashier to pay the check.

James visited Buffalo while Luna was home during winter break last year and charmed my mother, too. We all stayed home on New Year's Eve and ate a dozen different kinds of frozen appetizers baked on cookie sheets in the oven: spanakopita, tiny quiches, cherry turnovers, that kind of thing. It was exactly what we used to do when we were small, though back then we couldn't make it until midnight and had to celebrate at six o'clock, when the celebration happened in Paris or Madrid, or seven, when it was midnight in London. There were years in the middle when we celebrated at nine or ten, when it was New Year's somewhere over the Atlantic. Eventually we worked our way to midnight when Luna was thirteen and

I was eleven. We watched movies and ate a million tiny cream puffs and passed out on the couch after the ball drop. Sometimes Tessa came over if she could escape from the party her parents gave every year, especially the years it got rowdy and loud over there.

Last year, when James was in Buffalo with us, we started celebrating the New Year with Istanbul and Rome and Dublin and various places over the sea, blowing our noisemakers every hour on the hour. James joined right in, singing "God Save the Queen" during the London hour and making up several nonsense songs about whales and floating oceanic garbage piles for all the hours that didn't have a city attached. Sometime near midnight I saw my mother smiling at James. It occurred to me then that Luna knew what she was doing: trying to get our mother to like him before she could hate him later, when Luna told her she was taking a leave from school.

Outside, the air is cooler, the day's heat starting to soften. The sun has already slipped below the row of brownstones, the slight overhang of their roofs like hats pulled down low. We walk side by side without leaving shadows on the sidewalk. I feel helium light, fizzy around my edges. I can't wait for what's going to happen next.

There's a box of books resting on a low stone wall a few buildings down, and Luna stops to riffle through them.

"You wouldn't believe what people throw out in this neighborhood," she says, making a new pile of books on the wall so she can dig deeper in the box. "Pretty much our entire apartment has been furnished from the street. Which sounds gross, but the stuff is really nice." She pulls a beat-up paperback copy of *The Catcher in the Rye* out of the box, the same red-covered, yellow-lettered edition I read for school last summer, and puts it in her bag. "I think it's because people move so much and no one wants to carry a lot of junk with them. Not to mention there's no space."

Luna puts the rest of the books back in the box for the next customer, and we keep walking. The restaurant is down the street and over a block, and inside it's dim and cozy, gold-lit by candles that reflect on wall hangings woven with metallic thread. The walls are painted deep red, and ochre cloths line the tables. I take a breath and realize how nervous I feel, how aware I am of my own heartbeat thudding in my chest.

James is sitting with Josh and Archer. I've met those two twice, back in February and before that, in November, when the Moons were just starting out. Thinking of that first meeting now—a half hour, maybe, in a coffeehouse up near Columbia—it occurs to me just how quickly the band has found some kind of success. They released their first record, an EP called *Clair de Lune*, on a great indie label called Blue Sugar, and an even bigger label called Venus Moth is interested in the next one. They just want to hear it first.

All three of the boys stand up when we get to the table.

"What gentlemen," I say, looking at Luna.

"Yeah, seriously." She pulls her chair out. "Why don't you guys stand up when I come into a room?"

"It happens too often," Josh says. "You're always coming in and walking out. You never stay still."

Luna rolls her eyes and sits down, just as James comes around the table to hug me.

"The littlest Ferris," he says, and squeezes me so hard I exhale without trying.

"I'm not little," I say when he lets go.

I shake Josh's hand and then Archer's, which feels weird because I've met them already, but it goes with this whole politeness game we're playing at here. Josh is African-American, with light brown skin and dark eyes. His fingers are so long and slender that his hands look like sculptures when they're still (but he's a drummer, so they hardly ever are). Archer, who's three or four inches taller than I am, has dark brown hair that curls at the base of his neck. His eyes are seawater blue.

I sit down between him and Josh, then unfold my napkin and put it into my lap, just for something to do.

"How long are you staying?" Archer asks. He leans toward me a little as he says this, and I find myself doing the same thing in his direction.

My lips feel dry suddenly, and I have to stop myself from taking my lip balm out of my purse. "Till Tuesday," I say.

"Eighties band!" Josh says from across the table. I look at him. He's nodding enthusiastically. "The lead singer was Aimee Mann."

"Um, yeah." I smile.

"He's trying to impress you with his encyclopedic musical knowledge," Archer says.

"Do you actually think she doesn't know who Aimee Mann is?" Luna says to Josh. "Meg Ferris is our *mother*. We have both been schooled by the master." She shakes her head and corrects herself. "Mistress." She thinks for a moment. "Plus I think she was friends with Aimee."

Josh shrugs. "Okay."

"Anyway," I say. "As I was saying, I have to be home for freshman orientation."

"Geez, I thought you were a little older than that," Josh says. Luna laughs, one loud bark of a laugh that makes the couple at the nearest table look over at us.

"Sorry," Luna says to them, smiling with all her perfect white teeth, and instead of looking annoyed, they smile too. Luna Ferris's unstoppable charm strikes again.

"She's at least fifteen," James says in a loud whisper. Archer is smiling from his part of the table, but he doesn't join in.

"Ha-ha," I say, pronouncing it like a word instead of an actual laugh. "Is this the Luna and the Moons Comedy Show? Have you practiced for this?"

"Every day of our lives," Josh says, his voice dead serious. "So just how old are you, Little Ferris?"

"You can call me Phoebe," I say, just as Luna whispers, "Fifi," from behind her hand.

"Seventeen and three weeks, thank you very much. I'm not a freshman; I'm a senior orientation leader."

"Just like I was!" Luna says. "Adorable. Do you remember your orientation? You looked so tiny and pretty, like a doll. And now you're all grown-up." She pretends to cry into her napkin.

"Yeah, I remember. You terrified all my classmates, ordering them around." This is an exaggeration, but I want to see what Luna will say.

"I was trying to be *inspiring*," Luna says.

"You are, babe," says James. He looks at my sister when he

says it, and manages to sound both teasing and sincere.

"Awww," says Luna. She leans over to kiss him.

I turn to Archer.

"How do you put up with them all the time?" I ask.

"They're not usually so bad," he says. "We spent half the summer in a van together. We're bored with one another. You're new blood."

"We've been listening to Luna talk about you for weeks," Josh says. "Months, maybe."

I look at Luna. "Really?"

"I may have been a little excited about your visit," she says.

Sitting here with the Moons, it's hard not to wonder what it was like for my mother and father. Did Shelter go out for Indian food and laugh like this? My mother had been friends with Carter and Dan since they were teenagers, and they got along well enough with my father to play on several of his solo records after the band broke up. The only other person who might know—besides my father—is Aunt Kit, and I've never asked her. I'm not really sure why. When Luna was a baby and later, after I was born, Aunt Kit went on tour with Shelter to help take care of us. Nearly four years of touring, a couple of months at a time. Luna says she remembers, in flashes: sleeping in a hotel bed, watching the highway out the window of the tour bus, listening to sound check in a neon-lit club. I don't remember it at all.

Once, Kit showed me some photos from the shows when we were visiting her in DC. My mother was in the shower, and Kit laid the photos, loose, out on the table in front of us. The first tour after Luna was born ended on the West Coast, and my mother looked like an afterthought in some tourist's photos, baby Luna strapped to her chest. There was the Space Needle balancing its point up near the clouds, the jagged skyline of the city slick with rain. The ferries and the buildings and the water, all gray. In Aunt Kit's apartment, my mother came out of the bathroom before Luna and I could do much more than glance at the photos, but now those scenes seem like more than photos to me. They seem like memories, even if I wasn't there.

Now, James and Luna and Josh are arguing across the table about which Beatles record is the best (Josh and James think *Revolver*; Luna is pulling for *The White Album*) and I watch them with a smile on my face. I look over at Archer.

"Let It Be," he says, and I'm the only one listening. "It's sad because they're fighting, they're breaking up, but that's also what makes it so great." He smiles. "At least, that's my pick for this week." He looks at me. "We have this argument a lot."

"I can respect your choice," I say. "I might even be convinced. 'I've Got a Feeling,' 'Don't Let Me Down,' 'Let It Be.'" He nods. I'm showing off, but I want him to know I can hold my own with a bunch of music nerds. I want him to know that Luna is right: our mom taught us well.

"So what have you been doing all summer?" Archer asks.

"Working at a coffeehouse, mostly." I'm rolling my fork between my fingers and it clinks against my plate. "My mom dragged me to some galleries in the Finger Lakes. Toronto, too." I try to call the artwork up in my mind. "There was this one artist who kept painting her feet."

"Feet?" Archer raises his eyebrows.

"Yeah. She had pretty feet, I guess, but in the end, they were just feet." I don't know why I'm telling him this. My cheeks feel warm. "But more than anything I've been hanging around Buffalo making lattes."

"I like lattes."

"Lattes are fine. But you make enough of them and they stop seeming like something someone's supposed to drink. They don't seem real." I look down at the tablecloth. There's a runner in the middle, so intricately embroidered that it seems like it should be somewhere safe, where no one can spill chana masala on it. I run my finger over the stitching. "When I think about it, not much has seemed real about this whole summer."

Archer smiles. "I know what you mean," he says. "Right now doesn't feel quite real to me." He looks at me and my pulse kicks a little faster.

Out of the corner of my eye I can see the waiter walking toward us with a pot of chai tea and I look away, toward the waiter, toward the tea. When he puts the pot down, I'm happy to have something to do and I pour a cup even though I know it's too hot. Somehow I stop myself from drinking it right away.

The food is delicious, and I eat every bite of my dinner. Indian food is one of my favorites, probably because my mother started taking Luna and me to the lunch buffet at Star of India when we were tiny. There's a photo my mother keeps in her studio of six-year-old Luna and four-year-old me posing with one of the owners in her orange silk *salwar kameez*. The memory gives me a quick twinge of homesickness. I wonder what my mother is doing—eating cereal alone at our kitchen table? Or going out with her friend Sandra to the Mexican place around the block?

When we leave later the sky is a deep charcoal gray, but the streetlights are glowing so brightly that it doesn't seem dark at all. So far, summer in this city is like being in a terrarium built for creatures who don't need to sleep.

We stand in a loosely formed circle on the sidewalk, and I'm not sure why. Then it becomes clear that this is some kind of band meeting.

"The Tulip Club wants us there at eight thirty tomorrow," James says in a serious, Official Leader voice. It sounds even more official with his British accent. Presumably he's speaking to everyone, but he's looking straight at Luna. She's trying to balance perfectly still on her tiptoes, her arms at her sides like a dancer.

"Okay." She shrugs a little, almost imperceptibly, like she's knocking glitter off her shoulders. "Now it's time for the bet."

"What bet?" I ask. Luna smiles.

"We have a superfan," she says. "He's at every show we play around here."

"Even Jersey," Josh says.

"He may murder us all someday," Archer says, smiling.

"No," says Luna. "He's sweet. Anyway"—she turns to me—"he always wears one of two shirts."

"Maybe he only *has* two shirts," says Josh. His eyes are sparkling.

Luna ignores him and continues. "New Order and Superchunk. So before every show we make a bet, and whoever loses has to bring breakfast to the others in the morning." She looks at Archer. "Do you feel lucky?"

"Ladies first," he says. "You choose."

Luna closes her eyes and stands on the sidewalk, clasping her hands in front of her. She bows her head a little. We all wait.

Her eyes snap open. "Superchunk," she says.

Archer nods. "Okay." He glances at Josh. "That leaves us with New Order."

"Deal," Josh says. Luna and Archer shake on it.

"We'll know early," says James. "He'll probably be there waiting when our van pulls up."

It occurs to me then that I don't know how big their van is, and I picture myself traveling alone on the train to the show. I could end up in Queens somehow, or way up north in Washington Heights! "Uh, guys? Will I fit in the van?"

Luna smiles, shaking her head. "We don't need to fit." She curls her fingers around a lamppost and leans to the side, stretching. Her hair falls in a glossy curtain toward the ground.

"Luna doesn't take the van when we play in the city," Archer says.

Luna is still dangling sideways. "I like to have time alone before the show if I can."

"She doesn't want to help unload," Josh stage-whispers.

"Not true!" Luna pulls herself upright. She's trying to look indignant, but she's smiling.

"As long as you're *on time*," James says to Luna, "it doesn't matter how you get there."

"Now that we have a guest in town," Josh says, "we'll have to put on a kick-ass show."

Archer looks at me. My heart skips and stalls.

"We're always kick-ass," Luna says. She takes James's hand

and swings it back and forth. Both of them are smiling so wide they look like the "After" picture on a commercial for a dating site. *Have you met your soul mate? Try RidiculouslyCuteCouples.com! You'll be so happy, your friends and family will want to punch you, or puke!*

"'Heartbeat,'" Josh sings in his best Buddy Holly voice, "'why do you miss when my baby kisses me?'"

Luna and James start to dance on the sidewalk, managing to look as if there were a choreographer standing somewhere outside of our sight, directing them. This is when Archer leans close to my ear and whispers what I didn't even know I was waiting for him to say. He quotes part of my lyric right back to me—the one I texted him earlier in Luna's apartment. "'Sometimes happy is an accident,'" he says, "'and we forget not to give up on it.'" His voice is low, and when I look around, no one else is noticing us. It's like we're alone.

"That line's been in my head all day," he says, "and it's not even set to music." He smiles. "Yet."

I shake my head, but I'm smiling. This is another secret: that Archer and I are friends, or something. I don't even know what we are. We've been texting since I saw him in February, but I haven't told Luna. Somehow I know she won't like it.

"All right, Fifi," Luna says. "Let's go home." She's hand in hand with James, but she grabs my hand too, and starts to pull me toward her apartment. I turn back toward Archer, who's standing next to Josh, smiling at me.

I lift my hand, palm flat, in something like a wave. I smile back.

"See you around?" I ask. But when I say it, it doesn't really sound like a question. It sounds like I'm sure.

thirteen

BACK IN THE APARTMENT, Luna sits in a gray flannel armchair in a tank top and shorts, her legs over the side of the chair. Her hair is pulled into a messy topknot and she has already washed off all her makeup. She's flipping through her copy of *Rolling Stone*. I'm lying on the couch with my head on the pillow she gave me, looking up at the cracks running like rivers and tributaries through the ceiling plaster. The fan near the window drifts from side to side, pushing hot air around.

James is in the shower and I can hear the water running, plus little bits of him singing "Nowhere Man" from time to time.

"What's new at home?" Luna asks.

I think about it a moment. "I'm pretty sure Mom's sculptures are getting spinier."

"What do you mean?"

"Like, pointier." I try to make the universal gesture for *pointy* by stabbing my index finger into the palm of my other hand. "More dangerous."

"That could be bad for business," Luna says. "Some rich guy could lose an eye."

I shrug. "I'm sure that's the least of Mom's concerns."

When she was gone on tour, I tracked Luna through her Instagram account, those little squares of softly lit scenes I would never see in real life. Here was Luna drinking beer on a boat off Cape Cod with the water rippling behind her, one sundress strap falling off her shoulder and her mouth open, midlaugh. Here was Luna holding her sandals in her hand on a beach in Maine, stepping through the sand in her bare feet. Here was Luna, smiling in the window of their band van, a blue Plymouth Voyager from sometime last decade. Here was Luna, inscrutable but always happy.

I caught my mother looking at the pictures once, late at night when she thought I was asleep. I came down the back stairs to get a glass of water before bed, and she was on her laptop on the couch, bathed in silvery light. She had headphones over her ears so she didn't hear me, and since the kitchen lights were off, she didn't see me in her peripheral vision either. I watched her watch Luna for a minute, and wondered if she were listening to Luna's music too, streaming from the Moons' website, maybe, or her own iTunes.

Here in Luna's living room, I can hear people laughing down on the sidewalk, each group getting louder and then quieter again as they pass by.

"You could have called more," I say.

Luna looks at me. "I did call."

Three times in three months, I want to tell her. *Always when you knew Mom would be teaching her summer class.* But I just nod.

She tosses the magazine on the coffee table next to my mother's sculpture. "We text all the time."

"But that's not the same as actually talking," I say right away, without even thinking about it. Because it isn't. You can be so careful what you say when you're texting, and the other person might never know what you're thinking. You can be whoever you want to be.

She shrugs. "I think it's fine." She pulls lip balm out of her pocket and runs it over her lips.

"Are you sure this is what you want?" I say. She looks at me.

"What?" she asks.

"To give up school," I say. "To be famous."

"We're not famous yet," Luna says.

"But you're trying to be."

She shrugs. "Everyone wants to be famous. I'll worry about it when we get there." She picks her phone up off the table and stares at the screen for a second, frowning.

"Dad's living in Brooklyn now, you know." She looks at me, waiting for a reaction. "He got an apartment near the studio."

I take a quick breath, surprised she brought him up. "Have you . . . seen him?" I'm trying to test the waters here, before I tell her that I want to.

"No," she says, and then adds, "Of course not."

"Right. Where is he?"

"Williamsburg, I think." She scoffs. "Trying to pretend he's twenty-five."

I only know the Brooklyn I've seen so far with Luna, so I don't really know what she means about Williamsburg. But I don't want to ask straight out. "So what are *you* trying to pretend?" I say instead.

"What?"

"If every neighborhood means something, what does Brooklyn Heights mean?"

Luna thinks for a second, furrowing her brow. "Babies, I guess. The sidewalks are clogged with strollers." She shakes her head. "That's not me, though. I'm not Mom."

Except in all the ways you are, I think.

"You could try giving Mom a break," I mutter.

"What?" Luna says, but I know she heard me. Then, "Why?"

"Because you can't be mad at both of them at once," I say. "Right?"

Luna gets up then and steps onto the rug in front of me. She sets a folded sheet on my stomach.

"Sorry it's so hot," she says. "You might still want some kind of cover. I hate sleeping in just the air."

She drops her hand to the top of my head and lets it rest there for just a moment. I think of the little girl in the airport who tried to touch her skirt and the way Luna turned her full attention to the girl for a moment, and then walked away. Here in the living room, Luna takes her hand back and walks to her bedroom. She shuts the door.

I unfold the sheet and flip it out over my legs in one quick motion. It's an old sheet from our linen closet in Buffalo, one with tiny blue flowers scattered over a white background. I lift the hem to my nose to see if it smells like home, but it doesn't. It smells like dust and someone else's detergent.

Luna's copy of *Rolling Stone* is just out of my reach, so I roll closer to it and stretch out my fingers. Beyoncé is on the cover, and at first glance, no one I'm related to seems to be anywhere within. It's a Ferris-free issue, and I'm glad of that. It's only a matter of time before Luna and the Moons end up in there, and it wouldn't be her first time.

Luna first made it into *Rolling Stone* a few months after she was born, in a four-inch square photo with my parents, taken by Aunt Kit. The clipping was cut out and tacked to a bulletin board in our kitchen for most of my childhood, and I know there's a whole box of copies of that issue in our attic. In the picture, my mother holds Luna half-wrapped in a dark blue blanket, Luna's skinny arms and starfish hands free. She's sitting next to my father on a gray velvet sofa in their old West Village loft, one of his arms slung over my mother's shoulder. They look tired but happy. The headline reads, *Their Little Moon.*

This was five years after Kurt Cobain and Courtney Love had Frances Bean, when it seemed like the new cool thing was for rock stars to have babies. It was three years after Kurt, the world's most famous rock-star dad, shot himself. I suppose my family's story isn't so bad, compared to that. My parents just broke up: their marriage, their band. Other than that, everyone survived.

Now I want to text Archer—actually, I want to talk to him— but I'm not sure what to say. Here's the thing: Archer knows the girl who sends lyrics by text message, some other version of me. I'm not sure I can even be that girl in real life. But I'm going to try.

I'm nothing but a shadow, nothing but a silhouette. I lose all my certainty the farther away I get.

I wait a moment, and then send another. *I don't even know what that means.*

His reply comes a few seconds later: *Sometimes that's okay.*

I fall asleep with a smile on my face.

fourteen

MEG
OCTOBER 1995

IT WAS PAST MIDNIGHT WHEN Kieran came in. I was in the bedroom with a spool of twenty-six-gauge copper wire glowing like spun fire in my lap. I'd been trying to make a tree, an oak, a plan for a larger sculpture I wanted to make someday. If I ever had the time.

Kieran sat down on the bed next to me and kissed my forehead. He smelled like a distillery.

He leaned back on the pillows. I formed another copper branch with my hands, looking at him. "Hello, gorgeous," he said. "I'm sorry I'm so late."

"And that you're drunk?" I said, but I tried to sound playful. The metal was warm between my fingers, and I bent it, curved it, all without looking down.

Kieran nodded, smiling. He fell heavily on his elbow.

"Yeah, I'm a little drunk," he said.

This was the third night this week he'd been out with industry people. Guys from the label tonight, a couple of editors from *Rolling Stone* on Friday, and last Wednesday, two-thirds of the band we'd tour with that fall. I swallowed a sigh and looked down at my metal tree. I imagined it so much larger, as big as a real tree, maybe, two stories tall. If I could figure out how to use a blowtorch, and how to cut copper pipe.

"Hey," Kieran said. "Are you mad?"

I shook my head, but I didn't look up. I wasn't mad, not exactly, but I had thought he'd be home hours ago.

"I was with Carter and Dan," he said, his voice smooth around the edges, slow as syrup. He slid his hand up my thigh. "I missed you the whole time."

"Really," I said.

It wasn't that I was jealous. I knew the way girls got around him, their eyes widening, leaning into his airspace like they were crossing a border. But he wouldn't cheat on me. The truth was right there in the lyrics he wrote, the ones that were too sweet and sentimental for Shelter. Kieran liked to love. And the one he loved was me.

And, anyway, if he even thought about cheating, Carter and Dan would beat him within an inch of his life.

"You said you'd be home early tonight," I said. "It was just a party. Why couldn't you just tell them you had to go home?"

"Because I *couldn't*. We have to be a part of this world, Meg. Or at least I do." There was a sheen of anger on his voice, but it faded. "I told the label guys you weren't feeling well," he said.

"That's not true."

"Well," he said, but he didn't finish his sentence. He slipped his watch off his wrist and laid it on the bedside table. "We wanted you there, but you always want to stay home."

I could remember when Kieran had asked me to start a band with him. "We would be so good together," he said to me. I told him I wouldn't leave Carter and Dan, my friends since I was sixteen. "You'll have to be good with me and Carter and Dan at the same time," I said. "I can be that," he'd said. And he had been, ever since.

"Listen," Kieran said. "When we're on tour you say you wish we were at home. Now we're home, and this is our job when we're here. Making connections, keeping things solid with the people at the label." His voice was low, but there was an edge to it. "I don't know what else you expect me to do."

I looked up at him, and his face softened. "I'm sorry you're upset," he said.

"It's okay." I tried to smile.

He leaned forward and kissed me then, soft and slow, and when we parted he lay down on his back.

There was something I wanted to tell him, but when I looked down his eyes were closed. I watched him breathing, his chest rising and falling, and by the time I looked away I couldn't even remember what I was going to say.

fifteen

"HEY, SLEEPYHEAD."

Luna's voice pokes through my dream and for a moment, I'm fifteen again, sleeping past my alarm, and we're going to be late for school. That happened all the time when Luna was at St. Clare's with me. I'd pull myself out of bed at the last minute, brush my teeth and my hair, and eat a granola bar in the car while she drove. Luna, on the other hand, woke as soon as the sun poked through her curtains, showered, and usually had time to do her eyeliner, even.

She leans over me, throwing a shadow with the curtain of her hair.

"Seriously, Fee," she says. "Let's get moving!"

"No," I mumble, and pull the sheet over my head. I keep my eyes open, though, and the tiny blue flowers look like dark stars sprinkled over a white sky.

"Okay," she says, her voice a little farther away. There's a clattering sound, then metal scraping metal. Dishes, maybe? Pots and pans? I sit up, pulling the sheet tight around my knees. From my spot on the couch, I can see Luna in the kitchen, holding a skillet in one hand.

"Just trying to prove that I use the stove." She points with her free hand. "Sit down at the table. There's no breakfast in bed served at Chez Luna."

I move over there, but under protest, with the sheet still wound around me. Luna fusses in the cupboards and I hear butter sizzle in the pan.

When she brings me the plate, her expression is triumphant.

"Maple toast!" she says. Our mother used to make this for us when we were little. It's just wheat bread toasted in a skillet with butter and cinnamon, then drizzled with maple syrup.

"Real syrup," she says. "James tried to buy that fake stuff and I said no way." She wags her finger. "I think it cost at least a quarter of our grocery bill, though. It's expensive."

"And this has been another episode of 'Things You Don't Know When Your Mom's Buying Your Groceries,'" I say.

"Right," she says. "You want some yogurt and granola too?" She's already back in the kitchen, rummaging through the fridge.

"Sure," I say.

When Luna brings it over, the yogurt is in a delicate bowl with pink flowers. I recognize the bowl; in fact, I thought it was still in the cupboard at our house back in Buffalo.

"How did you get these?" I ask.

Luna sits down, squeaking her chair across the floor. "Mom sent them," she says.

"When?"

"About a month ago." She's looking at the bowl, not at me. "It was nice of her."

It's like some kind of code that I can't figure out how to break, my mother's sending of objects. What exactly are they supposed to mean?

That copy of *The Catcher in the Rye* that Luna picked up yesterday is on the table, pushed up next to the wall. I slide it over and open to the title page. *Happy birthday—1976—to Michael*, it says on the yellowing page opposite. *We come into the world alone. We go away the same. I'm glad that some days of our lives were spent together.* The inscription at the bottom reads, *Much love, Jackie.* The ink is ballpoint-pen blue, and the cursive is careful and small. I wonder where Jackie and Michael are now, and how the book made its way out into that box on the wall. I wonder how many days they got to spend together.

Catcher makes me think of Tessa, who wrote her AP Lit thesis paper on the carousel.

"There's the thing itself," she told me last spring, trying to explain her idea. We were in physics lab, and I was trying to measure the velocity of a spring-powered toy car. It kept falling off the table and Tessa wasn't helping.

"These horses that just go around and around in circles and never get anywhere at all," she said. "And then there's Holden, who has been looking for some kind of realness and sincerity through the whole book, looking at his sister on the carousel, feeling so happy, finally. He can't ride it, right?" She leaned forward. "Because he's not really a kid. But his sister can, and he can watch and feel her happiness, so it becomes his own." Tessa stopped and looked at me.

I held the car, spring wound tight, in one hand. She smiled. "Plus his sister's name is Phoebe."

If Tessa were dropped down in New York today, I know the carousel is the first place she'd go. She's obsessed. We had plans to come together to visit Luna, maybe after Christmas or next spring, whenever Luna was in town, but it doesn't look like that's going to happen anymore.

Still, Michael and Jackie's copy of *Catcher* seems like a good-luck charm. I study the creases in the dark red cover, crisscrossing like a map of roads in a mostly empty space, and then I put it in my bag next to my copy of *SPIN*. It fits in the pocket perfectly, no space left to spare.

sixteen

LUNA AND I SPEND THE day going to her favorite places, some of which I saw on my last visit when she was at Columbia, and some of which are new. It's a little dizzying, if I think about it. Last year she was a freshman in college and now she's, what? A musician? A girl in a band? Some kind of grown-up, anyway.

We sit at a tiny table in Bryant Park for an hour, just like we did last year. We sip what I have to admit are pretty decent iced mochas out of plastic cups with long red straws. We go inside the big library there at Forty-Second Street to say hello to the old and worn stuffed animals that inspired the Winnie-the-Pooh books. They sit together in a glass case, their black eyes shiny. When we come out, Luna makes sure we both give one of the stone lions a pat on its head.

For lunch we go to a perfect Japanese restaurant the size of a living room and eat cucumber-and-avocado rolls, edamame beans in their bright green, salty shells, and miso soup with porcelain spoons. We sit on the stairs at the Met for a while with a hundred other people and then use the membership my mom bought Luna to go inside and see the Egyptian tomb in its light-filled room. Before we leave we peek in to see Degas's dancers, which Luna knows I love.

We used to come to New York together when I was small, in those years where my mother and father were actually trying to coparent. I don't remember it, but Luna told me there was a time when we'd go together, all four of us, to an Ethiopian restaurant my parents liked on the Upper West Side. I was five, Luna seven. She remembered eating with her fingers, and with spongy pieces of bread that would come in a big basket at the center of the table. She said my parents actually seemed to get along then, that they'd talk about people they used to know and smile in each other's presence. I can't remember anything like that.

My first memories of my parents together come later, when my mother would drop us off at my father's old place on Ninety-Sixth Street, thrusting a bag full of snacks and books at him. After kissing us good-bye, she'd just sort of disappear behind us on the sidewalk. A few times, some random passing music nerd would recognize both my parents at the same time—maybe seeing them in context helped—and his head would explode. This ended with my father signing an autograph and my mother stalking off toward the train station.

My father would take our hands and lead us slowly up the stairs to his apartment, which was open and bright and full of records.

He'd play us songs all afternoon. I don't remember him telling us much about the bands, but it's possible that some of the information I attribute to my mother having taught us actually came from him. And later, he'd take us for hot chocolate or milk shakes, depending on the season, and French fries or pancakes for dinner. My mother would pick us up outside his apartment before bedtime. I remember him standing there waving as we walked away down the sidewalk, and the fact that he'd stay there until we reached the corner.

I asked Luna once what she thought had changed between them, why they'd gone from getting along to barely speaking.

"Mom was probably just pissed that she had to do everything by herself," Luna said. "I'm sure it was really freaking hard."

Maybe she's right. In the beginning, maybe my mother saw the divorce and Shelter's breakup as her own choice. She wanted a different kind of life for us. But as the years ticked on and she ended up doing almost everything alone, she must have gotten angry. I can see that. It drives me crazy, though, that I'm the only one in my family who doesn't remember a time when things were good.

Luna and I ride the 5 train back to Brooklyn, then walk for blocks down Court Street to BookCourt, her favorite bookstore. I buy a black Moleskine notebook and a tiny, beautiful paperback copy of Shakespeare's *Twelfth Night*. We read it last year and it's my favorite play, with its gender-bending heroine and tales of mistaken identity and improbable love. At six, when the sun is still hot but a little lower in the sky, and guys in suits start to come out of the subway stations, blinking like animals who live underground, we walk back to Brooklyn Heights. We eat falafel at a Lebanese place off Court

Street with deep orange walls stenciled with a lattice pattern.

"Is this what you do, all day every day?" I ask.

Luna shrugs. "I read," she says. "I do yoga." She folds her hands into prayer position. "We played a couple of shows with this singer who told me she never eats before she performs." She spears a falafel with her fork. "She says it makes her nauseous. Better to do it on an empty stomach, is her theory." Luna tilts her head to the side, considering this. "I would never make it. I need the calories if I'm going to do all that jumping around."

I dip a piece of pita bread into the bowl of hummus in the middle of our table. "Makes sense to me."

Luna smiles. "That girl's band is called Poncho, so she's not showing good judgment in other areas either."

I hear my phone chime in my bag just then, but Luna doesn't notice. I slip it out and look at the screen, hiding it under the table like girls at school do, with varying degrees of success, when they're trying to keep the teachers from seeing. It's a text from Archer: *Ready for another real-life sighting of each other tonight?*

What's the collective noun for *butterflies*? Because a whole flock—flutter?—of them have taken up residence in my belly.

We get back to the apartment after dinner, and a half hour later I'm kneeling on the floor in front of my suitcase, trying to decide what to wear. I've been taking out dresses and shirts and laying them out on the couch, but nothing seems right.

"Just go into my closet," Luna says. "Borrow something of mine." I'm frowning, looking at the couch, where it seems like a bunch of mildly fashionable teenage girls have been Raptured off to heaven, leaving their outfits behind.

"Seriously," Luna says. "You're making a mess." She scoops up a dress and a couple of shirts and drops them back into my open suitcase. She turns and crosses the living room.

I follow her into her room. She opens her tiny closet as wide as she can and sits down on the edge of her bed.

"I've already picked out my dress." She motions toward a black one laid across her pillow. "Take whatever you want."

"Okay," I say. "I'll avoid black." Luna laughs.

The problem with that, I quickly see, is that almost everything in her closet *is* black.

"You'd think you were some kind of Goth girl," I say, pulling a few hangers out. "A Victorian widow in mourning."

"Rock and roll," Luna says. "It looks good onstage, especially with pale skin like mine." She looks at me. "Ours."

"Right," I say. "That's why I don't want to match you."

The space is crammed with clothes, so it takes me a while to flip through. Eventually, somewhere in the middle, I find a sleeveless, jewel-toned green dress with a drawstring waist. I pull it out.

"This," I say, holding it up.

"Okay," says Luna.

I strip off my own shirt and shorts and pull the dress over my head. It flutters down over my hips. When I look at myself reflected headless in the vanity mirror I can see that the dress fits perfectly. I tie a bow in the drawstring and sit down on the stool.

Behind me, Luna swoops my hair into an off-center ponytail at the nape of my neck. She pulls too tightly and I wince.

"Ouch," I say.

"Beauty hurts," says Luna. "Now turn around and close your eyes."

"Why?"

"I'll do your makeup," she says. "Just like old times."

Luna used to practice on me when we were younger. I was just ten in the beginning, when she'd sneak handfuls of our mother's makeup from the bathroom and spread it out over the quilt on her bed. Later, when she had her own makeup, and even later, when I did, I'd sit in Luna's bedroom in front of my grandmother's beautiful old vanity table from the forties, the wood lacquered to a high gloss, lipstick spread like candy on a glass tray.

Now I can feel the eyeliner pencil just above my lashes, a soft, gentle pressure.

"I'm trusting you not to poke my eyes out," I say.

"I'll do my best." She dabs shadow on my eyelids, and then runs a soft brush over my cheekbones. It's hard to keep my eyes closed, but I do it because I don't want to see until she's finished.

"There," she says finally.

I open my eyes, and in the big oval mirror, I study my face. I've always seen myself as a less-pretty version of Luna. We both have my mother's ivory skin and blue-green eyes, but her cheekbones are higher, her face less round. Her hair is thick and wavy in a well-behaved way, while mine is wavy-curly-can't-decide-what-it-wants-to-do. But I like the way I look now, glowy and shimmery and sure of something.

"It's a teen-movie makeover miracle!" I say.

"Whatever," Luna says, shaking her head, her smile small and true. "You always look pretty."

She unzips her jeans, peels them off, and throws them on the bed, then pulls her black dress over her head. She stands there for a minute, spine completely straight, looking into the mirror.

"Do you think I look a little fat?" she says. She pulls her dress tight at the waist.

This is weird, because Luna has never been one of those girls who worries about her weight. My sister has always been thin. She's always been beautiful.

"Um, no," I say. "Not even a little."

She stands there, looking, for a few seconds more, and then she sits down at the dresser to do her own makeup. I wander away into the living room.

There's a light breeze coming through one of the windows and I sit on the floor below it and open her guitar case. I hold it the way I've seen my sister do a hundred times: left hand on the neck, fingers between the frets, pressing down on the strings. The other hand down low on the body of the guitar. I strum so lightly almost no sound comes out, just a tinny collection of notes that don't quite form a chord. It seems like this should be natural for me, should be encoded in my genes or sprinkled like calcium in my bones, but it isn't. I put the guitar down and go sit on the couch.

When Luna comes out of her room, her eyes are outlined in smudged black liner and her hair is loose over her shoulders. She's wearing that black dress, which turns out to be a tank dress made of jersey and panels of raw silk. I don't say it, but she looks like our mother on the cover of *SPIN*, without the '90s makeup. She looks like our mother—but she won't ever be her, I realize, because if Luna manages to make it as far as our mother did, she won't give it up.

seventeen

MEG
MAY 1995

AT A BOUTIQUE IN SoHo, Kit was holding an emerald-green dress in front of her.

"Too Kermit?" she said. She furrowed her brow.

"That's an entirely different shade from Kermit," I said. "Don't you know your Muppets?" I stopped to consider the dress.

"Well," Kit said, "I've heard that it's not easy being green, so I'm feeling a little cautious."

"I like green," I said. "I wore it at Lollapalooza last year, remember? One of only three dresses I wore."

"Well, if Meg Ferris wears it, then I guess it's fine." Kit was smiling but I saw a spark of something like hurt in her eyes. "If you're *famous*," she said, hanging the dress back on the rack, "you can wear whatever you want."

"Come on, Kit," I said. I pulled a charcoal-gray sweater off the rack. It was so light and gauzy it felt like a spiderweb in my hand.

"I'm just saying." Kit shrugged. "I wouldn't mind being famous myself."

"You practically are. You were in the *Post* just last week."

"My *sleeve* was," she said. "My elbow. Next to your whole body."

"Well," I said, "you have a very famous elbow."

At the counter, the two salesgirls were leaning together, whispering. I scanned my eyes quickly past them, the way I always did when I wanted to pretend I didn't notice people noticing me.

She held up her bent arm. "I do," she said. "It's a nice elbow, isn't it?"

I nodded. "Very." I put the sweater back. "Anyway, sometimes it's shitty," I said.

"What is?" Kit asked. "My elbow?"

I laughed, but it felt off-kilter. "This," I said. "Fame?" It came out like a question. "I was Meg Foster, art student and girl in a band, and then I met Kieran and became Meg Ferris, famous person and Girl in a Band."

"When is it shitty?" Kit asked, not because she didn't believe me, but because she wanted to know.

When everything is different, I wanted to say. *When the person you love changes and you're not even sure how.* That would make a decent song, actually, I thought, but I'd need a metaphor. Something about disguises, or doppelgängers. Or alien body snatchers, though I didn't think the people at the label would like it if I suggested a sci-fi concept album. But I didn't tell Kit any of this, because I didn't know how to say it out loud. Words failed me sometimes when I was not speaking through a song.

"It's just . . . not always as great as it seems. That's all."

I didn't want to talk about this anymore. I turned toward the salesgirls and shone my smile their way. The dark-haired one came out from behind the counter.

"I have to ask you," she said. "Are you Meg Ferris?"

I nodded and tilted my head just slightly to the side like I was posing for a photograph.

"Oh my god!" She turned to the blond girl still at the register, leaning on the counter. "Alexis, I told you!"

She lowered her voice to a whisper. "We can totally hook you up," she said. "Our boss loves it when famous people shop here. Would you let us take your picture for the wall?"

I looked behind her. The photos were Polaroids, so they were small, but still I could see one of Courtney in her red lipstick, hamming it up as usual, and another of Kim Gordon, looking cool and intriguingly beautiful. I could do something like that.

"Of course," I said. I grabbed Kit's wrist in mine and pulled her up to stand next to me. "This is my sister, Kit."

The girl nodded and smiled. "I'm Leah," she said. "Pick out something to wear." She gestured toward the racks. "You can totally keep it."

I took that gray sweater and a short black dress off the rack and Kit went back for the not-Kermit. She shimmied out of her jeans right in the middle of the store, so I did the same.

We stood and we posed.

Voilà—fame, of a sort, for my sister, and some new free

threads to go with it.

Sometimes this is so hard, and sometimes it's so easy. Maybe Kit is right. Maybe there's something to be said for being known, even if you feel like you're only playing a part.

"Thanks," Leah said, fanning the undeveloped photo in the air. "Our boss will go nuts."

She set the photo down on the counter and I stood there with Kit, my shoulder pressed to hers. We leaned on the counter, elbows on the glass, waiting to see ourselves appear.

eighteen

AT EIGHT, WE'RE OUTSIDE Borough Hall under a sky that's orange around its edges and still blue gray overhead. The buildings are radiating heat, so we duck inside, happy to find shelter. Luna carries her guitar and a black bag over her shoulder and I have my bag too, the copies of *SPIN* and *Catcher* tucked inside.

There's a long hallway to the train platform and it's even more humid underground. Luna's dress taps against my thighs as I walk.

"Why don't you let them take your guitar?" I ask. I touch the tiled wall without meaning to, and it feels smooth and glassy.

"It's a ritual," she says. "Whenever I take the train to a show. Just me and my guitar." She swings the case a little and its tip points toward the ceiling. "Or in this case me, my guitar, and my little sister."

When the 4 train comes, the air inside is so cool and

fluorescently lit it feels like a refrigerator. The car we choose is only half-full, and we find a row of empty seats across from the door. I drop my purse down on the seat between us, and Luna holds her guitar case between her knees. The train's doors slide closed with a whoosh of air.

"Where are we going, anyway?"

"It's called the Tulip Club. Weird name, but everyone plays there. It's in the Village." She pulls out her lip gloss and takes the cap off one-handed, holding the neck of the guitar case with her other one. "We can walk across Washington Square on the way."

Borough Hall is the first Brooklyn stop, so the next one is in Manhattan, on the other side of the river. The train lurches and screeches. Outside the window opposite us is only darkness, but all I can see is my reflection, not Luna's. I close my eyes so I don't have to stare at myself, and don't open them again until we're at Brooklyn Bridge and we get off to switch to the local.

As Luna said, the club is a few blocks from Washington Square Park, and we walk through the park even though it seems like it's a little out of our way to do that. I think about what James said about being on time, and I know we won't be. Luna stops for a moment at the fountain in the center and we lean together against the stone wall, watching the water and the people around it. There's a bulldog playing in the water, putting his big face right in the spray in the center. He's soaked and ridiculous, his open mouth a big grin. Seeing him makes me miss Dusty.

I look at Luna—to tell her that, I guess—but she's staring up at the sky. She sees me looking at her and drops her head.

"I feel nauseous," she says.

"That's probably normal," I say. "You're about to perform."

Luna shakes her head. She crosses her arms and hugs herself, and when she looks at me, her eyes are shiny with tears. I actually gasp a little when I see it. Luna doesn't cry. She never, ever cries.

"Hey!" I say. "You're okay. Don't worry! It makes sense that you'd be nervous."

Luna tips her head backward, trying to blink the tears away.

"I don't get nervous," she says.

I don't know what to say. I put my hand on hers and squeeze it. We sit for another minute or two, staring ahead. The bulldog has left the fountain, and now there's just the water, spraying up in a constant stream.

"All right." She takes a deep breath. "Let's do this."

She stands and I follow her, knocking my knee against her guitar case. We walk out of the park and down West Fourth, then stop at a pink neon sign that reads TULIP CLUB. There's a pointy blossom at the sign's end, and when I turn away from it, the shape lingers on my retinas.

There's a standing chalkboard on the sidewalk near the curb. TONIGHT, it reads, LUNA AND THE MOONS. The door is open and by the door there's a guy reading one of the newspapers handed out for free on the street. He looks at us with only a little bit of interest.

"We're the band," Luna says. He nods. I wait for him to ask what I play (possible answers, considering my musical talent or lack thereof: Tambourine? Triangle?), but he doesn't ask for any more information. Luna walks past him and I follow as if I know what I'm doing.

It's dim inside, mostly empty, lit by big gold bulbs on the stage and the hazy neon of beer signs scattered around the walls. Speakers somewhere—everywhere—are playing the Stones' "Beast of Burden" and I feel like I've walked right into the song.

The boys have already loaded in and are setting up their gear on the stage. Luna heads toward them, but I hang back by the bar for a moment. I'm not really sure what I'm supposed to do while I'm waiting. I perch on the edge of a stool and watch Luna hop up on the stage and kiss James on the mouth.

"You're late," he says—I can read his lips from here—but he's smiling. She's facing the back of the stage and I can't hear her reply. Someone switches the Stones off and the last note echoes around the now-quiet room.

Archer stands with his bass slung over his shoulder, adjusting the tuning pegs. I can hear the low notes, halfway between music and plain old vibration, like the rumble of a far-off train. He sees me and waves.

I wave back, but I feel a little silly about it. First of all, I'm not that far from him, and second, how are you supposed to wave and not look like Miss America, the Queen of England, or someone's crazy aunt? Archer motions to me to come up there, and for a moment, I wait. It would be easier to stay here, where nothing bad can happen. Where I'm safe. But then I see his perfect smile and the way he's walked to the edge of the stage to help me, and safety doesn't seem like the most attractive option. So I grab his hand and hop up.

Onstage, a galaxy of lights shine above me, and I tip my face toward them.

"Want to sing backup?" Archer asks.

"I don't think that would be a good idea," I say. I want to do something besides stand there, so I touch the microphone stand gently, running my finger down the metal. Luna opens her case and plugs a cord into her guitar, kneeling down near the edge of the stage. I see now that the soles of her sandals are silver. They don't even look dirty.

"Didn't inherit the voice, huh?" Archer is looking at me, but he's still moving his fingers, tuning his bass.

"No," I say. "I'm not sure what I inherited from our mom. Her neuroses, maybe?"

I face the room and look out. I can't see the windows to the street, just the neon signs above them. The few people inside the club now are just shadows moving around.

"You can't see much from up here." I look back at Archer.

"No," he says. "I like it better that way."

"Really?"

He shrugs. "I get nervous if I have to make eye contact. So this way I don't have to spend the whole show staring intently at the Sam Adams sign." He points at the blue neon sign in the back.

"Does Luna get nervous?" I ask. I'm still surprised at what happened at the fountain.

"No," Archer says. "I'm pretty sure she doesn't know what that word means."

My mother didn't either, as far as I can tell from the few live performances I've seen. My favorite is from a little theater in Austin,

Texas, one of the only times Shelter played that state. There's a guy at the front of the crowd in a cowboy hat and my mother sings right to him, sitting down on the stage and dangling her legs over the edge. Eventually she puts out her hand and helps him up next to her, still sitting. He's twenty, maybe, dark-haired and dark-eyed, and he looks embarrassed and completely happy at the same time. My mother looks totally comfortable, her guitar slung behind her back, charming the pants off everyone in the audience. By the end of the song, she's wearing the guy's hat.

Now, Archer leans forward, squinting into the lights. I can see a guy standing in the middle of the nearly empty floor, wearing a dark T-shirt with blue lettering. I can't read it from up here, but Archer knows what it says.

"Superchunk." He smiles and shakes his head. "Looks like I'm buying breakfast."

A half hour later, I'm standing next to the bar holding seltzer in a slim cylindrical glass and trying to look busy. The room is full now. I know that Luna and the guys must have friends here, but they've been busy setting up and no one has introduced me. I wish again for Tessa. I'd have someone to talk to, and I know she'd love this.

A Shins song blaring across the giant speakers ends and the room stays quiet. The sound of the crowd talking, which had been up to now a low buzz underneath the music, hushes too. You can't really make a dramatic entrance in a place without a curtain or a backstage, but when James offers his hand and Luna takes it, stepping up on the stage right at the front where her microphone is, where her guitar waits in its purple stand, something changes in the room. People start to pay attention; they turn toward her like they're sunflowers and she's the sun.

"Hello, New York," Luna says. Applause starts like rain might, slow and light at first and then heavy, heavier.

"It's so lovely to see you again," she says. "I see you every day, but this is different, isn't it?" Her voice sounds lower, smokier, but to me she still sounds like Luna.

"This is nicer," she continues, both of her hands cradling the microphone in its stand. "And now we're going to spend a little time together. So settle in. I'm going to tell you some stories."

She steps backward and picks up her guitar then, and as soon as she puts the strap over her shoulder and looks back toward Josh, he hits the first beat. James's guitar and Archer's bass and Luna's own guitar follow.

When she starts singing, I'm surprised as I always am that something so pretty and delicate and strong at the same time can come out of my sister. Not because I don't expect her to be capable of it, but because she's mine in some way. She belongs to me, and still, she can do *that*.

Luna's voice is like something golden, like light, filling the space from the scratched wooden floor to the ceiling rafters. Some songs are solid things, but movable, like sand, and others are completely liquid. Each one fills the room in layers. I've listened to the Moons' first record a hundred times, but the songs sound different here, live—ephemeral but resonant and part of this room, all the way to its corners. Right now, Luna belongs not to me but to everyone, and if I didn't know the music would eventually stop, that Luna and Archer and Josh and James would stop it, I'd be afraid of losing her to it forever.

She's not a person up there; she's a force.

More than anything, I wish I could be up there too. I want to make something that's fleeting and impermanent but so real and deep and loud.

Archer has a small smile on his face the entire time, and he looks toward me half a dozen times during the set. I know what it's like up there—I know the lights are blinding—but still, it feels like he can see me. It feels like he's looking right at me.

nineteen

An hour after their set started, I'm standing with my back to the bar, waiting for Luna and the boys to pack up their gear. I didn't want to hover, so I left the area next to the stage. I'm still holding that glass of seltzer— ice melted, bubbles flat—trying to look like I belong. The Pixies play in the background while I look down and riffle through my bag just for something to do.

When I look up, Archer is walking my way. When he gets there he leans toward me, puts his mouth near my ear. It feels electric. I swear my blood starts to spin in my veins.

"Do you want to come outside for a few minutes?" he says. He's nearly shouting, but still I can barely hear him. I look in Luna's direction but she's still up by the stage, talking with James and a girl I don't know, a tall redhead in a short purple skirt. Luna must be telling a story. I can tell because her hands are fluttering like birds.

I nod and say, "Sure," but I don't try to shout. I'm sure he can only see my lips move, but he turns and walks toward the door anyway. He says something to the bouncer as we pass, and then holds the door open for me.

Out on the street it's cooler. We lean against the building so we don't get in the way of all the people on the sidewalk, walking somewhere. It's like a parade, this nighttime foot traffic. Back home, you could walk all day on the sidewalks but you'd never run into more than a few people at a time.

It's a lot quieter outside the club, and I wait for Archer to say something. I can hear the next band doing a quick sound check, the thumping of a bass drum and a few jangly guitar chords.

"My ears always ring after we play a show," Archer says, "even with the earplugs." He puts his hands over his ears and shakes his head lightly. "Sometimes it's hard to wait around if someone's playing afterward. Rude to leave, though." He smiles a little with his mouth closed, and I find myself looking at his lips. I snap my gaze back up to his eyes.

"Quite the rock star," I say. "Worrying about rudeness and all."

"I'm just the bass player," he says. "James is the bad boy."

I'm surprised to hear him say this. "Really?" I shift my weight to my other hip and feel the scratchy wall of the building through my dress.

"No," he says, laughing. "He's a Boy Scout. Or whatever the British equivalent of a Boy Scout is. A Lad Scout, maybe." He looks across the street, where a girl in sky-high heels totters out a restaurant's front door. "If we had a bad boy, I guess it would be Josh, just because he doesn't give a shit." He shrugs. "Drummers."

I nod knowingly. "My mother always warned me about them."

"She did?" He opens his eyes a little wider when he says this, and I notice how long his lashes are.

I smile. "It sounds like something she'd say."

"She'd know, I guess." He shifts his weight to his shoulder and leans against the wall. "Did she say anything about bassists?"

I think of my mother's no-musicians rule again, glowing like another neon sign somewhere at the back of my mind. "I'm sure she'd extend the warning to players of any and all instruments. Clarinet, for example."

"Tuba," Archer says.

"Xylophone." I shudder for effect.

I'm ready to keep going, but he takes a pack of cigarettes out of his pocket.

"Do you mind?" he asks. I'm a little bummed, actually, that he's a smoker, but out here on the street, it doesn't seem to matter. I shake my head.

He flicks a silver lighter and touches the flame to his cigarette. His lips purse. He takes a drag and the end burns orange in a perfect bright circle.

For a moment, I feel so utterly unlike myself that I wish there were a mirror here so I could check. Am I me? Maybe it's because I'm wearing Luna's clothes: I've soaked in a little of her energy along with the dress. But a part of me I don't really recognize wants to touch Archer, the inside of his wrist, maybe, or his earlobe. It occurs to me that I might be a weirdo.

He exhales and the smoke floats toward the sky. "What was it like, having parents like them?"

"Oh, fantastic, for sure." I touch the sole of one foot to the wall behind me. I don't want to talk about my parents right now.

He looks at me without saying anything. He's waiting for me to answer for real.

"I didn't really have my dad around much at all," I say. "I'm sure Luna's told you that."

"Well, yeah, I know she's mad at him. He wasn't there when you were small?"

"We moved to Buffalo when I was two. He stayed here." I look across the street instead of at Archer, at the windows in the building opposite us. People must live up there behind those square windows, must sleep in those rooms while people out on the street stay awake.

"We used to see him a few times a year," I say, "but that just tapered off when I got to high school. I haven't seen him since I was fourteen and a half."

"That half really makes a difference," Archer says, teasing, but his smile is kind.

I shrug and look sideways at him. "I think it's okay to count things by halves," I say. "I'm seventeen now. Two and a half years sounds better than three."

He nods, looking out toward the street. "I can see that."

Of course, it's more like two and three-quarters years if you do the math.

We're both quiet for a moment, but it doesn't feel uncomfortable. It feels perfect with the street lamps shining down on the light-struck sidewalk, the building still faintly warm from the day's heat.

It feels like I could stay here all night.

"Luna's always so sure about everything," I say.

Archer taps his ash over the pavement. "Do you think so?"

"Don't you?"

He shrugs and slides down the wall to sit at the edge of the sidewalk, so I do too.

"I listened to Shelter all the time in high school," Archer says. "And when I met Luna, I couldn't believe that Meg and Kieran were her parents. But she sure doesn't make it easy. To be fans, I mean. Of them."

"She doesn't make much easy." I push a loose lock of hair behind my ear.

A tiny brown dog prances by, attached by her leash to a human, but down here, I really only see the dog. She sniffs Archer's shoes and then his fingers when he holds them out to her. I touch her silky ear.

Archer puts the cigarette to his lips again, breathes in. When he exhales, he blows the cloud of smoke away from me. I watch it spiral into the air and disappear.

"I'm not going to offer you one," he says, looking back at me. His smile is the slightest bit crooked.

"It's okay," I say. "I don't smoke."

"I figured. But I was afraid you might say yes anyway. Luna would be pissed." He smiles. "We're taking a big enough risk not telling her we've been talking."

"Texting," I say.

"Right."

I shake my head and look away from him. "Everyone's scared of Luna," I say.

"That's not it," he says. "I like it. That we have a secret." He pauses. "That *we're* a secret."

He's looking at me, and I feel myself blush. But before I can say anything Archer speaks again.

"Go easy on Luna," he says. "You're her little sister. I know how it is. I have a little sister too."

He never mentioned her while we were texting over the summer. Neither of us mentioned our families, which was probably part of what I liked about talking to him.

"What's her name?" I ask.

"Calista," he says. "And if some guy offered her a cigarette, I'd kick his ass." He smiles. "She's only fifteen, though." He holds up the cigarette and looks at it. The tip still glows orange and smoke curls in a thin line toward the sky. "It's stupid anyway. Sometimes I think I smoke only so I have something to do with my hands."

"And your mouth." I say this without thinking, and as soon as I realize how it sounds I feel my cheeks warm. But Archer just laughs.

"Right," he says, and stands up. "Who knows what I'd do if not for these?" He crushes the cigarette on the building behind him and tosses it into the can next to the club's door.

"Coming in?" he says. "I should make sure to see some of the next band."

"Such good manners," I say.

"I try." He spreads his hands out in front of him, palms up.

I look at him. *I know you,* I want to say, but that wouldn't be true. I don't, not really. Not yet.

"I'll be in soon. I have to call my mom." I pause. "That sounds dumb."

Archer laughs. "If my mom were Meg Ferris, I'd call her all the time." He opens the door wide and disappears inside. I feel like someone shut a stereo off in the middle of a really good song.

I walk out to a lamppost near the street and dial my mother's number. She answers on the second ring.

"Phoebe," she says, instead of hello. She exhales my name like a breath, as if she's relieved. As if she's been waiting for me to call since the moment I left.

"Hi." It's strange to hear her voice through the tinny speaker. Just yesterday we were standing out in the backyard, making jokes about kidnappers. "Where are you?"

"Out back."

I picture her sitting where she always does, with a book in her lap, in a beat-up lawn chair crooked in the grass under the crab apple tree. The tree she decides she'll cut down every fall, when the red pebbles of fruit clog the lawnmower and get smashed on the driveway, drawing bees, who get drunk on the juice. But she reconsiders every spring when the tree bursts into foamy pink bloom.

I look at the sky, which is charcoal gray, what passes for dark in New York. Tonight it's cloud-covered and luminescent, glowing right back at the city lights on the ground.

"Is it dark there?" I ask.

She laughs. "Fee, we're in the same state."

"I know that. I just wondered . . ." I stop. I don't even know what I wondered. There's a flyer taped to the lamppost. LOST, it reads, in wide black type, and at first I think it's about a pet. MY

YOUTH, MY HEART. Where there should be a picture of a cat or a dog is a picture of a woman with long brown hair. IF YOU FIND IT, PLEASE CALL JOELLE.

Huh. It must be some kind of art project.

"Where are you?" my mother asks. I look around, as if I've forgotten. Three girls are walking down the sidewalk across the street with their arms linked together, laughing.

"Outside a bar," I say. "In the Village."

She sighs. "Just what every mother of a seventeen-year-old wants to hear. Where exactly?"

"West Fourth. A few blocks from Washington Square." I glance back at the sign over the door, glowing soft and pink and neon above me. "The Tulip Club."

I try to picture her here, standing on the sidewalk outside or watching near the stage like I was when Luna was singing. I can't quite make her fit, even in my imagination.

"Luna and the guys just finished playing," I say.

I hear Dusty in the background, one quick bark like a warning.

"How were they?" my mother asks.

"They were great, Mom." A girl wearing a long striped maxi dress walks by and smiles down at me, her skirt fluttering around her ankles. I smile back. I could be anyone, any New York girl, standing on this sidewalk. I might not be Phoebe Ferris at all. "Really. Luna's voice sounds amazing."

"I'm sure it does," my mother says, and I can almost see her nodding as she says it. "Luna is better than I ever was."

Then why are you so mad about it? I want to ask. But instead I say, "You were great too." I say it like I mean it—I do mean it—but I'm not sure how to make her believe it. And I don't know why that seems so important to me in the first place.

My mother continues. "So Luna's still doing this?"

"Doing what?"

"Leaving." It's a weird way to put it, I think, because in a lot of ways, Luna has already left.

"She's still planning to go on tour, if that's what you mean. In September." The door opens and I look toward it, thinking it might be my sister. But it's a blond girl with a tattoo of a butterfly covering her collarbone, its ink lit up in navy and dark pink under the club's neon sign. "I haven't had a chance to talk to her about it much yet."

My mother stays quiet, and I press the phone closer to my ear. I want to hear the sounds of our backyard during a summer night, the cicadas' rattling hum, the mockingbird that tries on a dozen other birds' calls. But I can't hear anything, not even my mother's breathing, over the noise from the club and the street.

"Their show was pretty packed," I say. "They're . . . a little bit famous."

"The best kind," she says, but I don't really know what she means. I'm about to ask her when I hear a voice in the background, deeper than my mother's and farther away. I can't make out what he's saying.

"Jake's there?" I ask. Jake is my mother's best friend from the university, the one who named her Goddess of the Forge. He makes huge sculptures out of old things that have something to do with the sea. He'll stack a bunch of rowboats, or stretch sailcloth in strips across a whole park. He was in Germany a month ago installing a big, open-weave box made of oars in a town square.

I'm glad he's there with her. It means she's not alone.

"Just got here. He brought me Chinese from May Jen," my mother says. "He thinks I'll wither away without you." I hear the rustling of something—a paper bag, or the long red sleeve of a pair of chopsticks. "He might be right. It's so quiet in the house."

"I *am* known to be an exceedingly loud person," I say.

"Cacophonous." She's joking, but she sounds sad.

Both of us are silent. I want to ask her about my father, or Shelter, what it was like when she was the one onstage. I thought it might be easier to talk about things like this on the phone, where we could avoid looking each other in the eyes, but it's still not easy to speak to my mother now, here on the street, even though she can't see me and I can't see her. It's like I don't know where to start: the beginning or the end. And where do I fit in?

"I'll let you go," I say, though I know my mother hates that phrase. *If you want to get off the phone, just say so,* she always says. In fact, I say it *because* she hates that phase, because I want her to tell me to not to say it. But she doesn't notice.

"Okay, Fee," she says. "I love you and I'll talk to you soon. Give Luna my love." Then she hangs up—I hear the tiny click, the empty air—before I can say good-bye.

twenty

MEG
FEBRUARY 1995

KIERAN TOOK MY HAND AND I stepped out of the limo. We were
blocking traffic and I heard a taxi's horn behind us, a long thin peal.
I looked up toward the slate-blue sky and saw three pigeons flutter
down from the building above us.

Dan slammed the door and Kit took my other arm. Behind
me, the limo drove away to circle the block until we were done. It
made me a little dizzy to think about it, but that might have been
because the five of us had split four bottles of champagne on the
way over there. We'd had a ball. I normally didn't drink, but I felt
so happy-nervous—my lungs were fluttery and my heart thumped
off-beat—that I'd had three big glasses. Now, when I stepped into
the foyer, I realized that I might be drunk.

"Shit," I said. I wobbled on my heels and leaned hard on Kieran's arm.

"Babe," he said, "are you okay?"

I laughed. "Um, I think so." The world was tilted, I swore, because I couldn't stay straight up. Thank god my parents weren't flying in until dinner. Somehow I convinced them that the courtroom would be too small for all of us. I loved them—I really did—but it was too much pressure.

Kieran steadied me and slipped his hand onto the small of my back.

"If I didn't know better," he said, "I'd say you were drunk."

"But you *do* know better," I said. I tried to tilt my head coyly, but it just made me lose my balance. I held on to Kieran's arm. Who had invented high heels? *A man,* Kit always said, but hers were even higher than mine that day.

Kieran smiled. He looked so handsome in his dark gray suit that it almost hurt to look at him.

"Of course. But why don't you take this anyway?" He handed me a mint from his pocket. "Just so we don't give the judge the wrong idea."

"She's not drinking whiskey," Kit said. She fixed her hat, dark blue felt with netting and a bird. It was vintage, ridiculous and fabulous at the same time. "If anything," Kit said, "she'll smell like a fancy French lady."

Kieran smiled and shrugged. "Okay," he said.

Dan shook his head. "I think fancy French ladies smell like perfume," he said. "Not booze."

I ate the mint.

Carter was reading the signs in the hallway. "This way," he said. Kit grabbed his hand and tried to get him to skip, but he couldn't quite do it, so she let go and twirled in the middle of the hallway, laughing. Carter just looked at her, eyes wide-open like he was bird-watching or something. Kit was wearing a blue-gray skirt suit from the sixties, found, as usual, in one of her favorite vintage shops in the East Village.

"Thirty years ago, I bet some girl wore this to *her* sister's wedding," she told me when she bought it. "And now I'll wear it to yours." Kit was always doing this: seeing stories in her clothes. But Carter saw only Kit. He'd had a crush on her for years. Too bad for poor, sweet Carter that Kit's own crushes were on women.

Now, I saw a bathroom.

"I have to pee," I said. Kit turned around, curtsied to the guys.

"That's my cue!" she said. She took my hand and pulled me in.

Inside, it was all gray tile and wide mirrors, and this didn't do much for my vertigo.

"The world is spinning," I said. We stared at each other in the mirror, smiling.

"Not the world," Kit said. "Just the bathroom."

"Same effect," I said. I locked the stall door behind me. I sat for a moment and the world settled, coming to a stop beyond the door. For the first time all day, I felt a wave of panic rise up through my belly. What was I doing here? I'd wanted to marry Kieran since I accidentally became Meg Ferris, when a reporter for *Rolling Stone* got my name wrong. He thought we were already married, heard Ferris when I said Foster. He read my mind, or my wishes. And we let everyone think it was true.

But on my wedding day, this felt like some kind of time travel, because if we were already married, why were we there? And if we weren't married, then why did everyone think we were?

Drunk thoughts, I knew. But I still had that flickering feeling in my chest, and I couldn't quite catch my breath.

I got up and flushed. When I came out of the stall Kit was reapplying her eyeliner. I looked at her in the mirror. She looked at me too, sideways, without moving anything but her eyes.

"What if this is a mistake?" I said. Kit turned toward me.

"Margaret Maeve Foster," she said. "Are you kidding me?"

"Katherine Deirdre Foster," I said. "I am not." I shifted my weight to my other foot and held on to the sink for balance. "Everyone already thinks I'm Meg Ferris anyway."

She put her hands on my shoulders, still holding an eyeliner in the right one.

"Meg, you love him. He loves you. He can be a jerk and you can be a weirdo, but I've never doubted the love."

"Geez, Kit," I said. "You're really good at sentimental talk. Don't let anyone ever tell you otherwise."

She rolled her eyes, but she was smiling. She put her eyeliner back into her tiny purse.

"Everything is going to be fine," she said. "Breathe."

So I did.

Kit took my arm and we walked out the door and down the hallway. In the room where we would get married, Kieran stood next to the judge, a tall man who looked like a soap opera star. In a good way.

"Wow," Kit whispered. "I would hop on that train if I were more into men." I laughed then, and so did she, and I could feel my shoulders relax.

Kieran smiled at me and without even trying, I smiled back.

135

Kit and I started to march up the middle of the floor. Carter and Dan came up on either side of us and we all linked arms.

"Aren't you going to ask who gives the bride away?" Dan asked.

The judge blinked at him. "It's not required," he said. There was a woman sitting at a desk next to where he was standing, and she giggled.

"Well," Dan said, "it's all three of us."

"Noted," said the judge. "You have to sign some paperwork first, anyway."

"It's not like anyone needs to *give* her away," Kit said, punching Dan in the arm. "She's a free woman."

We finally reached Kieran, and he pulled me close and kissed me.

"This is out of order," Carter—the romantic—said. "Kiss the bride is later. After you're married."

"Sorry about that," said Kieran. "Couldn't help myself."

"Right," said the judge, but finally he was smiling a little. "Let's get down to business."

I didn't even care that we were making a spectacle of ourselves because now, standing next to this boy I loved, I felt really, truly okay.

twenty-one

WHEN I COME IN OFF the street, Luna is sitting on a stool near the front, holding a brown beer bottle between her knees. The second band has finished. I completely missed their set while I was talking to Archer and then my mom.

"Hey, Fee," Luna says. Her eyes are a little wider than they were earlier, her mouth softer. Her makeup is smudged, but on her it looks smoky. She tucks her hair behind her ear. "What did you think?"

"I thought it was amazing," I say. "Really." Luna smiles.

"Do you want a beer?" Josh asks. He's standing behind Luna, leaning on the bar. Even though I try not to, I look at Luna, and she is already looking at me. She's waiting for me to answer.

"Just a seltzer with lemon," I say. I figure that way it will at least look like I have an actual drink in my hands.

I sit down next to Luna, on a stool covered in beat-up brown vinyl. James is standing so close to my sister that their shoulders are touching. They fit together like a two-piece puzzle that snaps in the center.

"I talked to Mom," I tell Luna. "She wanted to hear about the show. I told her it was great."

A flicker of a smile crosses Luna's face, but that's as far as it goes.

"I'd kill to have seen your mom in action," Josh says. "Bonus points if it included your dad."

"Even *we've* never seen that in real life," I say, "and we're their daughters."

Luna looks at me and blinks. Then she opens her mouth and says something totally surprising. "You know, I used to pretend that my real father was someone else, someone from one of the other bands they used to play with. Paul Westerberg, I hoped. Maybe Dave Grohl. Hopefully not Perry Farrell." She wrinkles her nose.

"Just you?" I notice that I'm leaning toward her, and I pull myself back so I don't fall off the stool. The boys are watching Luna, rapt, like they're sighting something rare, a bird, or a comet streaking its way across the sky. Josh's mouth is open just the tiniest bit, and Archer's eyebrows are furrowed. I know then that she must never talk about our parents to them.

Luna nods, smiling. "Sorry, Fee. You have the same dimple as Kieran, in the exact same spot." She pokes her finger gently in the spot next to my mouth. "You're marked. Pure Ferris."

"I guess." The bartender puts my glass down on the bar, where the bubbles glow in the dim light shining above us.

"Anyway," she says, the spell over, "it doesn't matter. He's my father. I'm stuck with him." Luna runs her fingers through her hair, separating the waves. "But it's not like I have to see him."

There's an uncomfortable silence.

"Does Meg ever see any of those people anymore?" Josh asks. "Carter and Dan, I mean?" This must be the first time he's asked her this. I wonder how that could be.

"Once in a while." Her voice is flat.

I look at Luna to see if she'll say anything else, but she's staring toward the windows.

When we were little and got mad at our mother, Luna and I would sometimes tell her that we were leaving her, that we were going to New York to live with our father. At that point, we saw him only a few times a year, and most of those times weren't in Manhattan. He'd come to Buffalo and stay in the apartment over our garage, before our mother built her sculpture studio out there. He'd eat breakfast with us and then take us to the zoo or down to the marina. And then he'd go back to New York and a few weeks or a month might pass before we would hear from him again. When he was on tour we'd get postcards, sometimes, with postmarks from California and Vancouver or all the way from Berlin or Madrid. He didn't say much in his notes. He might mention the other bands he played shows with, or what he had to eat the night before. Luna would stare at his scratchy, scrawled handwriting for hours, as if she was trying to decipher something more than the words themselves. Then she'd never look at them again. I think I still have them in a drawer somewhere.

When we got mad and told my mother we were leaving, she

never said go ahead and go. But she never said what was true, either: that he didn't want us, that he never really had.

"You were the *real* mistake," Luna said to me once. I was thirteen. She was fifteen, with a pixie cut and cat-black eyeliner winging out from her lashes like a sixties starlet. Her eyes looked enormous against her close-cropped hair. It might have been one of the first times I realized she was beautiful.

"What?" My voice was small and a little panicked. Luna sat down on the bed next to me.

"Well, me, I was an accident. That can happen to anyone. But then they stayed together, and they actually *tried* to have you." She shook her head, as if she couldn't believe it. "That was really, really dumb of them." She shrugged her shoulders. "No offense." She got up then and she walked away.

Now Luna stands up and puts her bottle down hard on the bar. I can hear the leftover beer slosh around and fizz. It's still half-full.

"Time to go," she says. "So tired." She leans over to kiss James. "See you at home, babe?"

"Right," he says, and Luna turns to Archer and Josh.

"Don't forget to pay up the bet."

"We'll make good," says Josh.

On the way out, Luna gets stopped by the singer of the other band, a tiny Korean girl with spiky hair and a red-painted mouth, and they hug and start talking. The boys end up loading out right in front of us. Josh borrowed the other band's drums for the show so it doesn't take them long: guitar, bass, two amps, a couple of suitcases full of pedals and cables. I sit on a stool while Luna talks and every time Archer passes, he smiles at me.

When she's finally done, we push out through the door and the street looks the way I left it, only quieter and cooler. Luna leads me in the opposite direction of the park.

"Let's get on at Astor Place," she says. We turn the corner by the subway stop. The van is parked here near a corner, and Archer stands leaning against the back of it, another cigarette held between his fingers. I take a step toward him without meaning to do it, as if he has his own gravity, and in that moment, I wonder: Have I been acting like I'm a mistake? Like something that shouldn't have happened? Maybe it's time to make things happen instead.

I know right then that I'll kiss Archer before this week is over.

"Smoking kills," I say, because I don't know what else to offer beyond a public service announcement. I hear a train screeching to a stop in the station below.

"He already knows," says Luna. She grabs my hand. "Come on. We can make it if we go right now."

Archer says something behind us, but I can't really hear him because we're running. By the time his voice reaches us, we're already halfway down the stairs.

twenty-two

LUNA AND I RIDE THE train without speaking for five stops. I know this because I'm counting, trying to learn their names and figure out where the different lines meet up. Luna doesn't notice; she leans her head back on the wall behind her and closes her eyes. Her face looks pale in the fluorescent light. When the train stops at Spring Street, Luna lifts her head and turns toward me.

"Mom said you and Tessa haven't been speaking."

"You talked to Mom?" I yelp the words in surprise.

"She told me a couple of months ago, in a text." Luna makes a phone-and-texting motion with her fingers and her thumb. "You never brought it up, and I forgot to ask you about it. I'm a bad sister."

"It's fine." I look at the top latch of her guitar case, silver and perfectly square. I have the urge to reach out and flick it open, but I don't.

"What happened?"

I take a breath. "Just a mess with a boy."

"The best kind."

I hear in those words the echo of what my mother said earlier, about being a little bit famous. They have the same vocabulary, my mother and sister.

"Not really," I say. "There's this guy she's had a crush on for a long time. She took him to prom, and I went with his friend." I stop. Something flashes in the dark train tunnel like lightning past the window. "He kissed me."

"Her crush or the friend?"

"Her crush." My heart beats faster at the memory of it. "But he's . . . my crush too. I didn't know she liked him when we met. It was . . . kind of a mix-up. He likes me too." The train screeches to a halt and the doors open. I can feel the hot, wet underground air flow into the train car.

"Rough," Luna says. I see that we're at Brooklyn Bridge/City Hall, and she stands up. "We have to switch to the 4/5," she says. I follow her out.

We stand on the platform waiting for the next train, Luna leaning on her guitar case, and I start to tell her the story.

When I think about the way it happened, the first thing I remember is the sky. It was wide and black and sprinkled with pixie-dust stars. We were out in the country, and I couldn't believe how visible the stars were, with all the streetlights so far away. There were more than I'd expected, filling in the spaces between the regular constellations I already knew. We'd left prom at midnight and taken our trolley bus to Chelsea's backyard, or what passes for a backyard out there. Thick dark woods edged the open grass behind Chelsea's big white house, and a three-quarters moon hung fat and silver in the sky above them.

When Tessa asked Ben to prom, she convinced me to ask Tyler instead of my friend Tom. I still wasn't sure why I had agreed. I didn't want to be anywhere near Tyler or Ben at all, and I certainly didn't want to be around Tessa and Ben together. I think I was afraid Tessa knew somehow, and maybe I said yes because I thought it might throw her off the trail. The trail of what, I didn't know. I had given up on being with Ben before I'd even tried.

I was standing at the bonfire trying to look like I was really concentrating on roasting my marshmallow (gelatin-free ones just for me—Chelsea thought of everything) when Tessa appeared at my side. She handed me a plastic cup of something pink. Wine from a box, I figured.

"Chelsea says there's a clearing in the woods." She pointed toward the trees. "It's not far, and she says the stars are really beautiful there."

"They're beautiful here," I said, flicking my wrist and my marshmallow stick toward the sky. "And it's warm and relatively bug-free." Tessa formed her mouth into an elaborate frown, but I shook my head. "Why don't you and Ben just go?" I said. I knew Tessa wanted Ben to kiss her, and I didn't want to be there for it. What was I supposed to do? Count all those stupid stars? Kiss Tyler? Not likely. I'd already have to deal forever with the fact that Tyler was holding on to my waist in my junior prom pictures. He was absolutely good-looking but just so obviously obnoxious. Something about his smile and his pretty white teeth.

I took a big swallow of the wine.

Tessa stood in front of me and shook her head, then her whole body: head, shoulders, hips. Her hair, set in big, perfect waves, rippled over her shoulders. She'd already had two glasses of wine, easy.

"All of us!" she said. Ben and Tyler walked up behind her then and I looked at first Tyler, then Ben. His smile was sweet and half-formed. It looked like some kind of apology.

"We're going!" Tyler said to me, leaning forward emphatically. "You and Ben go ahead."

Tyler took Tessa's hand and held it up like she was a prize-fighter at the end of a victorious match. She giggled. "Tessa and I will bring some provisions," he said, and dragged her away, still laughing.

There were cupcakes on a table in Chelsea's family room, but I was pretty sure by "provisions" Tyler meant "bottles of liquor," which could potentially only make this whole situation worse. Still, I drank the rest of my wine right then, chucking the cup in the garbage. I ate the stupid marshmallow. I even decided to bring the whole bag with me.

"Okay," Ben said. He looked at me and his smile went past halfway. I tried to make my own mouth smile, but I'm not sure how successful I was.

"Sweet tooth?" Ben asked, as we walked toward the edge of the yard. There was a soccer ball near some bushes, and he kicked it back onto the grass.

"They're vegetarian," I said, as if that was an answer. I lifted the bag up to show him. "I mean, Chelsea bought them for me. I don't eat gelatin because it's made of boiled cow hooves. Or something."

"Gross," he said.

"Yeah," I said. "So I don't want the rest of those creeps eating them while we're gone."

Ben laughed. "I can see that. And in a pinch, we can throw them at attacking bears."

In the fairy tales my mother used to read to Luna and me, everything important happened in the woods. I could see why, now, because when we stepped inside, something changed. It was dark beyond the trees, even with the big white moon shining overhead. We followed a soft path strewn with pine needles for a few minutes. I had taken off my heels hours ago and was wearing silver flip-flops beneath my dress, so some of the needles flipped up between my feet and the soles. I stumbled over a root peeking out of the ground like a horseshoe, and caught myself just before I fell into the dirt.

"Whoa," Ben said. He took my hand to steady me, and I let him hold it. That was the first thing I did wrong: I didn't let go.

When we found the clearing I felt dizzy. The stars swirled gently overhead, like they were at a bottom of a lake and I was running my hand through the water.

"The sky is spinning," I said. "I'm not sure I like it." I let go of Ben's hand and lay down on the grass, feeling its prickly dampness beneath my shoulders. The stars settled. I closed my eyes for a moment and when I opened them, Ben was lying flat beside me. I turned my face toward him, my cheek touching the grass. He was already looking at me.

"I asked Tyler to give us some time if he could find a way," Ben said.

"What?" I sat up and turned toward him. The sky shifted above me; the stars went back to swirling. Ben stayed flat on the ground. "Who is *us*?" I said.

"You and me," he said. He was fidgeting, rubbing the palm of his hand with his thumb. "I know this isn't the right way to tell you this. I just feel like everything got messed up." He sat up and turned to face me. "I wanted *you* to ask me to prom. Not Tessa."

"What?" I said. It came out in a whisper-shout.

"Stop saying that," Ben said. His smile was lopsided, hopeful. "You can't tell me that you're surprised."

Was I? I wasn't sure. "It doesn't matter what I think," I said. "Tessa has liked you forever."

"Forever?"

"Since the fall, at least." I pulled up a handful of grass and let it fall. "She used to see you with your lacrosse stick, riding around on your bike." I brushed grass off my dress's satin skirt. "She almost ran you over once." I had a flash of almost—almost—wishing she had, so I wouldn't be here in the middle of the woods with a guy I liked who also happened to be my best friend's prom date.

Ben's smile faded. "So she had first dibs?"

"Basically," I said. There was a feeling in my chest like the fizz in a soda bottle.

"That doesn't seem fair." His voice was calm, rational. "I don't get a say in it?"

"I don't think so." I pulled out a marshmallow and held it between my fingers, squishing it. I wished for a bear so I could throw it. So I could stop talking. I considered putting a whole hand-ful into my mouth. "It doesn't work like that."

We sat for a minute without saying anything. I strained my ears to listen for Tessa and Tyler, but I could hear only the soft chirpy noise of a cricket, and the far-off laughter of the rest of our friends around the bonfire.

Ben pulled his legs up to his chest. "I'm going to lodge a com-plaint with the front office," he said.

"Be my guest." My heart was pounding. I would have wel-comed the liquor bottles at this point. I figured if things were fuzzier, maybe this would be easier.

Ben looked toward the trees. "All I can think about is that I want to kiss you." He was speaking very softly.

I shook my head, but I kept looking at him. "That's because you're drunk."

"Maybe," he said, turning toward me. He put one palm flat on the ground to steady himself. "But I'm going to do it."

He moved closer, putting his other hand on my cheek and tilt-ing his head a little. He looked at me like he was really seeing me. Or maybe I was finally letting him see. I couldn't move. Then his lips were on mine, soft and sure, and I kissed him back before I could stop myself. I could hear something, a low humming sound, my heart maybe, or the stars burning through the sky above us. All at once, I felt like I couldn't breathe.

I pulled away, putting my palms flat on the dewy grass.

"We can't do this." I said it and at first it seemed like a ques-tion, and then like some kind of prayer to the sky or the stars or whatever might save me from screwing over my best friend.

I heard Tessa's voice in the woods then, as if I had summoned her with my mind. She and Tyler were laughing as they came from the path into the clearing, and they both ran to us, collapsing onto their knees on the ground, clinking a bottle of Grey Goose against a pebble in the grass.

"Provisions!" Tessa said. She looked so happy I felt better for a moment. Tessa didn't know what had just happened. I could still save this.

Ben kept trying to catch my eye as Tyler poured vodka I wouldn't drink into a red Solo cup. I looked at Tyler, made myself smile, but I wouldn't look at Ben. I pretended I was cold and we went back to the bonfire after twenty minutes or so. I left the marshmallows in the clearing, and I still feel bad for littering. Maybe some nice vegan bunnies found them and had a sugar party.

I didn't tell Tessa, not that night, not any of the next—but she found out anyway. Because just like in the fairy tales, a kiss can change things: fix them or break them right open.

We're on the train under the river when I finish the story. Luna sits with her perfect posture, swaying a little as the train does. She's quiet.

"How do you feel about him?" she asks.

"It doesn't matter." I run my fingers across my forehead as if I have a headache, but I don't.

Luna's voice is kind. "Of course it does."

I loosen my muscles and let the train move me back and forth as if I'm in the water.

"I liked him," I say. "I did. But now none of that seems worth it." I look at Luna. "Tessa and I have been best friends for twelve years. And I'm so pissed at him for telling her what happened."

"Yeah, but he must just really like you," Luna says. "You can't blame him for giving it a shot. He probably thought she'd get over it. Maybe he just didn't want to lie."

Lie, like I did. But can I blame him? Yes, I guess. I do. But still, when I think about him, I always take a deep breath. I remember the way it felt to kiss him. I remember how sweet he was.

"And anyway," Luna says, "Tessa's mad at you for kissing him? Or she's mad that you didn't tell her?"

I think about it a moment. "Both, probably, but mostly that I didn't tell."

Luna draws her knees to her chest, balancing the soles of her sandals on the very edge of the seat. Her toenails are painted navy blue.

"Do you want to know what I think?" She looks at me.

"Of course."

"Okay. For one, it's easier for her to be mad at you," Luna says. "Rather than at Ben. Or herself." She touches her hand to her heart. "Plus, I bet she got sick of you getting extra attention."

"Attention for what?"

"For being a Fabulous Ferris." Luna laughs. "You know, having our parents as parents, among other things." She rakes her fingers through her hair. "You know how people are back home. Starved for celebrity. Even the B-list kind." She looks toward the window, and I can see that we're stopping at Borough Hall. "Why do you think Rachel Johnson spread those rumors about me when I was a junior?"

I don't remember much about that, or maybe I didn't know much about it in the first place. I was only fourteen. I remember Luna in tears on our Metro ride home, and her furious, fierce posture in the hallway the next day when she passed Rachel's locker. They had been friends once. Then they weren't anymore.

Luna gets up and I follow her off the train. The station is bright enough that it could be any time of day. It feels like such a long time since I've slept, but right now, I can't imagine falling asleep.

"It's not about Mom and Dad with you, though," I say. "You have your own thing."

She holds her guitar up as we go through the turnstile. "First of all, yes, it is. Everyone wants to talk about Shelter." In the hallway, I can hear her footsteps echoing louder than my own. "Second, you have your own thing too. It's just not music."

"Let me know when you figure out what it is." I take a deep breath. Suddenly, my limbs feel so heavy I'm not sure how I'm going to make it through the walk back to Luna's apartment. "Tessa did tell me to have fun with my famous family," I say.

"Ha! See? Exactly what I said."

"I don't know. I think she's just upset."

We come out of the station then onto the same street we left hours before. Cars still move slowly down Court. Luna steps up to the curb and starts crossing just as the light turns.

"I like Tessa," she says. "I always have. And this situation sucks. But I think you have to let yourself off the hook a little. You're not dating the guy. You said you were sorry. She'll come around." She glances at me. "And you're the one who gave up a guy you really liked."

I smile. "He *was* pretty great."

Most of the storefronts have their metal grates rolled down, and the street looks different. Lonely. We turn at Schermerhorn and the bookstore is lit up but empty.

My mind makes a connect-the-dots further back in our conversation. "You think Dad is B-list?" I say.

Luna considers this. "I don't know. He did pretty well with the critics on the last one. Pitchfork says he's a 'musician's musician.'" She makes the air quotes. "I think that means he's good but a lot of people don't notice."

"Some people do, though."

She nods. We pass the wall where the *Catcher* book box had been, and I see that it's gone.

"I'm pretty sure junior prom is supposed to suck," Luna says. "Like, it's a law or something. I went with Rob Markham. Do you remember him?"

I do, a little. He was tall with blond hair, and he wore a dark blue vest that matched Luna's dress, which had a beaded top and a full chiffon skirt. She'd found it in a vintage shop. When she'd put her hair in a bouffant and done her makeup, she looked like a time traveler from the 1950s.

"He put his hand on my ass during the first dance and after that, I spent most of the rest of them in the bathroom with Leah." She smiles. "It's not that I have a problem with guys putting their hands on my ass. But I have to really like them back." She hops down the stairs toward her apartment door, the guitar case still swinging next to her. She puts her key in the lock. "I learned an important lesson, though."

"What?" I follow her through the door into the glow of the foyer.

Luna lowers her voice. "Hiding out by the toilets can be preferable to spending one more minute with an idiot." She turns and starts climbing the stairs.

What was my lesson? I wonder. That you can't trust things that happen when the sky is starlit and you've had too much pink wine? Or maybe it's that secrets aren't permanent, that they break open and spill out before you can stop them. Maybe things would have been different if I'd returned Ben's texts in the days after prom, but I just turned off my phone and tried to pretend it hadn't happened. I imagined stopping those messages somewhere up in the satellites, above the atmosphere, like I should have stopped him from kissing me.

twenty-three

WHEN I WAKE THE NEXT MORNING, it's past ten o'clock and the apartment is full of light. I've stretched my legs out onto the arm of the couch, crossed at the ankle, and my left foot is completely asleep. I sit up slowly and then stand, my whole leg tingling. I hop on one foot, trying to shake life into the other. The living room is empty, and Luna and James's bedroom door is still closed.

When I fell asleep last night, I was thinking about Tessa and Ben, so now that I'm awake my brain is still trying to put that whole story in order. Three weeks after prom, after dark on the last day of exams, Tessa texted me at ten thirty and asked me to meet her at the swings. I knew she must have sneaked out by trellis in order to get out of the house that late, but I didn't have to do that. My mother was at a conference in Toronto.

I didn't bother to change out of my sleep clothes, so I walked down the quiet street in ballet flats and yoga pants. I took Dusty on her leash and she tried to sniff every tree on the way, but I pulled her along. The street lamps threw pale halos of light on the sidewalk, which made the spaces between seem darker.

In the park, Tessa sat on the curved rubber seat of a swing, holding on to the chains with both hands. She wore jeans and a long sweater, and her nail polish was chipped and ballerina pink.

"Hey," I said. "What's up?" I dropped the leash and Dusty snuffled over to the pole of the swing set. "I was already in my pj's. You're keeping me up past my bedtime." I sat down on the closest swing and twisted it so I was facing her, but she kept looking ahead toward the street.

"He told me," she said.

I dug my feet into the sand so I'd stay still on the swing. "Who told you?"

"Who do you think? Ben. I called him."

I felt a chill and wrapped my sweater tighter around my waist. "What did he say?"

"He says he likes you, and that he's sorry." The word sounded harsh in her mouth. "He says he told *you* that at prom, when you guys were in the woods. He says you kissed."

My heart was thumping behind my ribs. "Tessa, I—"

"Don't." She raised one hand like a stop sign. "I get that you're the pretty one—"

"No!"

"—and you're the interesting one." She looked at me then. "But how could you not tell me?"

I let myself twist on the swing again. I had to look away from her. "I thought it would ruin prom for you. He was drunk. He didn't know what he was doing." I said this, but it was a lie. He knew.

"I don't give a shit about Ben. This is about you, Phoebe." She stood up in the sand in front of me. Dusty lifted her head and walked over to Tessa, sniffing her hand. Tessa didn't seem to notice. She didn't move her hand.

"You can't pretend things just happen to you," she said. "You're the one living your life. You're the person."

She looked at me for one second longer and then she turned away. I didn't follow her. I sat on the swing and watched her walk down the street until she was just a tiny figure on the sidewalk somewhere near her house. She could have been anyone.

I sat on the swing for a few minutes more, and then I picked up Dusty's leash and walked back home. The house seemed quiet and empty and though I thought about texting Tessa, or Ben, even, I didn't do it. I didn't do anything. As I tried to fall asleep I went through the Morse code letters in my mind, all those dots and dashes, and thought about the messages I could send by flashlight to Tessa in her window, if I only knew what to say.

I take a shower in Luna's tiny bathroom, and then I come out, hair still wet, and stand in front of the refrigerator. This is the only place in the apartment with any photographs, but it makes up for the lack: the whole front of the freezer door is covered. Here's Luna and my mother and me in Ireland three years ago, standing in front of a sapphire bay. Our hair whips around our shoulders, the exact same shade of dark brown in the sun. Here's Luna going to kindergarten in our old red wagon, with three-year-old me next to her, clutching my stuffed bear, Fuzzy. Here's Luna in her prom dress with Amala and Pilar, hitching up their skirts to show their garters. As far as the pictures show, her prom was perfectly fun: no ass-grabbing Rob

Markham, no hiding in the bathroom. I wonder what I'll remember if I look at the pictures from mine in a few years. Marshmallows and stars, probably.

I open the fridge and take out the carton of vanilla soy milk, then a box of Rice Krispies from the cupboard. I'm about to sit down when I hear Luna's phone chime a text message, and across the room, James's phone does the same. Luna's is right there on the table, and so I lean toward it. Without touching it, I can see that it's from Archer. The screen goes blank before I can read it, and I have a short argument with myself about whether it's ethical to read other people's text messages. Then I stop arguing and click the screen back on.

Going to Madeleine's, it says. *Any requests?*

The bet. Archer's getting breakfast. I Google Madeleine's and see that it's a French bakery down Court Street in Cobble Hill. I could be there in ten minutes.

"You're the one living your life," Tessa told me months ago, standing in front of the swing set. "You're the person. You can't pretend things just happen to you." Here's what I'm wondering: Will things turn out differently if I run straight toward trouble? If I go after the boy instead of floating around, letting him come to me? There is, as they say, only one way to find out.

I put the milk back in the fridge. I find a takeout menu from a burrito place in a clip on the counter and a purple pen in a drawer, and then I write Luna a note in on the back: *You're asleep. I'm awake. Going out for a walk.* I leave the note in the center of the coffee table. When I close the door, I do it as quietly as I can.

twenty-four

OUT HERE, I DON'T HAVE to be Phoebe Ferris, sister of Luna, daughter of Kieran and Meg. I can be just That Girl on the Street in the Blue Dress and Wet Hair. That's what I like about New York. There are so many people that the chances of you seeing anyone you know at any given time are slim. You can disentangle yourself from your story. You can be whoever you want to be.

Except then I open the glass door of the bakery and I have to be Phoebe again, because I see the boy I came to find. Archer is standing in front of the glass counter in his black Chuck Taylors, wearing a dark gray T-shirt and the same jeans as last night, I'm pretty sure.

It takes me a minute to catch his eye because I don't want to scare him, or seem like a baguette-buying weirdo who lurks around French bakeries. When he sees me he looks surprised, a question forming in his eyebrows, and then he smiles. It's like a light goes on in his face.

"Hi," he says.

"Hi." I let myself smile.

He walks toward me, holding a brown paper bag. "You found me," he says.

"I got your text," I say. He looks puzzled. "I mean, the text you sent Luna. I peeked." I point to my eyes then, as if he needs the extra clue. "I'm a text peeker."

"You can peek at my texts anytime," Archer says, smiling.

I feel my cheeks get warm. "Thanks," I say. "Luna and James are still asleep."

"Really?" He glances at his watch. "Well, I'm just here to pay off the bet." He holds up the bag.

I look up toward the counter. "Where's Josh?"

"Oh." He gestures over his shoulder. "He's going straight to Luna's. He's a little slow in the morning. Plus he wants me to buy the pastries." He smiles and pats his front pocket, and I stare at his pants a little until I realize he's tapping his wallet. "Which is fair. I slept on his couch last night. You could pay a hotel bill in chocolate croissants from this place."

He holds the bag open for me and I take one out, half-wrapped in wax paper, a drizzle of dark chocolate on the top. I take a bite. The crust crackles, and the chocolate is smooth and bittersweet.

"This is amazing," I say, chewing, my mouth full of buttery pastry and chocolate. I pretend to swoon, sinking into a wooden chair at a tiny table by the window. "God, can I live here forever?"

"Sure," Archer says. "Well, probably not in this bakery." He sits down in the other chair and takes a bite of his croissant. There's one golden crumb beneath his lower lip and I want to brush it off with my thumb. Somehow I restrain myself. But then I knock my purse over on the table and my lip balm rolls out onto the floor. Which would be fine if I had only one tube, but I have at least four.

Archer bends down to help me gather them. He raises his eyebrows at me under the table.

"Is that all you have in that bag?"

I laugh. "No," I say. "I just always lose them. I buy a lot."

We both sit up and I snap my bag shut so nothing else goes rolling out. I look at Archer.

"So what are you doing this morning?" I ask. My phone chimes then and I look down to see a text message from Luna.

Hey, early riser, it says. *What's going on?* I slip it back in my purse.

"I have to head to my parents' apartment," he says. "My tuning pedal keeps shorting out, and I need to pick up my old one."

"So you don't actually live with Josh?"

"Not officially," Archer says. "I crash on the couch a lot. He lives with three other guys and it's actually kind of gross there. But it's closer to the practice space, so after gigs I always sleep there. Going from Brooklyn all the way to the Upper West Side is no joke." His eyes widen. "Once I fell asleep on the train and ended up in Washington Heights. It was a long ride back down."

"Can I come along for the ride?" I ask. Why not? Except that Luna might kill me for bailing on her. "I feel like I need to get out for a while," I say. "I need an adventure." I feel silly for a moment, as if the subtext here is: *And you, sir, can you provide one?*

But Archer smiles, wide and warm. "Well, I'm not sure that going up to my parents' place is an adventure, but you're welcome to come along."

It would be easier if we could bypass Luna's altogether, but Archer has to drop off the pastries. When we get back to the apartment, Josh is leaning against the front door.

"Hey," Archer says. "Luna and James are still asleep." I stand there silently, not volunteering the information that Luna is, in fact, awake.

"Damn," Josh says. He looks at his wrist, but he's not wearing a watch. "It's like noon."

"Well, no," Archer says. "It's actually ten thirty."

"Right," Josh says. "Whatever."

I unlock the door for Josh and we all step inside for a minute.

"Can you take this up?" Archer asks. He hands him the bag.

"Where are you guys going?" Josh says.

"To get my other tuning pedal," Archer says.

Josh looks at the bag of pastries. "Did you get the kind with the almonds and the chocolate?"

"Yep," Archer says. "But if you want one you have to deliver the rest upstairs."

Josh shrugs. "I guess that's worth four flights." He turns and starts up the stairs.

I type a text to Luna then: *Ran into Archer outside.* Which is sort of true, in that I was *outside* her apartment when I saw him. In a bakery, sure, but who cares? *Taking a subway ride uptown with him to get his tuning pedal. Be back in a bit.*

"Come on," Archer says to me. "Let's get out of here while we still can." He touches his hand to the small of my back, but I'm already moving, over the tiled foyer and past the mail table and up to the heavy wooden door.

When we step out onto the sidewalk, I feel as if we're getting away with something. I look up at Luna's bedroom window expecting to see—what? Her face, maybe, her waving hand. But I see only the curtain fluttering in the breeze.

twenty-five

MEG

SEPTEMBER 1994

I PUT THE RECEIVER BACK in the phone's cradle and rested my hand on the rotary dial.

"How's your dad?" Kieran asked. He was standing at the edge of the kitchen table, holding on to the back of a chair. Our air-conditioning had broken the night before and the old box fan we'd propped in the window hummed behind him, blowing in hot, humid air. It was September, but the heat still wouldn't let up.

"They don't really know yet," I said. I pulled my hair off my neck, twisting it up onto my head. It was damp with sweat. "It was a heart attack, but he's awake. He's talking."

Kieran knelt in front of me and put his hands on my bare knees. "That's good," he said.

"He's going into surgery in the morning." I heard my voice start to waver. "I have to go to Buffalo. Kit's already there."

"Of course you do." Kieran stood up. "Why don't you pack a bag and I'll call the airline?"

I nodded, staring at the smooth and glossy surface of our kitchen table. My dad was a carpenter who did custom work in people's houses: bookshelves and cabinets, sometimes a built-in table or bench. When we'd still lived in Buffalo, he and Kieran had built this table together. It took them a whole weekend, basically, because my father hadn't just done it while Kieran watched. He'd shown Kieran how and let him do most of the work himself.

"Will you come with me?" I asked.

Kieran pulled out a chair and sat down. "Meg," he said, "you know I can't come today. One of us has to be at the VMAs or it'll look like we don't care."

"It's MTV," I said. "I *don't* care." We had gone to the Video Music Awards the year before, and though it was fun to see the spectacle (Madonna with her backup dancers in lingerie, dancing like strippers, for one), I could definitely have lived without going again.

Kieran sighed. "Meg." He held my gaze. "We need them to play our videos."

"Carter and Dan can do it."

"Carter and Dan aren't Ferrises."

"Neither am I." I looked down at the black-and-white tile of our floor.

"You are," he said, tipping my face up toward him. "You know you are. And someday we'll make it official."

"Anyway, they're honoring Kurt." His voice was soft. "You know that." I was surprised to hear him mention this. We hadn't talked about it since we'd agreed to go to the show. After Kurt died in April, Kieran could barely say his name for months.

"That just makes it worse," I said. "Everything's too sad." A memory flashed into my mind then: Kurt and the rest of Nirvana backstage after the Video Music Awards a year before, being interviewed in front of a camera. On Kurt's lap was Frances Bean, eating a cookie and clutching his beer bottle in her tiny hand. When the interviewer walked away, I caught Kurt's eye. He waved, but another interviewer sat down just then, so I didn't go over.

"One of us should be there," Kieran said, talking to himself as much as he was talking to me. I knew he loved Kurt, but at that moment, I wasn't sure if he said this because of our dead friend or because of the cameras that would pan over the audience to see our tears while the memory reel played. "You don't have to worry about it, though. Just go see your dad."

"My dad likes you," I said. "He gave you a label maker." I said this last part quietly, and as the words came out, it sounded a little ridiculous. But it was true.

"Meg, I love your dad. And I love that label maker." He smiled. "Just look at my record cabinet. You can always find the punk or the sixties soul." He squeezed my hand. "I'll be there as soon as I can."

"I wonder what Madonna will do this time," I said. "How can she top last year?"

Kieran smiled widely, happy that I was willing to make a joke.

"Maybe she'll come out naked," he said, smiling. "I promise I'll cover my eyes." He stood up. "I'm going to get you a plane ticket."

I knew I needed to get up and pack, but I sat for a moment, listening to the fan's whirr and then to Kieran on the phone with the airline. He was trying to do the right thing—I knew that—but sitting here at the kitchen table, it felt wrong.

twenty-six

IT'S A LONG RIDE ON the train, and when we come up from the station the sky is sun-bleached and strewn with wispy clouds. Archer's parents live up near Columbia, where his dad teaches economics. I remember the neighborhood from being there with Luna. We even pass the diner where I first met James.

We walk a few blocks past the train until Archer stops in front of a tall gray limestone building. The doorman sees him and steps back to open the gold-framed glass door, beyond which I can see the dim lobby. He's wearing a light coat even in the heat, but he's smiling, his eyes crinkling at the corners.

"Good morning, Archer," he says, and then looks at me.

"Hey, Rafael." Archer turns to me. "This is my friend Phoebe."

"Hi," I say.

"Hello, Phoebe," Rafael says.

I smile and let him hold the door wide for me, but it feels a little strange to have a guy to open the door for me. I don't think I've ever been in a doorman building before.

Inside, the lobby floor is made of smooth gray marble, and light from the wall sconces seems to slide along it like molten metal as we walk.

"Fancy," I say.

Archer presses the button for the elevator. It glows golden, an up-facing arrow dark in the center of it.

"Yeah, it's all right," he says. "We've lived here since I was in ninth grade. That's when my dad got the endowed chair. My parents wanted someplace they could give parties." I imagine the party-goers walking across the lobby, the women's heels clicking on the marble.

The elevator opens. It's big. The inside is dark wood, with a big silver mirror running the length of the back wall. For just a second I look at Mirror Archer next to Mirror Phoebe and I like what I see: a matched pair maybe, if you squint your eyes. Then I turn to face the door. Archer hits the button for floor twelve and leans against the wall. He even slouches cute.

"Your mom must have a nice place, right?" he says.

"It's pretty," I say. "We have a Victorian—a farmhouse, basically, but it's on a city block. Super old. She hired some guys to paint it yellow." I picture the big windows, the shaded porch. The two downstairs in the front have these fantastic arched parts filled with leaded glass in shades of blue and gray. I know my mom had this guy who calls himself the Glassman repair them when we moved in.

"It was a mess when my mom bought it, and houses are pretty cheap in Buffalo. But I bet it's worth a lot now." The elevator chimes and the door opens. The hallway is painted deep blue with glossy wood wainscoting running along the wall.

"I'm not really sure what my parents' arrangement is," I say. "For money, I mean. I know my dad sends something. My mom just makes her art and sells it to rich people. And teaches at the university."

"I'm sure there are still royalties from Shelter," Archer says. He stops in front of a door and pulls his keys from his pocket, finds the right one.

"I never thought about it," I say, which is true. My mom talks a lot about "rich people" as if they're very different from us, and I'm sure they are, but it's not as if we're poor. "You're probably right."

Archer shakes his head. He looks a little embarrassed. "I don't even know why I'm talking about this. I get anywhere near my dad," he says, opening the door, "and I just start thinking about money."

There's a foyer inside the apartment, and beyond it, I see a kitchen with a huge, gleaming stove and granite counters. There's a man in the kitchen, leaning against the counter looking at his phone. He's tall with graying hair and ice-blue eyes, and he looks toward us when we come in.

"Archer," he says. "You're home."

Archer nods. "I was at Josh's place. We had a show last night." He stands straight, his posture stiff, as if his bones are connected by wire. Archer looks at me, then back to the man. "This is Phoebe. Phoebe, this is my dad."

169

"Dr. Hughes," Archer's dad says, and he shakes my hand. "A pleasure. How do you know Archer?"

Behind him, I can see that the front of the refrigerator is completely bare, no photos, no drawings. Nothing. "My sister is in his band," I say. "She's Luna. Um, obviously."

He looks at me as if he's not sure what I mean. Then he says, "You're a musician too?"

"No," I say. "I'm not anything yet."

"Archer is a musician," Dr. Hughes says, and he turns his gaze to his son. "As for what he'll be in another ten years, we'll see."

"Thanks a lot, Dad." Something goes brittle in Archer's voice. He turns away from his father just a little, but I notice. "As always, your support is overwhelming."

"I *am* supporting you." Dr. Hughes slips his phone into his pocket and picks up a briefcase from the counter. "Not in the way in the way you hoped, I suppose."

Archer doesn't say anything, just exhales softly and fidgets in place. Sunlight streams into a golden square on the tiled floor next to his feet, and the room stays quiet.

"My mom teaches at a university too," I say, just to fill the space. I'm not about to tell him that she used to be in a band as well, and she gave it up.

"Really?" he says. "Which one?"

"University at Buffalo. She's in the art department."

"Art history?" His eyebrows rise as he says this.

"Studio art," I say. Then "Sculpture." I hope he doesn't ask me what medium, because I don't imagine he's much into metal. What would my mother think? He doesn't look like he has the constitution for it. *This guy,* she'd say, *would never be able to stand the heat.*

He nods as if he's considering my answer. I can almost see him make the decision: art history would have been better.

Archer moves in something like a shudder, his limbs going loose. "Okay, well, we're just here to pick up my tuning pedal," he says.

Dr. Hughes nods. "Right," he says, "and I have a meeting. I'm leaving now."

Archer is already walking away toward the back of the apartment, and I stand there only a second before I follow him.

"Nice to meet you," I say before I go.

"Likewise." He smiles, and in that moment, it seems sincere.

Archer goes through a doorway down the hall. His room is large, I suppose, by New York standards, and painted a deep gray blue, a vintage roll-down map of North America on the opposite wall. He has a poster of the Beatles' *Let It Be*: John, Paul, George, and Ringo, each in his own square. There's a wide window that looks out on the black-edged windows of the sandstone building across the street. I can see an Irish flag in the window opposite, and some kind of palm tree in the one next to it. Archer turns on his stereo and puts the needle on the record he's left on there. It's the Kinks.

"Nice," I say.

"You're a Kinks fan?" he asks.

"Of course," I say. "People think the question is 'Beatles versus Stones,' but it should be 'Beatles versus Kinks.'" This is my mother's riff and I'm just paraphrasing, but Archer doesn't have to know that. Besides, she's trained me, and Luna, too, given us a full musical education. Sure, she left out the Shelter lesson in Nineties Music 101, but I'm catching up on that.

Archer is smiling at me, and I feel my cheeks flush. "So who would win?" he asks.

I smile too. "Oh, the Beatles, of course, but at least it would be a real contest."

Archer kneels down on the floor in front of his bed and pulls out a box. I stand in the center of his room, not sure what I should do. There is a cluster of photographs on his desk and I try to look at them without him noticing. There's at least one of Archer and a pretty dark-haired girl.

"I like the color," I say.

"What color?" He's rummaging through pedals and cables, pulling some out and lining them up on the rug.

"Of your room. It's like a whale."

I'm positive that I'm making no sense. Any power I've had over words is failing me. You get me in a cute boy's bedroom and I fall apart, apparently. But Archer smiles again.

"Definitely the look I was going for," he says.

"Really?" I almost feel relieved.

He laughs. "Well, no, not really. But I like whales."

Archer starts digging through the boxes under his bed and I don't really know where to sit, so instead I go over to stand by the window. Down on the sidewalk I see Rafael helping a deliveryman with a huge box of groceries. An orange falls out and rolls to the curb without either of them noticing.

In my normal life, I'm never this high up. People are never this small, enacting whole scenes in miniature down on the street. The cars slide by, the yellow taxis switching lanes. Suddenly I notice the silence of the space between songs, the record crackling like radio static. Then "Strangers" starts, Dave Davies singing with a voice like gravel at the bottom of a clear cold stream. I close my eyes and take a deep breath. I feel like I'm in a movie, but I'm not sure what the plot is. I'm not sure what happens next.

"Is there a better song than this in the world?" I say. I turn back toward Archer.

He smiles. "Maybe not."

"Right now, it sounds like the best thing I could possibly hear."

I hear Dr. Hughes say something from the other room, maybe *good-bye*, and the door shuts hard behind him. Some kind of spell is broken, like a radio dial going off station when you drive too far to get the signal.

Archer turns and sits down, leaning against his bed. I notice that it's made carefully, the gray coverlet tucked under his pillow and creased in a straight line. I wonder if Archer did it or if they have someone whose job it is to do that. I'm not sure, yet, if he's the kind of guy who makes his bed.

"My father drives me crazy," Archer says. He's looking up at me, so I drop down and sit on his rug too.

"Maybe he's just jealous," I say. "Economics is not very sexy."

Is this what I'm supposed to say? I wonder. *Am I doing this right?* I have no idea.

Archer laughs. "I've thought about that." He picks up a green bass pedal and moves the knobs absentmindedly. "You know, we used to talk about music. He was the one who first introduced me to sixties soul. He had all these records when I was a kid: Otis Redding, Sam Cooke, Ray Charles. But then we moved, and my older sister started having problems.

"Does she live here?" I ask. I had peeked inside the first room down the hall, which had long purple curtains and a bunch of satin toe shoes hung in a clump from the door. If Tessa were here, she would have stuck her whole head in the room, gathering intel like a spy.

"No," he says. "Only Calista does. I don't know where Natalie is. Boston, as of a couple of months ago." He pushes the box back underneath his bed, where it fits neatly under the bed skirt. "She was a dancer, but she got hurt. And then she couldn't stop taking the pain meds."

He takes out his wallet then, and I expect him to hand me a picture. Instead, it's a driver's license. *Natalie Hughes,* it says. I study her picture: she's the girl from the photo on Archer's desk. She's pretty, with a narrow face and high cheekbones, sky-blue eyes and wavy dark brown hair like his.

"She left that in her room. Right in the middle, like a message." He shakes his head. "I mean, what is she doing without her ID?"

"Maybe she has a fake." *Eyes: blue,* the license says. *Hair: brown. Height: 5 feet, 7 inches.*

"Maybe. But why? She's twenty-two. It's like she just wanted to leave her whole life behind." He rubs his fingers across his forehead. "And she wanted us to know." He squints a little, as if the light behind us is too bright. "What am I supposed to do with that?"

I don't know how to answer, but it's okay because I don't think he's really looking for one.

"When I dropped out of school, my dad just lost it," he says. "He doesn't even know how to talk to me anymore." He rubs his forehead. "It's not like I can't go back. He'll still be there. He'll be there forever. They're going to have to drag him out of that endowed chair. No matter when I go back, he won't have to pay my tuition."

Archer is still sitting on the woven rug, leaning back against the side of his mattress. I reach out to touch a striped wool camping blanket folded at the end of his bed, but I want to touch him. His knee or his shoulder. I want to feel the warmth of his skin through his clothes.

"Do you want to go back?" I ask.

"What?"

"To school, I mean. Someday. Do you think you will?"

He pulls up a corner of the rug and lets it drop. "Maybe. I like the idea of being in school; I'm just not sure I need a degree at the end of it. It depends what happens with the Moons." He shrugs. "I should move out, I know. We're just gone so much lately it hasn't seemed worth it. We won't be back for a month this time. And Calista likes that I still officially live here."

"What do you think will happen?" I ask. He looks at me. "With the Moons, I mean."

He thinks for a moment. "I don't know. I know Venus Moth is really into us, and that would change things. For the next tour, I mean. We'd probably get to leave the States, even. Play Europe."

"Be famous," I say.

"Eh," he says, "I don't really care about that. I just want to get out of this house. Get my dad off my back."

"My mom wants me to talk to Luna," I say. "Try to convince her to go back to school in the fall."

Archer looks at me, waiting, so I keep going.

"I haven't said much yet, and she's not going to listen anyway." I turn toward his desk, touch the milk crate full of records on the top. "The two of them drive me nuts. First of all, my mother is mad at Luna for doing the same thing she did. And Luna's, like, following our mother's every move and doesn't seem to realize it at all."

Archer smiles, but his eyes look serious. "I think it's hard for her to see that," he says. "She wants to believe she's making her own choices."

"Don't worry," I say. "Luna always makes her own choices."

I start to flip through the records in the crate. There are three more crates like it on the floor by my feet. I see Otis Redding, the Eels, Talking Heads.

"That one is signed by David Byrne," Archer says. I can see the signature in the left-hand corner. "My father bought it for me." He sighs. "A long time ago." He stands up to open a tall cabinet by the window. "This is all records too," he says.

"I think you have a vinyl problem."

He slips an album from the middle shelf. "I know I do."

I keep flipping, the album sleeves smooth and papery under my fingers. I'm almost through the second crate when I find it: the record that stops me midflip. I didn't even know I was looking for it, but when I see it, it's as if some kind of search is over.

twenty-seven

MY FATHER HAS COME OUT with one album in the three years since I've seen him, and I bought it myself on vinyl six months ago. *Rolling Stone* did a piece about it, even put a small headline on the cover. I saw my mother looking at it at the grocery store, squinting, and when she walked away to put orange juice in our cart I pulled a copy off the stand and crouched down on the floor to read it. *Gimme Shelter,* it said. *Kieran Goes Back to the Studio with* Promise. Considering that my father *owns* a studio, I'm not sure how he went "back" to it, but I figured it wasn't really worth writing a letter to the editorial department.

I picked it up at Spiral Scratch, an indie record store in our neighborhood. When I brought it up to the counter I expected there to be some fanfare involved in the checkout, but of course the clerk didn't know who I was.

"We've been listening to this one in the store," he said. He pushed his dark-framed glasses up on his nose. "Finally this dude did something right."

I smiled and might have shrugged, then walked home clutching the record in its paper shopping bag. I didn't listen to it while my mother was home, and I didn't put it in the cabinet with the rest of the albums in the dining room. I guess I had given up on trying to get her to talk to me about my father. I kept it in the narrow strip of space between my dresser and my bookcase, resting on the hardwood floor, and sometimes at night I'd slide it out and disassemble it as if I were diffusing a bomb. The cardboard sleeve, the envelope, the lyrics, which came printed on a paper thin and transparent as onion skin. The black vinyl record itself, its concentric rings like the inside of an old tree. The album came with a digital download, of course, and I had it on my iPod. I'd listen before I went to bed, trying to figure him out from his lyrics, his voice. What was this "promise," and who was he making it to? There was a song about a breakup and one about a girl named Laura. I didn't know anyone named Laura. There was a lyric about a girl with blue-green eyes, and I wondered if it was about my mother. But my father had been touring without her for fifteen years, and he might have picked up a hundred blue-green-eyed girls since.

There was only one picture of him on the album, a small one on the back where the recording information was, and the credits for the other musicians. He stood in profile, shadowed, black-and-white. He was smiling widely, his mouth open. This was my father in gray scale, compacted. And even in photographic form, I couldn't get him to look at me.

Now, in Archer's room, I find myself looking at the photograph of my father again. It's so small I can't see the dimple that matches mine.

"Is it weird that I have that?" Archer asks. He's standing behind me, so close that I can feel his breath on my shoulder.

I turn to look at him. "Why would it be weird?"

"Because you guys don't talk to him. And Luna's so angry."

I shake my head. "It's not weird."

Archer's brow furrows. "Are you?"

It seems like his sentence is missing an adjective. "Am I what?"

"Angry."

I think about it. "I'm confused. I just don't know where he went. I mean, he was never around all that much, but now he's just totally gone." I lift the album sleeve up. "Except for this." It's paper, it's pictures, but I feel like it carries the music inside of it somehow.

I fit the record back in its spot in the milk crate and sit down at the edge of Archer's bed.

"What is weird," I say, "is being the only one in my family who doesn't, you know, do music." I've always felt this way, but I don't know if I've ever said it out loud. And then I do say it, and nothing happens except Archer sits down next to me.

"You never tried?" he says.

"A little. My mom didn't push me, but she was open to it. Surprising, seeing as how she acts about Luna now. I mean, what was she expecting would happen?" I pull one leg up on the bed and hold my ankle. "Anyway, I didn't have any talent. My voice is fine, but it's nothing special. I couldn't really pick up an instrument. I even tried the flute. I figured that would be totally different, and I could have something that was just my own. But I hated it. And I wasn't any good. Or maybe I was afraid to be really bad at something they're so good at." I stop, feeling my cheeks flush. "I don't know why I'm telling you this."

Archer smiles, a slow, wide smile that takes its time moving across his face. "I asked."

A pigeon flies past the window, a fluttery blur of gray wings. "I always thought I'd find something else," I say. "I have the smart thing, the grades thing, but that's pretty much it."

"Are you kidding me?" he asks. "Phoebe, you are an incredible writer. Poet, lyricist, whatever." He reaches toward me and takes my wrist between his fingers. His thumb presses right on my pulse and I feel as if I might melt straight onto the floor.

"Thanks," I say, and suddenly I feel very aware of the space between us. You could measure it in inches, not feet, not yards, not miles. I can see the amber flecks in his blue eyes, and I'm wondering what he can see in mine.

The record ends, and I hear the needle return to its stand. That's how quiet it seems. Archer lets go of my wrist and goes to put a new one on.

There's an Elvis Costello concert poster on the wall next to me. It's from his *Brutal Youth* album, and Elvis looks serious and maybe a little disapproving. *Yeah, I don't know what I'm doing here, Elvis,* I think. *But maybe it's not too late to turn back.*

My heart starts to beat harder against my rib cage. The idea blooms inside me like one of my mother's daylilies: beautiful, star-shaped, for a limited time only. I lean toward Archer a little bit.

"I need to go someplace," I say, "and I don't want Luna to know." I don't know what to do with my hands, so I put my palms flat on my thighs. I take a deep breath. "It has to be today. Will you come with me?"

twenty-eight

I KNOW WHERE MY FATHER'S studio is. I know because Luna took me
there once last year, when I visited her at her dorm during her first
semester in New York. It was early November, chilly, and when we
got off the train, the wind smelled like blue sky and dry leaves. The
trees in Brooklyn burned red and gold. We stopped first at a tiny
café for hot chocolate in cardboard cups, and then we walked three
blocks with the warm cups in our hands.

When we got there, we stood across the street and looked at
the building for a while, then crossed in the middle of the block and
climbed up on the stoop: one, two, three stairs up. There was a small
white doorbell and above it, printed in tiny letters on the green tape
of a label maker, it read KIERAN FERRIS STUDIOS. I wondered
if my father had made the little sign or if he had some kind of secretary. I leaned against the railing and Luna stood crookedly and

stared at the sign, rubbing one of her tall brown boots against the other. I took a sip of cocoa. Standing there, I thought we might as well ring the bell and see if he was there, but that was never part of Luna's plan. When I reached out toward the button she stopped me, grabbing my hand and pulling it back. She shook her head.

She turned and stepped onto the sidewalk, then started walking toward the train.

"We're leaving?" I asked. I was still up on the stoop looking down on her. Her red scarf blew across her shoulders.

"I just wanted to see it," she said.

I didn't try to convince her. I just walked down the stairs and followed her past the café, onto the subway, back uptown to her dorm. We didn't talk about it later, and what I wondered most was why she'd taken me along. She was in the city all the time; she could have come alone and no one would have known. Instead, she'd brought me on her strange pilgrimage, just to stand on a stoop and then turn around and walk away. Maybe he hadn't even been there.

It feels different this time, with Archer, because the stakes are lower. If my father isn't there, or even if he is, I don't have to worry about what Luna will think. I don't even have to tell her.

There's something so steady about Archer, starting with the way he walks next to me, keeping pace with me exactly even though we aren't saying anything to each other. It's only now I realize that when I walk with Luna on these city streets, I feel as if I'm always a half step behind, even when I'm moving as quickly as I can.

Here on the sidewalk, I want to take Archer's hand, but something stops me. After talking with Luna last night my head is still a jumble of Tessa and Ben. I wonder, if I take Archer's hand, is Tessa right about me? Do I even know what I'm doing?

My phone buzzes then, at the corner of my father's street, and I pull it out of my bag. It's a text message from Luna: *Be back soon, okay? We can go to the grocery store. I'll make pasta for dinner.* I stand still and text back, *Okay.* Archer stands exactly next to me on the sidewalk and waits while I scan the street for my father's building. I point when I see it.

"That's it," I say. It matches up with the picture in my memory: an old factory building with huge windows and wrought iron railings out front lining the four separate doors, four stoops. I recognize the one where I stood with Luna last November.

"Should we do this?" Archer asks. He must sense my hesitation because he puts his hand out and waits for me to take it. I do, and he squeezes my fingers gently. We walk together toward the door.

Panic spreads through my body like ice. I haven't seen my father in almost three years and now I'm just going to show up, without Luna and with Archer, and I don't even really know what's going on with us. I've been more honest with Archer about this than anyone except Tessa, even if I haven't told him everything. For one thing, my father is playing a show at the Bowery Ballroom tomorrow night and I'm planning to get myself invited.

But Archer is still holding my hand, and before I know it we're up on the stoop, my finger pressing the bell. The same green tape label is stuck over the buzzer, and I look at all the letters in my father's name until the door opens.

twenty-nine

MEG
JUNE 1994

IT WAS ONLY WHEN KIERAN turned on the lamp that I realized I was pretty much sitting in the dark. My guitar was on the floor in front of me, but I hadn't touched it in at least an hour. I had even picked up a brand-new composition notebook at the drugstore down the street, but it wasn't helping.

"We're screwed," I said. Kieran sat down on the arm of the couch.

"I don't know what to write." I shut my notebook. "They've rejected three songs so far."

"I know," he said. "It's okay, babe."

"*Too wordy,* they say. *Needs a hook.*" I tossed Rick's notes on the floor. "You know, Rick has terrible handwriting."

Kieran laughed. "We probably shouldn't tell him that."

I raised my chin and glanced up at him. "I might."

"Breathe," Kieran said. He kneeled down behind me and slipped his hands over my shoulders. When he pressed down with his fingertips, I realized how tight my muscles were. I sighed and dropped my chin to my chest.

"This isn't how I thought it was going to be," I said. I ran my toe over a scratch on the hardwood, one Kieran made months ago sliding his amp over the floor. Our cat, Patti Smith, walked over and bopped my knee with her head. I reached out to touch her fur.

"So here's what I think," Kieran said. "You're trying to do this on your own, but we're a team, right? Let me see what you're writing."

I handed him the notebook.

"'You're at the edge of the sky and falling,'" he read. He looks up. "That's good."

"Yeah, but I don't even know what it means," I said.

Kieran picked up my pen and started writing, just a few words. He handed me the notebook, and I read what he'd written.

But the world's not flat anymore.

He was watching for my reaction. I smiled.

"You have terrible handwriting too," I said. But I liked what he had scrawled there. It wasn't bad.

Kieran shrugged. "There's a reason Lennon and McCartney did their best work together. Don't go rogue, Paul." He poked me in the shoulder.

"Come on," I said. "I'd be Lennon. You're the McCartney, Mr. Sentimental."

"Fine." Kieran stood up and pulled me close. "I can handle

that. You can make sure I keep my edge."

"You'd have to have an edge to keep it," I said. He shook his head, smiling.

"Shut up," he said, and kissed me.

thirty

WHEN HE OPENS THE DOOR, my father looks pretty much the same as he ever did. He's wearing a dark blue T-shirt and jeans with a pair of black headphones around his neck, the cord looped around his hand like a lasso. His hair is a little shorter than it used to be, but he still doesn't really look like anyone's *dad*. Which is fine, because he isn't. Not really.

For a moment, he squints at me as if he's trying to place me, or maybe to make sure it's actually me. Maybe he's looking for identifying marks, just as I'm searching for the dimple I know is there in his right cheek, mirror-matching my own. I feel like a specimen dropped off on his doorstep, ready to be examined. Then his face breaks into a smile.

"Phoebe," he says. "I didn't know you were in town."

Right, I think. *How would you have known?*

"I am," I say. "Um, obviously. I hope it's okay I stopped by." I fidget, rubbing the fingertips of my right hand together. I dropped Archer's hand sometime before the door opened, and I feel unmoored and unsteady. My father is nodding, smiling like it's any old day.

"Of course it is," he says, and his voice is warm and friendly. This whole long-lost-daughter thing doesn't seem like a big deal to him. You'd think we had seen each other a couple of weeks ago.

"You answer your own door," I say. "I wasn't sure if I was going to have to explain who I was."

"Nope." He shakes his head. "I have a couple of other engineers who work with me sometimes, but it's only me here now. I'm recording Prue Donohue today." He motions with his head behind him and says this as if I know who she is, but of course I don't.

I reach to my side and touch the wrought iron railing, which is warm and smooth. "We don't want to interrupt."

"We're just finishing up," he says. "Come in." I step into the foyer just as he looks past me to Archer. I realize I haven't introduced him yet.

"This is my friend Archer." I angle my body back toward him.

"Hi, Archer." My father puts his hand out, and Archer shakes it.

"He's in Luna's band," I say.

"Oh, right. You play bass? I saw you guys at the Mudroom." My father backs up into the foyer and then begins to lead us down a narrow hallway into the studio. The walls are lined with framed records: my father's four solo albums placed in chronological order the way we're walking, along with other records I don't recognize on the opposite wall.

"I remember," says Archer, behind me. "Thanks for coming."

"Sure." My father glances back at us. "I was hoping to talk to Luna afterward, but she disappeared."

I don't look back at Archer, but I hear him hesitate before deciding, as I expect, to cover for Luna. "She wasn't feeling well," he says.

My father nods, but I can see only the back of his head, so I can't tell if he believes Archer's story or not.

The studio is sunny thanks to a huge window on the right side, looking out onto a courtyard behind the building. It's not very big in here, though what space it occupies is crammed with instruments and amps and cables.

There's a pretty girl in her late twenties sitting at the soundboard, pink streaks in her dark blond hair.

"Hey," she says, her voice low and sweet.

"Hey," I say. I feel like I'm echoing her. "I'm sorry to interrupt." I glance at my father, who sits down next to her.

"No," he says. "We were just listening back."

"I'm Prue," she says.

"Phoebe." My father gestures for Archer and me to sit on a low leather sofa against the wall. Archer sits, but I don't. I lean my hip against the couch.

"My daughter," my father explains to Prue. He says it easily, as if the word doesn't feel strange in his mouth.

"Nice," she says, nodding. "I played a show with your sister. She's great." For the first time since I walked through the door I wish Luna were here, if only so she can tell me what I'm supposed to think of this girl. Prue leans a little closer to my father than I would to a guy twenty years older than me, but maybe it's a trust thing, artist to engineer. Maybe he's a father figure. He's certainly not busy fathering anyone else.

"I'm in the Moons," Archer explains. "Archer Hughes." He leans forward and puts out his hand. She shakes it, her smile spreading even wider across her face.

"Great," she says. "I thought I recognized you." She looks back toward me. "Luna's not with you?"

"No," I say. *Obviously*, I think. *Unless she's invisible.*

There are three guitars on stands next to the sofa, one the sleek Fender Jazzmaster I know my father likes best, its edges asymmetrical as an amoeba. The sound booth past this room is the size of Luna's bedroom on Schermerhorn, and I can see a stool and a microphone in the center. On the far wall are a bunch of posters from my father's solo shows, each framed carefully in black and matted in three inches of creamy white paper. I can't keep myself from walking closer to them. One is from his first solo tour, when I was two. He stands with his guitar slung over his shoulder, his eyes cast off to the side, trying to look serious.

"I'm out, Kieran," Prue says. I turn back toward her. She slings a huge purse over her shoulder. "I've got to pick Alexei up at four." I wonder if Alexei is her boyfriend. But just as easily he could be her kid or even her dog. A little dog, I decide, but maybe a rescue, at least.

My father nods at Prue. My father is always nodding. He starts to sing the Beatles' "Dear Prudence."

"Yeah, yeah," Prue says, but she's smiling. "I've already been

191

out to play. Nice to meet you guys."

"You too," I say. She seems perfectly nice, but I still can't quite make my mouth form a smile. I sit down on the couch then because I don't know what else to do. I want to reach out and touch Archer's hand or his knee, but that would probably be weird. He's looking at me, though, asking some sort of question with his eyes. *Are you okay?* or *Do you want to go?* or maybe *Should we stay a little longer?* I give a little nod to all three of the imagined questions.

Archer looks around the room. "You have a nice setup here."

"Thanks," my father says. "It's small, but it works. I get some great musicians because I'm willing to give them attention but be hands-off when they need it."

Ha! I think. *He has a lot of experience in being hands-off.*

I almost laugh. My interior voice is a bit of a brat today.

"Can you fit a whole band in there at once?" Archer asks.

My father shakes his head. "It would be tight. I don't usually record whole bands live. Mostly solo artists, or bands done one or two instruments at a time. Come on, I'll show you."

They pass through the sound booth's door and I watch them through the glass of the windows. My father is taller than Archer by several inches, and as they bend with their heads together I have this sudden panicky feeling that I don't really know either of them at all. I wish for Luna again, or for my mother or Tessa to be here with me on this black leather couch. But then they turn and I feel better. There's my father, who is finally within yards of me after three years. There's Archer, who came with me willingly and even held my hand.

As they're coming out, my father asks Archer who recorded the Moons' last record.

"We recorded with Greg at Jackson," Archer says, and though

it sounds cryptic to me, my father knows the studio he's talking about. He smiles.

"Greg's a great engineer," he says. He sits down at the sound-board but swings his chair around to face the sofa, and just then I'm closer to him than I've been this whole time. I look at his face without trying to hide it. I can see faint wrinkles in the outside corners of his eyes, which deepen when he smiles. He takes the headphones from around his neck and sets them down on the desk. "Are you looking to record again soon?"

"We have enough material," Archer says, sitting down next to me. The sofa sinks a little, and I feel calmer knowing he's so close. "Just trying to raise the funds."

My father leans back in his chair and it creaks, a short, crickety sound beneath him. "I'll do it for free," he says. "I'd be happy to."

I look at Archer. His mouth has dropped open and his eyes are wide. I feel woozy, and certain that I've made some kind of mistake by coming here. This is spinning out of my control.

"Luna likes to do things on her own," I say. I sit forward, holding the edge of the sofa with both hands.

"Sure," my father says. "But I'd like to help if she'll let me."

Archer looks at me and then back to my father. "It's so gener-ous of you," he says. "Luna doesn't tell anyone she's your daughter." He smiles sheepishly. "Though people keep figuring it out."

My father seems to consider this. He picks up a pen from the desk absentmindedly, without turning his head to look at it, then rolls it between his fingers.

"I admire that," he says. "But it's silly not to use my studio. I can ask another engineer to do the recording, if she wants. Hell,

Greg can do it. But why pay for studio time when I have the place right here?"

"You make a good argument," Archer says. He looks at me. "We'll talk to her."

I take a breath, but my lungs don't feel big enough for how deeply I want to breathe. My father looks at me.

"I'd like to see Luna, Phoebe. Will you tell her that?" My father is looking right at me, and this close I see that his brown eyes are flecked with green. Something in his posture reminds me of Luna, and maybe it's because they're both used to being in a room full of people looking back at them. "And I'd like to see you again too," he says.

For a second, I look at him and I think, *Um, I'm seeing you right now. Are you kicking me out?* But I don't really know how to do this either: how to hang out, how to be together.

My father puts his hands on his knees. "I have a show at the Bowery Ballroom tomorrow night. I can put you on the list. With Luna, maybe? And Archer, of course."

"You're playing tomorrow?" I say. "I didn't know that." I feel as if I were reading from a script. I wonder if Archer can tell that I'm lying. I wonder if my father can. "Sure, we'll come. I don't know about Luna, though."

"Great." My father writes down his phone number in dark blue ink, even though it's the same one he's had for years and I still know it by heart. He writes his address below it. He hands me the paper and I look at it.

"Okay," I hear myself say.

Later, Archer walks me down into the train station even though he's planning on meeting Josh at their practice space in Dumbo in an hour. We stand in the swamp-like heat of the train tunnel waiting for the light and the rush of the next train way down the track. I feel a little dizzy, and I can't tell you what time it is, really, or whether it's light or dark outside.

"I should go back to the apartment," I say. "Luna wants me to go grocery shopping with her. She's making dinner." I'm looking forward to it, strangely: Luna's tiny kitchen and old dishes and tomato sauce from a jar.

"That should be interesting," he says.

"I think she's just making pasta," I say, and as if it's necessary, "from a box."

He's smiling. Then he presses his lips together. "Are you going to tell Luna we saw him?"

"No way. Are you crazy?" I say it like I'm joking, but I'm serious. "I'll figure something out." I studied the map on my train ride earlier, and I know where I'm going. "I'll meet you outside the Bowery stop at seven tomorrow."

"You're not going to tell her where we're going?"

"No," I say. "I'm just gonna go."

We stand for a moment, facing each other, and I've never been so aware of the air. I pull my phone from my purse without looking away from him. A smile starts to play at the edges of his mouth, and he nods.

"Okay, Phoebe. I don't know how you're going to pull this off, but I'll be there. Text me if you have a problem."

When I reach out and take my phone back from him, our fingertips touch. I want to grab his hand, but I don't. Not yet.

"I'm sure I'll have lots of problems," I say, "but I'll be there."

thirty-one

IN THE MORNING, LUNA AND I head to a bagel shop on Montague before the sun starts to get hot. We order honey-wheat bagels toasted with cream cheese—they make their own, Luna says—and wait for them, leaning at the end of the counter. The guy at the cash register looks at Luna carefully while he hands back her change.

"You're Luna," he says. He tilts his head, but his carefully messy hair stays still.

"I am," she says. She smiles a Mona Lisa smile and straightens her shoulders.

He takes our package of bagels from the girl who toasted them and hands them to her. "Of Luna and the Moons," he says. His coworker puts her elbows on the counter and looks at Luna as if she thinks she should know her, but doesn't.

Luna shakes her hair over her shoulders. "That's the one."

He's smiling now, nodding. "We saw you at the Tulip Club the other night," he says.

"Cool." Luna's own smile widens. "What did you think?"

"It was awesome."

"We had a great crowd," Luna says. "Thanks for coming." She smiles again like she means it and we pass through the glass door. It closes behind us with the tinkle of bells and I'm thinking, That's it? It can be that easy, but every time my mother is asked who she is she plays complicated games of pretend and deny.

Luna and I head down to the Promenade to eat our bagels. We sit on a red bench in the shade of a spindly tree and look out over the blue and sparkling river. The Statue of Liberty rises green and spine straight from the water, holding her torch aloft. She's much tinier than I expected, out there all alone.

Luna holds the perfect circle of half a bagel and points the toes of her left foot. She traces a line on the ground. "What's Archer's parents' place like?" she asks.

"Kind of fancy," I say. I look across the water so I don't have to look at Luna. "But his dad is kind of a jerk."

"Well," Luna says, "so is ours." She makes a wide gesture with her arms like she's in a musical. She's performing, though no one but me is close enough to hear. This is Luna's "breezy" act, where nothing matters much and everything is funny, even dead-beat rocker dads.

The wind lifts my hair from my shoulders and drops it back down. I can hear a ship's horn, a low moaning sound that could be an animal. An elephant, maybe, or a walrus, something with big lungs and a spectacular nose. It's comforting somehow, that the ship just shouts its warning as it travels. I wish everything in life had a warning sound like that.

Next to me, Luna sighs. "I'm sorry, but I'm going to have to shut this whole thing down."

"What?" I snap my gaze toward her, but she's looking out across the water. Unless she's been training as a spy—or Archer told her—there's no way she could have known about my visit to our father.

Luna looks at me. "No Archer." She shakes her head for emphasis.

"What do you mean?" I ask. I'm so disoriented by my panic that I can't make sense of what she's saying. A teenaged girl runs by, chasing a little dog who has slipped its leash, and I turn my head to follow her. Her flip-flops slap against the ground and the dog runs just far enough ahead to stay free.

"Consider him off-limits." Luna's voice is firm. "I mean, I know he's cute, and I love him, but he's a mess."

I turn back to her, nearly sighing with relief. This doesn't have to do with our father at all. "First of all, who said I was interested?"

She looks right at me with eyes as blue green and clear as my mother's.

We stay quiet for a moment. The buildings on the edge of Manhattan look like a stage set, or someone's scale model. They're too perfect, too geometric to be real.

"What kind of mess?"

Luna crushes the foil wrapper in her hand and puts it back in the bag. She extends her legs and looks at her shoes. "The kind that can't be cleaned up in the next few days." She takes a breath and lets it out slowly, like she's demonstrating a meditation technique. Then she looks at me. "Me too," she says.

I have no idea what she means. "You too what?"

"I'm probably that same kind of mess." She smiles, but it's a wavering smile that seems as if it could collapse at any time.

I notice that I'm holding on to the edge of the bench hard enough that I can feel the ridges in the wood. "So maybe I should warn James against you," I say.

"I don't think he'd listen," she says, shaking her head a little.

"So why should I?"

"Because if you don't," she says, "I'll tell Mom. And then you'll have to hear it from her." She seems back to normal, sure of herself and certain she's right. "She'll jump in the Volvo and be here by dinnertime."

I could picture it: my mother and Dusty pulling up to Luna's apartment on Schermerhorn, ready to save me from acquiring a musician boyfriend or whatever. You know, the kind of boyfriends/ husbands they've both had. *Because you're basically living Mom's life*, I think.

"Well," I say, "you'd have to talk to her to tell her."

Luna shrugs. "I'll send a text."

There's a cloud above us in the perfect shape of a turtle, floating like a balloon across the sky. I tip my head back to look at it. "What's wrong with Archer?" I say. "He seems great."

Luna nods. "He *is* great. But he's had a tough time this year, since his sister left." She unscrews the cap of her water bottle and takes a sip. "For a while I thought we were going to have to kick him out of the band."

I know what this is code for. There's been trouble with booze or drugs or girls or *something*. But I can't quite put what she's saying together with the Archer I've known so far, so polite and responsible. "So what happened?"

"Well, we had a big talk. All of us. He stayed with Josh for a few weeks, without going back to his parents' place." She presses her lips together, remembering. "He's been better since then."

So what's the problem? I think. "Well, we're just hanging out." *And, um, texting all spring and summer.* I wave my hands in front of my face as if I were brushing away a cloud of gnats. "If I stay with *you* for every minute of the next few days, we'll kill each other." I look at her. "Let me have a friend. He's really nice." I can feel my own voice start to tremble. "Things have been so crappy, and yesterday . . . helped."

Luna reaches out and touches a lock of my hair, just over my shoulder. "Fine," she says. "Friends. That's all, though."

I nod and I smile, starting small but then growing wider. I might as well be crossing my fingers behind my back. I don't know how Archer feels, but I don't want to be just friends with him. It feels good, finally, to have a secret that can't hurt anybody. Maybe one is enough.

So I almost tell Luna then, that we went to see Kieran, and that he wants to record their record. That he seems to miss us, in his own way. But then Luna stands up and walks to the metal railing at the edge of the concrete and pulls herself up on it, standing between the slats on the bottom rung. The sun comes back out from behind a cloud and her hair shines like lava must, when it cools back to black. I squint my eyes and watch her turn to a silhouette against the wide blue sky.

thirty-two

MEG

DECEMBER 1993

I HAD TORN MY TIGHTS, but the wardrobe woman—I thought her name was Julie—wasn't worried.

"I like them that way," she said. She was standing with her hip cocked to one side, tilting her head. Her blond hair was dyed purple at its ends, like she'd dipped it in grape juice. "It makes it look like you don't care. Like everything's an accident."

I almost told her that it *was* an accident, ripping my tights— and that my entire life felt like one too, lately—but Kieran appeared in the doorway in a T-shirt and jeans.

"They're ready for us," he said. "Are you dressed?" He looked me up and down. "You look amazing."

"Thanks," I said. I'd been too nervous to eat all morning, so I felt light-headed and dreamy, like I was moving though water instead of air. If there were butterflies in my stomach, they were the prehistoric kind, with wingspans three feet wide. I let Kieran take my hand and pull me into the hallway.

"That's what you're wearing?" I asked. "Did you even change?"

"What?" he said. "They want me to look normal. I have a natural sense of style, you know." He twirled me around and leaned me back like a salsa dancer, and he was just about to kiss me when I heard a shriek behind us. It was Julie from wardrobe, again.

"Don't mess up her lipstick!" she said. Kieran pulled me upright, spun me away from him. He smiled.

"That's not all I want to mess up," he said.

It was so bright in the studio it felt like we'd landed on a different planet, just by walking through the door. Near the back of the room was a huge black backdrop, a moon printed in the middle, shadowy with empty seas. Carter and Dan were already there, staring at the ceiling and wandering back and forth a little. They looked relieved when they saw us.

"We don't know what to do here," Carter said.

"You're doing a good job standing around so far," I said.

The photographer's name was Christian, and he barely looked older than I was. He was also wearing a black T-shirt and jeans, so he might as well have been a member of our band.

"There's a uniform," I whispered to Dan, "and I'm the only one not wearing it."

He smiled. "Yeah, where's your purple hair?" He picked up a flannel shirt from a table just out of the light space. "I'm supposed to put this on."

The four of us stood close, Kieran and me in the center, Dan and Carter on the sides. The lights shone on us like blazing suns. I could feel myself start to sweat under the long-sleeved black dress Julie had picked out for me.

"Do we smile?" Carter asked.

"No," said Kieran, at the same time that I said, "They'll tell us." He shrugged.

"All right," Christian said. "Let's do this. Meg, come up front."

I glanced at Kieran, who was frowning, then I took a couple of steps toward Christian.

"Two more steps," he said. He looked toward Kieran. "And guys, why don't you move to the side, right at the edge of the moon." He pointed to the backdrop, then whispered to his assistant. She led them to a spot on my left, pushed and pulled them, her hands squarely on their shoulders, until they were standing where she wanted. I couldn't have reached them even if I had stretched my hand out as far as it would go. But for some reason, that didn't bother me too much just then.

I could tell that every person in the room was looking at me: the lighting guys, the hairstylist, Wardrobe Julie. The lights didn't feel uncomfortably hot, just soft and warm, like they were melting me in the nicest way. I smiled and shook my hair out a little. I almost laughed—this was not a shampoo commercial—but Christian seemed to like it.

"You're a fucking natural," he said. "Beautiful. Just keep looking at me."

I did, at first, but then I couldn't help looking sideways at Kieran. He looked serious, even wary. But when I caught his eye he smiled slightly, barely turning up the corners of his mouth. I couldn't tell if he meant it.

"Stay serious, guys," Christian said, and Kieran frowned. I turned back to Christian, opened my lips just slightly, and took a deep breath. He peeked around his camera for a moment, looking at me.

"First girl on the moon," he said, and then I couldn't see anything for the flashes.

thirty-three

I TAKE A 4 TRAIN to Brooklyn Bridge/City Hall and then I walk underground to the J line. When I get off at Bowery station, I'm pleased with myself. I feel like some kind of subway expert, even though all I did was take two trains without getting lost. I look around for someone to notice, but everyone continues his or her own subway rush, moving up the stairs or down the platform to the open-door train. No one notices.

My mother has been texting on and off all day, and I've tried to answer quickly, seem busy. She asked what I'm doing tonight and I told her what I told Luna: that I'm going to see a reading given by a poet I like. It's true that there's a reading, and true that I like the poet—we read her in AP English last year—but obviously I'm not going to see it.

I'm wearing my own clothes tonight, dark skinny jeans and

a long, gauzy ivory top, but I still don't feel quite like me. I catch my reflection in the window of a shoe store and I see a pretty girl, hair loose, shoulders straight, layered over the high heels on display behind the glass. I smile and keep going.

At the Ballroom, Archer is waiting outside, leaning against the stone front of the building. A curved window rises two stories high beside him and I look up to see it, all the way to the top. I've seen this place only in photographs, when I looked it up after seeing the date on my father's show schedule. I guess I imagined even then what it would be like to stand here on the sidewalk knowing my father was inside, but now that I'm here, I feel an effervescent anxiety rise through my body. I don't know how I'm going to make myself go inside.

Archer pulls me into a hug, wrapping me tight in his arms. We press together, hips and shoulders, and I feel the nervousness recede a little like low tide. I feel safe. Then he lets go and looks into my face.

"What did you tell Luna?" he asks.

"I told her I wanted to see Rebecca Hazelton read at McNally Jackson," I say. Luna took me there the last time I visited, and we saw another writer, a soft-spoken poet whose voice was like music. "It's on Prince Street. Close." I can feel my voice turn a little defensive on that last part. I'm not sure who I'm trying to convince that what I'm doing is okay, Archer or myself. "I told her you were coming with me, though," I say. "I actually kind of wish we could go see Rebecca, too."

Archer is twirling an unlit cigarette between his fingers. "There's still time to change your mind," he says, smiling.

I shake my head and look toward the door. "This is where I have to be," I say.

Archer nods. "You sure you don't want to tell Luna where we're really going?"

"I'm sure," I say, even though I'm not.

"Okay." He puts the cigarette back in his pack and we walk toward the door. There's a guy in a black T-shirt with a clipboard standing in the doorway, next to the short line for people with tickets.

"Phoebe Ferris," I say. He runs his pen down the list and makes a check. He looks up at Archer, waiting.

"Archer Hughes."

"Yep," he says, using his pen again. "You're here."

He doesn't ask me for an ID, which is good, because mine says I'm seventeen. I guess if you're on the list it doesn't matter. Archer has a fake ID, he told me yesterday, just in case he needs it.

"You can go up to the balcony," the guy says, and he hands us each a small badge. "VIP."

I hold it in my hand and look at it. "Do I have to?" I ask. "Go to the balcony, I mean."

The guy blinks. "No," he says. "You can go down on the floor, too."

I nod. I look at Archer. I'm afraid he'll be disappointed, but he's smiling.

"We can always go up later," he says. "If you want to."

I already know I won't want to. I want to watch this show with everyone else. I don't want anyone to wonder who I am.

I start to walk through the door, then I stop and back up.

"Is there a Luna on the list?" I stand on my tiptoes and try to look without being too obvious about it. I don't even know why I'm asking this.

His eyes scan the list. "Luna?" he says, still looking.

"Yeah. Can you just look? Luna Ferris."

"She's on here." He glances at the empty space behind me and the sidewalk beyond. "Is she with you?"

"No," I say. "She's not coming." I fall back on my heels, bounce a little. "I mean, I don't think she's coming. But leave her on there."

He looks at me as if I might be crazy, as if he might have to calm me down. He smiles with half his mouth.

"I'm not taking anyone off the list," he says, lifting one hand, palm facing toward me. "Don't worry." And then I see him realize who I must be.

"Are you related to Kieran?" he asks.

My first impulse is to lie, but I'm here and he has my last name on the list in front of him. And part of me wants to claim my father, even if he's never really claimed me.

"Yeah," I say. "I'm his daughter."

"He's a cool dude." He's nodding while he says this. "But you must already know that."

I look at Archer and he smiles at me. I glance back at the guy.

"Sure," I say. "Thanks."

Archer takes my hand, lacing his fingers through mine, and we pass through the door. We walk through the basement and the bar, and then take a set of stairs to the ballroom itself. It's like a labyrinth. The room beyond has an underwatery glow, and I feel right away that I'm moving through something. The room is full of people with pockets of space in between. The crowd hums low, like the sound power lines make if you're standing close enough to them. I look at faces as we walk from space to space, toward the stage. There are plenty of people my parents' age, but just as many who are closer to Archer's age or mine. Archer is still holding my hand, so when I stop halfway through the room, he stops too. I don't want to be right in front. He looks at me and smiles. I notice his slightly crooked canine tooth and the curve of his lips. I hold his gaze for a second and then I take out my phone. With both thumbs I type a text to Luna: *Don't be mad. With Archer at Dad's show at the Bowery. Come see? You're on the list.*

But I don't send it. I don't want to find out that she won't come. I hold the phone up in front of my face, watching the screen glow like a nightlight in this big dim room. Then—even though I know I'm a liar—I delete the message and turn off my phone.

thirty-four

I'VE NEVER SEEN MY FATHER play a show before. Not in real life, anyway. I've watched YouTube videos of his shows, I've seen him on *Austin City Limits*, and of course I've seen all of Shelter's music videos. Even the one where they play "Three Days of Rain" on an empty beach in the gray middle of March and if you watch closely, you can see my mother shiver in her long black coat. Behind her, my father leans his foot against his amp, half-sunk in the pearly sand. This year, the week *Promise* came out, he played on Jimmy Fallon's show and even sat in the chair next to Jimmy's desk for a few minutes. They talked about their favorite pizza place in New York, which was apparently the same wood-oven place near the Brooklyn Bridge. I read reviews on Yelp for an hour before I realized I was looking for one signed, *Kieran*.

I can even remember my father playing his guitar on the couch when I was a kid and he'd visit, singing Beatles songs, with Luna and me curled next to him on the cushion. But I've never seen my father live, playing in front of people besides me at an official show.

When my father enters the stage, he walks forward to stand in a pool of light, that same Fender Jazzmaster I saw at the studio slung over his shoulder. He waits for the current of applause to die down, and he smiles steadily and sincerely. There's a really beautiful backup singer standing to his left, her skin lit red and gold by the lights, her Afro surrounding her head like an aura. Farther back on the stage is another guitarist and the drummer behind his sparkly blue kit. The bassist has a dark red Fender, and it seems to me that's where Archer is looking right now.

I stand there and wonder if my father will say something about me. I wonder if he'll say my name.

"Hello, New York," he says. A cheer rises up from the crowd, rippling through the room like a wave. "We're so happy to be here." He's smiling, and he glances back toward the drummer, who raises his sticks. "There's no place I'd rather play than my hometown, even though it's true that almost everyone here comes from somewhere else." He steps forward and touches the mike in its stand. "I came from somewhere else," he says, "but it was so long ago I can't remember where that was."

"Not so long!" someone yells out.

My father laughs, a clear sharp sound in a room full of hum. "I think it was," he says, drawing out the last word. "But it doesn't matter. The best thing is when the people you love show up right where you are, right?"

I glance at the people on my left, but they're looking up at the stage and my father. I feel like I might be glowing, as if there were a sign over my head, but no one knows I'm his daughter except that guy at the door. I'm not sure if I want anyone else to know or not.

"I know what you're thinking," my father says, and I turn my head back to him. "Get to the point, Kieran. Okay, okay." He strikes a chord on his guitar. Without thinking about it, without looking at him, *I* take *Archer's* hand, lacing my fingers through his. I can see him out of the corner of my eye, smiling at me.

I know the songs. I know *all* the songs. I've listened to them on my iPod while running with Dusty and on our turntable when my mother is at work. So even though I'm standing in the same room as my father now, even though he's playing right in front of me, the songs still sound a little lonely to me in a way that they most likely don't to anyone else in the room. They sound a little sad.

Everyone else is here to see a show, to see this guy they might have loved when he was in a band called Shelter twenty years ago. Maybe they've followed his career through the decades and bought each album, on vinyl and tape and CD and vinyl again. But for me, this is just field research, helping me to understand my father. This is the part where I watch him, and I watch other people watch him, and I listen to these songs in a room with the guy who made them.

Luna's music seems to be in a hurry, trying to get somewhere, trying to fill all the space around you. My father's songs are different. They take their time. They're just moving around the room, filling it up the same as Luna's, but so slowly you don't really notice.

I look at the crowd when I'm not looking at my father. The light from the stage reflects on their faces in shades of gold and silver. They bob their heads in rhythm with his songs, or they sing along, sometimes loudly, opening their mouths wide and smiling while they sing, and sometimes quietly, doing not much more than mumbling the words.

It occurs to me that he can do no wrong onstage in his favorite city. There's a kind of safety to what my father is doing, going up there to be supported. He knows everyone here loves him. It doesn't seem as brave as what Luna does now, since plenty of people seeing her are seeing her for the first time. I guess she's seeking the same thing, and she's confident enough to know she'll get it too, eventually. They have something, my father and my sister, and I know my mother has it too.

He plays a long time, close to an hour and a half. I stand there and I hold Archer's hand. I shift my weight, but I don't sing along. Then finally he plays one more song and says, "Good night," softly and directly into the microphone. He leaves the stage so quickly I'm certain it isn't really the end. Applause starts up around me like the roar of the ocean when you first get out of your car and step out on the beach. It comes from nowhere in particular, but still it's everywhere at once. People shout his name, shout names of his songs, and they clap as if they're trying to call him from very far away. Archer and I start clapping too, softly at first and then just as hard as the rest of the crowd. Three minutes of this and he's back, and the applause settles into something satisfied, punctuated with cheers.

He starts to play the song I've been waiting for without realizing it, a song called "Lost Girls," about which I've wondered since I first heard it. Maybe he's lost plenty of girls over the years since he left, but I can't help but hope that it's about my mother, my sister, and me. "Lost girls," he sings, "waiting at the edges of my dreams.

213

I wish I could tell you my love wasn't what it seemed."

I've thought a lot about what he meant by those words. Does he wish he could tell the girls, but he can't because they're lost? Or is he saying that he wishes his love were different, but he knows it *was* what it seemed? That it wasn't enough, the way he loved. I wonder if he's singing that lyric differently now because he knows I might be here. I can't tell, but I realize I'm clenching my hands into fists so I try to loosen my fingers, stretching them out into the air at my sides. That's when I feel Archer take my right hand in his again and I smile without looking at him.

When my father is done, he doesn't leave the stage right away. The house lights come up and he bends down to pack away his own guitar and pedals, even though I'm sure he could ask someone else to do it for him. A few people in the crowd press forward and stand at the edge of the stage, talking to him. He seems happy to talk with them, and he manages to mostly keep eye contact even while he's packing things away.

"What do you want to do?" Archer asks. It's still loud in here and his mouth is close to my ear, his breath warm and soft on my skin. He's still holding my hand.

I turn toward him. "I don't know."

"We should let him know we're here, right?"

I don't move much closer to the stage, but there are larger empty pockets of space in the room now. I see my father look out over the dwindling crowd, squinting a little in the lights that still shine down on him. I raise my hand into a wave, just above shoulder height, and somehow my father sees it. His mouth breaks into a smile, a real one that goes into his eyes, too, and he raises his hand in return.

I turn away then, because I'm not sure what else to do. Archer follows me, or maybe I lead him, holding his hand.

The guy from the door is standing in the hallway where people are milling around. His job must be mostly over, because he doesn't look too interested in what's going on around him. But then he sees me and his eyes flash like a light is switching on. He smiles at me and I smile back, pretending I'm the girl he must imagine I am, the one who has just watched a show performed by her (B-list?) rock-star dad and who must, just must, have something like a perfect life. I wave to this guy too.

Ahead of us the double doorway frames a wide square of incandescent light. I take a deep breath, and I'm still holding Archer's hand as we step out onto the street.

thirty-five

WE WALK DOWN THE BLOCK QUICKLY, finding our way around Kieran Ferris fans still talking in groups on the sidewalk. Archer follows my lead. I feel as if I have to put some distance between the Ballroom and me. At the corner, we stop.

Sara D. Roosevelt Park is ahead of us, a narrow sliver of green in the middle of the Bowery. It's dark but the grass still seems to glow, maybe in contrast with the dingy grayness of the streets around it, or because the air above it is fresher.

"Want to go sit down?" Archer asks, squeezing my fingers with his own. I nod and we walk toward the park.

Most of the space in there is taken up by basketball courts and a soccer field, and both are still full of players even though it's late. Their shouts and laughter carry straight across the ground to my ears, and the thumping of the basketballs sounds like footsteps, as if a dozen giant people were running across a wide-open floor.

We find a low wooden bench and I drop my bag down next to me. It feels heavier, as if I were carrying something extra after that show, but I didn't buy or pick up anything. No one even gave me a ticket stub. It's just that same copy of *SPIN* and the one of *Catcher*, which I haven't shown to anyone in New York yet.

"Shit," Archer says. "That was awesome." He's smiling. "I hope we get to play there someday."

"You will," I say, and for some reason, in this moment, I think about Ben. Would I have gone to shows with Ben? I know he loves music, but somehow I can't picture it. So where would we have gone? Lacrosse games? Someplace where there are rules and two sides to choose from. Where there's a clear winner at the end of the night.

I lean back on the bench and slip my left foot out of my sandal. I touch my toes to the ground. It's been dark for hours, but I can still feel the sun's heat stored there.

"The pavement is warm," I say.

Archer reaches down to touch the concrete with his fingers. "It was hot today."

"It takes the pavement hours to forget," I say. "The day, I mean."

Archer is looking at me, waiting.

"Just . . . It keeps the heat." I start playing with my purse's strap to keep my fingers busy.

"I know what you meant," he says. A boy on a skateboard slides by in front of us, his wheels rattling on the cracks in the side-walk. "I liked the way you said it."

My pulse is humming in my ears and I have to look away. For the first time since I've been with Archer in real life, I feel a little like that girl I was in my texts. I feel like maybe I can make words work for me.

I look up at the sky, but there's nothing to see, really. It's graphite-colored, as dark as it gets here. There's a small round moon glowing over the other edge of the park, just above the smooth, straight tops of buildings across the street.

"It's a little awkward in the city," Archer says.

I look at him. "What do you mean?"

"All the light pollution." He pointed upward at the charcoal sky, gray and free of stars. "I went to camp when I was a kid, and there were so many stars. It was like someone added them to the sky while we were driving upstate from the city. I just couldn't believe it." He's looking up and squinting as if he'll be able to spot one if he tries hard enough. "If you ever felt a lull in a conversation with a girl," he says, "you could just try to find a constellation."

The tiny blinking light of a plane comes into view and starts to cross above us. I smile. "Talked to a lot of girls, did you?"

He laughs, a small laugh that sounds like an exhale. He turns toward me and I feel a catch in my own breath. "I've come around since then," he says. "Polished my conversation skills."

I look at him. "I can really tell," I say. I say it with a flirty edge to my voice, the way I've spoken to a dozen other guys I've liked, but this feels different. "I thought you meant there are always other people around. So it's hard to find the right moment—to try to kiss someone."

He smiles and looks right at me and I—I lose my nerve.

So I look up at the sky. "How many constellations can you point out?" My heart thumps behind my ribs. This is the way I'll regroup. I can point them all out, or all the famous ones, anyway, after a whole childhood of being taught their shapes by my mother.

Archer laughs. "Mostly I just made them up," he says. "The Big Platypus, that kind of thing. The Little Toaster."

I shake my head. "And here some nice girl thought she was getting an education." I touch his arm lightly, and I can feel how warm his skin is. "The Little Toaster?"

"It would be"—he draws a square in the air with his hands—"like this."

"We all know how the ancient Greeks loved their toasters."

"Big *or* little, yes." He pushes a lock of hair away from my face and I hold my breath. "I should have stuck with the Man in the Moon or something," he says, and points toward the moon in the Manhattan sky, still waiting over the tops of buildings.

"It's not a man," I say, before I even think about it.

"What?"

I look down at the bench. Someone has carved the name Audrey into the wood between Archer's and my knees, and I reach down to touch the letters. "My mother always said it wasn't a man up there. She said it was girls."

"Girl*s*, plural?"

"Yeah." I say this and try to remember what my mother used to say. I was seven, nine, twelve, sitting out in our backyard, looking up at a dusty, shadow-covered moon. Those smudgy features weren't some guy's face, she told us, and everyone who thought they were was wrong.

"So what's up there?" Luna would ask, looking at the moon as intently as I was.

"Girls," my mother said. "Girls just like you two."

I accepted it when I was small, in the same way you accept the Tooth Fairy and her dental obsessions, Santa Claus with his sleigh pulled by bejeweled flying deer. But now I wonder what she meant. Maybe they're scooped out like the lunar seas, all those craters that might hold water if there were any water up there. Or are the girls just sitting in the moondust, leaning back on their hands with their legs crossed in front of them?

Now, sitting on this bench with Archer, something clicks and I finally put together what my mother might have meant.

"I never considered this before," I say, "but I think it has something to do with this." I slip the copy of *SPIN* from my bag and hand it to him. He takes it from me as if it's something very fragile. He holds it up to the light coming from the street lamp behind us and looks at it, quiet.

"This is amazing," he says, after a few moments have passed.

"I know."

He looks at me. "Where did you get it? Your mom?"

I shake my head. "No, eBay," I say. "I used my friend Tessa's credit card. It finally occurred me that I could just buy it, if my mom was never going to talk about this stuff." I look at Mom on the cover in Archer's lap, the so-certain set of her mouth, her wide blue-green eyes. "Though maybe she was talking about it all along."

Archer is flipping through to find the article. "Have you shown Luna?"

"No," I say. "I want to. I just haven't found the right moment.

I don't know what she'll say." I gather my hair behind my head and twist it so it stays back. The cooling night air on my neck feels perfect, like something I forgot I wanted. "I don't want her to say the wrong thing, I guess."

"I'm going to read it on the train," Archer says, "if that's okay. It's too hard to see in this light." He hands back the magazine. "Plus, there's something I want to say."

I notice my heartbeat behind my ribs then, as if someone just switched it on.

"I was just thinking about Luna, before you showed me this."

"Why?" I wonder for a moment if I've read all of this wrong. Maybe it's Luna he likes, just like practically every boy who's ever met her. "Do you have a crush on her?" I ask.

Archer laughs. "No! Luna's my friend. And so is James. It's not that." He squints a little then, as if he's trying to see me in the half-light. He takes a breath and I wait. "I keep thinking that she'd kill me if I kissed you."

Those last few words give me a tumbling feeling, as if the bench has dropped out from beneath me. But all I'm thinking is that I want to keep falling.

"So let's not tell her," I say. My heart feels like marbles in a box, shaking around so hard I'm afraid he can hear it. Another plane, a bigger one, flashes its light overhead. There are a couple hundred people up there reading or eating pretzels or falling asleep with their heads against the window glass, and they have no idea that we're down here, that this is happening miles below them.

I turn my face toward Archer. "What about time travel?" I say.

He looks at me and smiles. "Explain."

"Well, it's a long shot, but if you had already kissed me, then it would be done." I wave my hand. "Luna would kill you or she wouldn't, but I'd already be kissed." I'm looking at his lips, and I don't care about hiding it. "There's no taking it back. It's already happened."

He nods as if I just made a serious scientific proposal and he's mulling it over. "Interesting," he says. "Seems very logical."

"Logic isn't my strong suit, but I'm making an effort here." I slip my fingers out of his and turn myself so I can completely face him.

"I'm convinced." He says this so softly I have to listen hard to hear him, and he doesn't do anything, doesn't lean forward or take my face in his hands. He just looks at me. But then his head tilts slightly, and it's like I can see what's going to happen before it does. Maybe this is how time travel works after all. His lips find mine, like they're searching for something, or asking a question. It makes a racket in me, a hum that starts in my belly and spreads in all directions like sound waves traveling through water.

The last person to kiss me was Ben, a kiss I wasn't allowed to want. A kiss that wrecked my friendship with Tessa, the rest of my school year, my summer until now. This time is different. This time, when we pull apart and I open my eyes there are no swirling stars in the sky, just Archer on a bench and a bunch of kids playing basketball somewhere behind him. I'm here on this bench, but some other part of me is spiraling away, time-traveling.

My parents must have had a first kiss somewhere, before the band, the records, the tours. Before Luna and me. I wonder if they felt sure in that moment, like I do now, in that slow heat that enveloped them, that everything was going to turn out just fine.

Or even if they knew there was a chance it wouldn't, they'd still have chosen to do it anyway.

thirty-six

MEG

OCTOBER 1993

OUTSIDE THE DINER, DRY LEAVES skittered across the pavement. The heels of my boots clicked on the sidewalk and I could hear the swish of traffic from Broadway, but otherwise, the street was quiet and we were alone.

I took a deep breath and tipped my head back. The sky was a washed-out shade of blue, crisscrossed with bare branches. The trees were my favorite thing about that block, besides the Flamingo Diner. We used to come here in the middle of the night after our shows, with our friends or alone, exhausted and wired and sometimes a little drunk. Now we'd been on tour for two months, and the Flamingo felt like a place from some other life.

"We've been gone so long," I said to Kieran. I turned to face him.

He was smiling. "And now we're back."

"Yeah," I said. "For two weeks. And then we have to leave again."

"Come on, Meg," Kieran said. He reached out to hold my hand. "You want this too. We have to work for it."

"I know. I just miss home," I said. "I miss you."

He pulled me close and kissed me then, and I could feel all the molecules in my body come loose and float toward his. I remembered the first time he kissed me, outside a bar on Allen Street back home. It was January in Buffalo, freezing and gorgeous, the stars bright pinpricks in a velvet sky. I wanted to keep kissing him forever.

"I miss you too, babe," Kieran said now. "But I'm always here. We're always together."

"I know."

He looked up at the pink neon of the Flamingo's sign. "Let's eat, and then we'll go home. Just the two of us."

He opened the glass door and the bell jingled above us. Our favorite waitress, Gina, waved to us from behind the counter. Her bright red hair was exactly the same, and so was her blue uniform, her Doc Martens.

"You guys are back!" she shouted.

"Finally!" I said, smiling, but she was too far away to hear.

"And the Flamingo is our first stop," Kieran said, his voice louder than mine. He squeezed my hand.

"We're honored," Gina said. "Give me a second. I'll clean your table."

I leaned back on the wall, covered in a palm tree mural, and closed my eyes. I could hear the pleasant racket of the diner's kitchen, plates and silverware clanking and the hum of the dish-washer.

"It sounds the same," I said, opening my eyes.

"And I'm sure it tastes the same," Kieran said. He leaned toward me. "Do *you* taste the same? Let me see." He kissed me, wrapping his arm around the small of my back. My blood started to thump a new rhythm through my veins.

When we pulled apart, there was a girl standing in front of us. She was maybe nineteen, blond and brown-eyed, wearing jeans and white T-shirt. She looked friendly.

"You're Kieran and Meg, right?" she said.

Kieran looked at me, smiling. "That's us," he said.

"I'm Annabel." She turned toward a table on the opposite side of the restaurant and nodded. Her friends—lots of them—stood up and came over. There were at least six, and they formed a semicircle around us.

"We saw you guys at the Knitting Factory last year," Annabel said. "It was incredible."

"Thanks," Kieran said. "I remember that show. We just got back from a tour."

They started to ask questions, but I wasn't really listening. I put a smile on my face, but it felt like a mask. This wasn't the way it was supposed to be. The Flamingo was our place, and we weren't supposed to have to talk to anyone but each other. And maybe Gina, while we ordered our pancakes. But now everyone in the restaurant was looking our way, either recognizing us too, or figuring we were people worthy of staring at. I could hear Cat Stevens's "Here Comes My Baby" on the speakers overhead, tambourine jangling happily, and I wondered what would happen if I just danced right out the door. *There goes my baby.*

From there I could see the booth I liked best, empty against the window. Blue vinyl seats, Formica tabletop lined with a sugar bowl, a pitcher of cream, a ketchup bottle. We'd sat there at least a hundred times since we'd moved to the city, eating pancakes and eggs and grilled cheese, milky coffee so sweet it hurt my teeth. The table was right there, twenty steps away, but I didn't know how to get there at that moment.

thirty-seven

WE LEAVE THE BENCH AROUND MIDNIGHT. An hour ago the moon slid beneath the buildings across the street and now I have this sleepy, dreamy feeling that makes the world around us seem high contrast and vivid, even in the dark.

"One more thing," Archer says, as we reach the edge of the park. "I want to show you something." He steps out on the sidewalk and looks around to orient himself, then starts walking west.

We walk without talking, holding hands. I wonder what the people we pass see when they look at us, if they notice us at all. It feels different now, being with him, after the last few hours. Some of the questions we wanted to ask have been answered. A connection like an electric current runs in the air between us, and through our fingertips when we touch.

"Where are we going?" I ask.

"SoHo." Archer checks a street sign and leads me over the curb. "It's just a few more blocks."

He stops a while later in front of a redbrick building and pulls me up on the stoop.

"Look," he says, pointing to the list of names next to the buzzers for each apartment. He watches me as I read them. I consider them like puzzles or riddles, but none of them mean anything until I get to the fifth: *D. Byrne*. I look at Archer.

"Really?" I say. "As in David Byrne of Talking Heads? He lives here?"

A wide smile stretches across his face. "It's his studio," he says. "I just like looking at his name. When I feel crappy, sometimes I walk down here." He looks a little embarrassed, then shrugs. "I do a lot of walking. It gives me somewhere to go."

I think about what Luna told me earlier, about the Archer of a few months ago, screwing up and missing shows. I want to ask him about it but it doesn't seem like the right time. Maybe it's that I want him to tell me without my asking.

"Sounds like meditation," I say, and I sound to myself like my mother. I step closer to the buzzer and look at the letters of the musician's name. "You've never wanted to press it?"

"Of course I have," Archer says. He doesn't step any closer. "But it wouldn't be right."

I kiss him then, again, on David Byrne's doorstep, and then we step back to the sidewalk and walk toward the train.

"Josh walks by Walt Whitman's old house in Fort Greene sometimes," Archer says. He slips his hand into mine and I'm surprised at how natural it feels. "Same reason."

It surprises me that Josh, with his sarcasm and his music facts, would choose a long-dead American poet to calm him. "Really?"

Archer nods. "Josh is a complex man."

We pass a coffee shop, still open and glowing through its big front windows. There are two old men sitting in a booth in the front, leaning forward over their ceramic mugs.

"Want a latte?" Archer asks, smiling. "Or any other coffee-shop food prop?"

"Ha-ha," I say. "You know, I actually do like that job. My coworkers tease me for being so straitlaced, but I feel like part of a family there." I say it and I realize that it's true. "They all have nicknames. It's like a club."

Archer glances at me and waits for me to keep going.

"I'm the youngest," I say. "They called me Lolita until I explained to them that the character was a victim of a pedophile. So now they just call me Phoebs."

"That's okay," he says.

"I don't know," I say. "I would like to have a really great nick-name."

Archer points to the subway sign a half block away, and we turn toward it.

"I could try to give you one," he says. I glance down into the open hole of a basement in front of a market. The narrow stairs and all that darkness makes me feel a little dizzy.

"Go for it."

He steps around a box of lettuce on the sidewalk. "All right. A phoebe is a kind of bird, right?"

"Yeah, but I'm named for the moon goddess."

"You already have a sister named Luna." He waves his hand. "Too many moons. Let's go with the bird phoebe. How about Bird? Or Birdie."

We walk under the awning of a flower shop and I smile in the direction of the roses in the window. I can see his reflection, watching me. "I like that," I say. "Birdie."

"Truthfully, there are probably a bunch of toddlers running around Brooklyn with that name actually on their birth certificate," he says.

"There are worse things," I say. "How did you know that, anyway?"

He looks at me. "How'd I know what?"

"About the phoebe bird."

He flips his palm up toward the sky in a *Who knows?* gesture. "I'm a man of much hidden knowledge."

"I see that." I take my first step down the stairs. "Fake constellations, rock-star doorsteps, that kind of thing."

Archer smiles. "I have it all," he says.

Archer insists on riding the train with me back to Brooklyn Heights.

"I don't have anything better to do," he says, swiping his MetroCard through the reader.

"It's one o'clock in the morning," I say.

"I'm not tired."

He stands with me on the platform, our shoulders touching, while the train pulls in after a rush of air that comes first.

A half hour later, when we come out on the street in front of Borough Hall, the air smells like rain but the pavement is dry.

"We better hurry up," he says.

On Luna's street, it's almost perfectly quiet except for the sound of someone in one of the brownstones listening to Otis Redding. I hold Archer's hand and close my eyes for a second, knowing that next time I hear "Try a Little Tenderness" I'll think of this moment, right here.

In front of Fourteen, a car slides past on the street. I look up to the window of Luna's bedroom. It's dark.

Archer leans in to kiss me there on the sidewalk, but I turn my head away.

"Not here," I say, and grab his hand. "Come on." I pull him down the stairs to the front door. His lips are on mine before we get all the way down; my back presses into the wall and his hands find their way into my hair. I feel like I'm made of embers, like I'm burning. I have no idea now long it is before he pulls back just a little, and our lips separate. He looks at me.

"I should go upstairs," I say. I'm breathless. "It's so late."

"Okay," he says, but he kisses me again, his fingers gently pressing against my spine. And then he lets me go.

When the door clicks shut behind me, I want to open it again immediately and go wherever Archer is going. I stand for a moment in the foyer waiting for my heart to slow down. The ceiling light shines brightly on the pile of mail, which has fallen in a small avalanche over the table. There are half a dozen magazines amid the white envelopes holding bills or whatever and I'm happy to notice that no one in my family is on their covers.

thirty-eight

"What the hell, Phoebe?"

It's so dark in the apartment I can't really see Luna at first. When my eyes begin to adjust I can just make her out, standing in front of the window. She's a shadow with nothing to stick to, the glow from the street surrounding her like an aura.

"What?" I say. Luna turns on a lamp and the room fills with light.

"Where have you been all night?" she asks. She's wearing a black tank top and pink gym shorts, her hair loose around her shoulders. Her hands are moving, as they always are, fingers splayed and palms facing one another. If you took a picture of her right now, she'd look like she was clapping, cheerleader-style. But angry.

As for me, I just don't want to get any closer to Luna. She's like a dangerous wild animal, a panther maybe, or some graceful and terrifying wild dog.

"I was with Archer," I say. I'm trying to keep my voice calm. "I told you that."

She shakes her head. "It's nearly two in the morning. You couldn't call?"

I look at my purse, which I'm still holding. "My phone ran out of battery." It seems safe to say this, since my phone is switched off in the bottom of my bag and I'm reasonably certain she won't ask for proof.

She takes a step toward me, barefoot on the worn wood floor. "So *Archer* couldn't have sent a text?"

"I didn't ask him to. You're not Mom. And you knew where I was."

"I didn't, actually." She switches her weight to other hip. "That's the point."

James comes out of their bedroom then, hair rumpled, in a white T-shirt and pajama pants. He leans in the doorway, looking sleepy and a little worried. I smile at him, partly so he'll stop worrying and partly so he'll be on my side, at least a little.

I walk over to the table to put down my purse and catch a glimpse of myself in the mirror. My hair has curled into loose ringlets from the humidity and my lips look bee-stung, kissed. It's likely Luna can guess what I've been doing. I wonder if James can too.

"Luna," he says, his accent just cool enough to make him sound like an alien in our superheated Ferris-girl galaxy. "She's back. She's fine. It's okay."

"I know, J. I just—I need to talk to her." She lowers her voice to a purr. "I'll be nice. Go back to bed." I can see how tense her shoulders are. Her stance is so tight it seems as if she's ready to pounce.

James stands in the doorway for another moment, looking at me. I give him a half smile to let him know it's okay if he leaves. I almost mean it. He nods almost imperceptibly, then steps back and closes the door with a soft click.

Luna walks over to the turntable and puts the needle on the record she left on there earlier. It's white vinyl, so I'm not surprised when the sounds of Vampire Weekend fill the room.

"We're *not* going to do this," Luna says, her voice a low whisper. The music, I can see, is a cover. She doesn't want James to hear.

"Do what?" I try to make my voice sound bored, but my heart is racing. I flop down on the couch.

"This . . . role switching. You are not going to be the bad one." She's walking toward me, taking measured steps in her bare feet. She perches on the edge of the gray armchair, her posture rigid.

"Why?" I ask, angling my shoulders toward her. "Because you're so good at it?"

"Because it's bullshit." She practically spits out this last word. "Because you're a kid."

"I'm only two years younger than you." I uncurl my fingers, my hands at my sides. I can't remember the last time I argued with Luna, but that's because I usually just let her have her way.

"Exactly," Luna says. "Two years is a long time. You're still in high school." Behind her, framing her head, is one of her narrow bookcases, and I figure some of the thick books must be her college textbooks. She was studying psychology with a music minor. Then she quit, and now she wants to pretend she has all the answers.

"Right," I say. "You're so old and so wise." I shake my head. "How'd you get that way? Because you dropped out of college?"

"I didn't drop out," she says, "I'm going back." But her voice is unsteady. She doesn't sound sure. She shakes her head and looks at the bedroom door, then takes a deep, slow breath.

"Right," I say. "You're on leave. That's why I should listen to you?"

"You should listen to me because I'm on my own." Her voice is softer now, steady again, but a surge of anger runs like electricity through me.

"Are you?" I say. "Because I'm pretty sure Mom pays your phone bill, *at least*. And you're living with your boyfriend, Luna. You're in a band. Like Mom was. With your boyfriend. Like Mom. You moved to New York. Like Mom!" I take a step closer to her. "You named your band the Moons! I don't know why you don't get it. You want to pretend that you're nothing like her, you act like you hate her, but you're practically trying to live her life."

She shakes her head and looks away from me.

"Mom's not perfect, you know." Luna's looking at the robot flower, which is shining cheerily in the lamplight, fake blooming forever.

"I have never, ever considered her perfect," I say, but Luna just keeps talking.

"First of all, she's not as independent as you think she is."

I roll my eyes and she delivers the rest of it quickly, like a punch line she doesn't expect to be funny.

"She's sleeping with Jake," Luna says.

"What?" I feel my face get hot. "No, she's not."

It's true that Jake is around a lot. They've been friends for years. But he's not her boyfriend.

"Of course she is," Luna says. "Mom wants to pretend she doesn't need a man or whatever, but that's only because Jake basically *is* her man. Has been for years." Luna leans against the back of the chair as if she's exhausted. "But she won't talk about it. I suppose she thinks it's better to be known as the patron saint of fortitude."

I can't make myself say anything, so instead I look down, inhale the night air, cool and fresh, coming in the window. I suddenly have the urge to go back outside, where the sky is open and there's more air than anyone can possibly use. The apartment seems so small right now. I look at Luna.

"Everything is so easy for you," I say. I mean: her life, her talent. I mean the way she always knows what's going on or just convinces herself that what she believes is right. She'll rewrite the story if necessary, and she can make herself believe it.

But when I lift my eyes to Luna, she looks stricken, shocked. I cannot for the life of me imagine why.

"Nothing is *easy*," she says. With the fingers of her right hand she's worrying a thread on the chair cushion below her, making the same movement over and over until she finally rips it free. "Nothing." Then she stands and turns and goes back into her bedroom. I expect her to slam the door, but she closes it quietly with the same click James made a while earlier.

The moment she's gone I hear the rain, dripping on the fire escape, twangy and metallic. Its scent comes in on a whiff of air: green and wet, almost like seaweed. Maybe it's been raining this whole time. I turn off the light and picture Archer coming up from the 2 train stop near his parents' apartment, and later, making wet footsteps across the marble floor of the foyer. Now I know what his bedroom looks like, the walls and the bed and the chair over which he'd drape his wet jeans and T-shirt.

I lie on the couch until the record stops playing and the needle returns to its stand, and then I lie there longer, until it starts to rain so hard the street sounds like radio static, just a solid wall of hiss and fuzz. Then in the lull of that comforting white noise, I sleep.

thirty-nine

IN THE MORNING, LUNA SEEMS FINE. She's awake before me again, putting cereal boxes on the table when I open my eyes. Her hair is still wet from the shower and twists in large curls down her back, dampening her shirt. She's singing, but so softly I can hardly hear her. She's mumble-singing. And I'm staring at her, which, eventually, she notices. She stops what she's doing and looks at me.

"Hi," she says. Then "Morning." She stands there, holding a cereal bowl, as if she were posing for a painting.

"Hi." I sit up and pull my legs underneath me, still wound in the sheet.

"Cereal," she says, and motions toward the table. It's like there's a language barrier between us, as if I were an exchange student and it's her job to make sure I understand the basics of life.

I run my fingers through my tangled hair. "Yep," I say.

She pours some granola in her bowl and places the spoon on top carefully, like a garnish. "Are you coming to practice with us?"

This is a good sign, I figure, since she just spoke a full sentence to me. Also, she's not trying to keep me as far as possible from Archer.

"Sure," I say. "I'd like to see the place. And I think my schedule's pretty free."

I mean this last part as a joke, but Luna just nods. She winds her hair into a bun and secures it with a rubber band, so she looks like a ballerina or maybe a librarian. She looks like she means business.

Luna points past me, across the room. "You'd better get into the shower, then."

She sits down at the table and I grab a handful of clothes from my suitcase near the door: a gray tank top and a navy striped skirt. When I close the bathroom door behind me I can hear Luna singing again, but through the walls I can't make out any of the words.

The Moons share a practice space in Dumbo with two other bands, in an old paper bag factory a few blocks from the river. They have a complicated schedule worked out, written in blue and green and red ink on a piece of notebook paper and pasted up on the door, and they can't practice late at night or people in neighboring buildings complain.

The stairway is dark and narrow, but their second-floor room has a huge iron-framed window looking out on the street. Josh and James are already there, Josh fiddling with his hi-hat cymbal and James unpacking his guitar.

"You know," I say to him, "for a guy who lives where I'm staying, I see very little of you."

"Early riser, most of the time," he says, smiling. "And you are a sound sleeper."

Luna unlatches her case and takes out her guitar, plugging it into an amp by the window. The amp hums softly like an insect.

"Where's Archer?" she asks, which means I don't have to. I try to read her, but she's poker-faced.

"He's coming from his parents' place," Josh says. "Be here soon."

I sit down in a chair between the window and Josh's seat at the drums, and put my feet on top of Luna's guitar case, gently, as if it were fragile. As if it were a cocoon, maybe, or some kind of papier-mâché sculpture made of newspaper strips and dried paste.

Luna and James start trying to work out a melody, their heads bent together over their guitars. Josh looks out the window and then sits down again, drumming his sticks on his knees.

"Archer said your dad is a musician too," I say.

He squints a little. "Yeah," he says. "You'd know his name, if you knew jazz."

"I know Charlie Parker," I say. "Miles Davis. Not new jazz."

Josh nods. "I think my dad wishes I would just join his band someday, but it's not my scene." He reaches out to touch the edge of his crash cymbal. "He comes to our shows sometimes. I don't hide in the back room like Luna does." He taps his sticks against each other. "But it is a little awkward when he and I are the only black people in the room. It makes it hard to explain why I'm here and not with him."

"That sucks," I say.

"Yeah. He looks past me, then smiles. "And whenever I see him in the crowd, it throws off my timing."

The door opens then, and Archer comes in.

"Hey," he says to everyone. He kneels down to open his bass case and looks at me. "Hi," he says.

"Hi." I can't keep from smiling, though I'm sure Luna is studying me.

"We're trying 'Open Road' again," James tells Archer.

"New song," Josh tells me.

Luna sighs and slumps back in her chair. "I don't even like this one anymore." She holds up her rumpled notebook and looks at the page. "Is it lame to write a song about touring? I mean, is that too meta?"

"*You're* too meta," Josh says, and she sticks out her tongue at him. He does the same back to her.

"Glad to see you guys keep things mature," I say, but it's good to see Luna be silly.

She sits up straighter and sings the first lyric: "Lean back and see the star-strewn sky." Her voice sounds so big in such a small room. She makes a face. "It's not right," she says. "Too many *S*s. And the rhythm is off."

"Star-bit," I say.

Everyone looks at me, and Archer breaks out into a full-on smile. I'm not sure what made me think of it, or what made me say it, but I know it's right.

"What?" Luna asks.

"*Star-bit*. Like, bitten by the stars? It's surprising, a little startling. It's a word you wouldn't expect." I look at James and then back to Luna. "When you put them together, those two words have . . ." I look for the right verb and then settle on it. "Fizz."

It's the kind of thing my favorite English teacher, Ms. Stanton, would say. I had her last year, and she was always trying to get me to work on the literary magazine. I haven't yet, but I'm considering it for next year. Especially since I'll have no friends at school and nothing to do. (Ha. Except seriously.) Anyway, what I like about songs is that the lyrics don't have to make sense. They just have to sound good. It's like poetry. The stars can't bite the sky, I guess, except when it seems like they do. It sounds right.

Luna smiles, slow and surprised.

"Let's try it," she says.

James and Archer step into their places, the same spots as when they were onstage at the Tulip Club. Josh gets this focused look on his face, as if he were going to run a mile or fix a car engine, and he hits the first beats. And then, in front of me, they make a song.

It's a quiet one, and Luna exhales the words like breath. She blows the song into the tiny room and it seeps out the open windows to the street. I think about all the people passing by and what they'll hear of her, on their way to wherever they're going. I wonder if they'll stop to listen for a minute. And when she sings my line, it sounds perfect, as if the words were meant to fit together just like that.

When they finish, Luna smiles.

"Yep," she says.

"Yep?" I say.

She nods, still looking at me like she's looking at something new. "Thanks, Fee."

I can feel the smile on my own face. "Glad to be of service," I say.

She looks down and fiddles with her guitar and Archer comes over to me. He crouches down next to me.

"Finally your lyrics got some music," he says. He touches my bare knee gently, and the way it feels, he might as well have tiny firecrackers in his fingertips. "They deserve it."

"You're leaving tomorrow," he says, his voice low.

I nod.

"What are you doing later?"

A sparkling feeling spreads up from my stomach. Really I just want to kiss him again, right now, but not in this room with my sister watching.

"We're busy later," Luna says, ten steps away.

I look at her. "We are?"

"And anyway . . ." Luna stands up. "She's seventeen, Archer." There's a hard edge to her voice, a broken asphalt heat and scrape.

I step toward her, and I can hear my sandals on the wood floor.

"And you're nineteen," I say. "And *living with your boyfriend*." But Luna isn't looking at me. She's standing with her shoulders angled straight at Archer, and now he's standing too.

"I know she's seventeen." Archer is shaking his head slightly, as if he can't believe they're having this conversation. "I'll take care of her, Luna."

Luna purses her lips. "She's my sister. *I'll* take care of her."

I look at James, who is sitting, but still clutching his guitar as if he's afraid to put it down.

"I can take care of myself," I say, but no one is listening to me. I feel invisible and mute, and if I've slipped through a doorway to some other dimension. I don't know how to make this stop.

Archer's shoulders are straight and square in his T-shirt. "Have you thought about what Phoebe wants, Luna?"

"What do you mean?"

"You're so mad at your dad, but maybe Phoebe wants to see him."

"What?" She turns away from him, shaking her head. "Our father isn't interested in us."

"Luna, this is crap," Archer says. "Your dad *wants to see you*."

I'm trying to catch Archer's eye, trying to stop this, but he won't look at me.

"You act like he couldn't care less, but he does. He'd be *happy* to see you."

Luna won't stop shaking her head, her hair brushing her shoulders. She looks fierce but small, and she's starting to look a little less sure. "If that were true, he'd have made it happen."

"He tried, Luna! He came to our show." Archer doesn't say: *and you hid in the back room*. He takes a breath and lets it out through his nose.

Josh is watching the conversation like a tennis match, following Luna and Archer with his eyes. James puts his guitar in a stand and sits down on a folding chair near the window.

Luna kneels down by her bag and starts rummaging through it, but what she's looking for, I don't know.

"This is a guy who has been gone, completely missing from

our lives, for three years," she says. "Now I'm in the city and it's convenient enough to see me? Because he only has to take the train?"

"Fine," Archer says. "Be mad. I get it. But we could use his help. He'd record us, for free, I'm one hundred percent sure."

I gasp without meaning to, but Luna doesn't hear it.

"How?" Luna asks. "How are you so sure?"

Archer looks at me. Finally. But now I don't really care anymore. I throw up my hands.

"Why the hell not?" I say to him.

Archer turns his head toward Luna. "Because I know," he says.

"You're going to have to elaborate," James says. He's sitting up straight in his chair.

"Because we saw him," I say.

Luna snaps her gaze toward me. "Who did?"

"Archer and me. I was the one who wanted to go. I convinced him to come with me."

"I'll bet," Luna says.

"Hey," says Archer. "This isn't even about me."

She whips her head toward him. "I say no, so you go through my sister?"

"I wanted to go!" I say. "It was me!"

Luna shakes her head. She's pacing now, like a wild cat, near the window. I can see a strip of sky over the roof of the building across the street, glossy blue like bright tile. Like the skies children draw in their pictures. I figure it's time to tell the truth, or whatever part of it I can get out right now.

"We went to his show last night, Luna. He invited us." I'm trying to get her to look at me. "He put us on the list."

Luna opens her mouth and then closes it. She blinks.

"Okay," James says, and his calm voice sounds like river water. It runs over stones; it rounds sharp edges. "Let's all take a breath." He says this and I do, but I might be the only one in the room who's breathing.

"Archer has a point," James says. "We're working really hard, Luna. And you have this connection that could make everything easier. It's frustrating sometimes." He presses his lips together and waits for her to say something.

"So you want me to call up my dad, who basically abandoned us, who doesn't give a shit about us—"

"He does," I say. And it's true, isn't it? He must care, at least a little. He was glad to see me. I know he was.

"Think about it this way," James says. "We're planning on recording in some crappy little studio, when your dad is *Kieran Ferris*."

"So that's why you want me around?" Luna says this, but I can't believe she really thinks it. It's so obvious James would love her no matter who her father was.

"No," James says. "I think it should be pretty clear that that isn't why I want you around, since I've never even met the guy. I want you around for yourself. But it pisses me off that you won't even consider it."

Luna stands and faces him. "Well, then you'll just have to be pissed."

James looks at her then, a long look like he's trying to

remember who she is just then. Then he stands up too.

"Okay," he says. "But you should think about telling the truth." He turns and walks out the door.

Luna's face is still stony, but I can see her mouth start to crumple. The room is so quiet we can hear James's steps as he walks down the hall and down the stairs. We hear the door shut.

Josh clears his throat. "I'm hungry," he says. "Anyone feel like tacos?" He waits for a moment and when no one says anything, he turns and follows James out the door.

"No one's asking you to make a decision today, Luna," Archer says. He's right, he's being reasonable, but I can't stand the way she looks right now, lost and sad. And right now, I can't stand the fact that some boy thinks he knows what's right for me—for Luna, too—even if he's right.

"Let her be," I say to him. "If she doesn't want his help, then she doesn't."

Archer puts his bass back in its case. He clicks it shut: one, two, three latches.

"Sure. What do I know?" Archer says.

He stands up then, leaving his bass on the floor, and steps over it. He walks through the doorway to the hall, to the street, to wherever.

The whole time, he doesn't look at me once.

forty

LUNA DOESN'T SAY ANYTHING FOR the whole walk back to her building. She carries her guitar case without swinging it, most of the time managing to keep it parallel with the sidewalk. It keeps bumping my leg until I move a little closer to the street. I touch some of the lamp-posts as we walk, for luck or out of nervousness, I'm not sure which. I try not to look at Luna. I look at the sky, clear and blue, golden light collecting around the tops of buildings. I haven't checked my phone, but it has to be close to dinnertime, since the subway was full of commuters in sneakers or flip-flops with their skirt suits. When we pass people, I make eye contact because I know she won't. I imagine her gliding along next to me like some kind of hovercraft, fueled only by her anger.

At the corner of Court and Schermerhorn, a tall, thin guy with a few days' worth of beard leans against a newspaper box across from the bookstore.

"Hey, girl," he says to Luna. "Smile a little."

Luna stops. She turns toward him, standing flat against the window so I can see the reflection of the back of her head. She angles her shoulders in his direction and it seems like the air shifts around us, whirling in a miniature tornado. I hold my breath. I'm waiting to see an impromptu demonstration of the famous Luna Ferris Fury.

But then she whirls back the other way, the air shifts back, and she keeps walking. It takes me a couple of steps to catch up.

She glances at me sideways, looking at me for the first time on our entire trip home. "I really fucking hate it when guys tell me to smile."

I sidestep behind her to avoid a garbage can on the sidewalk.

"They never tell me that," I say. "Which can only be because I'm always smiling, or because no one notices I'm not." I look at Luna and I can tell I'm chattering to no one. She unlocks the front door to her building and swings her guitar and herself inside the foyer, then starts to climb the stairs. I just follow.

Upstairs, she opens the door to her apartment, sets the guitar case on the floor, and sits down on the couch. I figure that since she's lounging in what's basically the middle of my bedroom for the week, she doesn't want to be alone. So I take off my sandals and walk over to sit down in the armchair across from her. I pull my legs to my chest. She doesn't look at me, just keeps her eyes trained on the ceiling.

I think about putting on a record, but I don't want to move from this spot until she talks to me.

"Maybe you can tell me how you do it." I run my fingers over the arm of the chair.

"How I do what?" She sounds tired, and her voice is so quiet I tip my ear closer to her without meaning to.

"How you're always so sure about everything. You always know exactly what you want. You always know what the right thing is for you." She doesn't say anything, doesn't even move, so I continue. "You can leave home, no problem. You can tell Mom you're quitting school." I take a breath. "You would have told Tessa if Ben had kissed *you*."

"Who knows what I would have done?" she says. "Sometimes it's easier to just shut up."

I scoff.

"What?" She sits up to face me, swinging her legs onto the floor. Her eyes look enormous, green and blue and gray all at once.

"You never just shut up."

She purses her lips. "I shut up," she says, "if it's necessary."

I shake my head, feeling my hair swing over my shoulders. "Nope."

"I do!"

I smile. "You are literally proving my point right now."

She takes a deep breath, a loud breath.

"You can't even breathe quietly," I say. I'm trying to make her laugh, but she doesn't. Instead, she just keeps looking at the coffee table, at the robot flower my mother made. It catches the sunlight still coming in the window and seems to glow, silver and spiny.

I suddenly feel like telling Luna the truth about something.

"I've been talking to Archer," I say. "Texting, I mean. Since I was here in February."

Luna looks at me. "What?"

"I like him, Luna. I don't know what this is, but it isn't nothing." I look down at my mother's bracelet and twist it on my wrist. "I'm sorry I didn't tell you."

She shakes her head. "Okay," she says. Her voice sounds small. My first thought is, *That was too easy.* I look up and see that she's shivering.

"I think I've screwed everything up, Fee." Luna presses her fingers to her eyes, and I notice that she's wearing three rings, all silver ones made by our mother. Her fingers have been bare for days before this, and I can't remember if she was wearing them earlier today.

"James will come back soon," I say, leaning toward her. "It's so obvious that he loves you."

"It's not James," she says. "I know he loves me. Even when I'm a bitch." She looks at me. "I think . . . I'm pregnant."

I forget to breathe for a moment. Sparkly lights pass before me and I think I'm seeing stars, that I'm hallucinating or passing out, maybe. But then I realize it's the lights of a passing police car twinkling blue and red on the living room wall.

"H-how?"

"How do you think?" She leans back on the arm of the sofa. She looks weak. It's the first time I've seen her look like this, maybe ever.

I'm shaking. "That's not what I mean." I speak slowly, enunciating every word. "How could you be so stupid?"

Luna doesn't say anything for a minute. I can hear the sounds of the street, passed up by the summer air through the open window. A dog barking. Cuban music from a tinny-sounding radio.

Someone throwing glass bottles into a garbage can. I have this feeling like I could just walk outside right now, toward that dog, toward that radio. I could walk away from Luna and none of this would be my problem tonight.

But I don't move. Every instinct is telling me to run, but I stay.

Luna tries to smile, but she doesn't quite make it. "That's a good question."

"Have you taken a test?"

She shakes her head. "I keep meaning to buy one, but I can't seem to make myself go into a drugstore." She rolls one of the silver rings between her fingers. "I chickened out at CVS and Duane Reade and even a Rite Aid in Manhattan." She looks toward the window. "I don't know what's wrong with me."

"Does James know?"

She takes a long breath, a deep breath, one that comes out like a sigh. "No," she says.

I stand up from my chair, my bare feet flat on the smooth wood floor. Her worrying about being fat makes more sense now, and so do the tears after her nausea at the fountain. The barely drunk beer. I marvel at my own stupidity for not figuring it out before now.

I walk over to the counter, where James keeps a bottle of whiskey from which I've never seen him drink, and I pour a shot's worth in one of the tiny jam-jar juice glasses. I'm not sure what I'm doing, what kind of show I'm putting on here, but it seems like the right thing to do. This whole thing already feels like a memory, going fuzzy around the edges like a Polaroid developing in reverse. I think of my mother twenty years ago, taking a pregnancy test. I wonder where she was.

The whiskey tastes terrible, like wet stinging fire, but I swallow it. I set my glass down on the counter harder than I mean to, and I see Luna's shoulders jump a little. If someone else were here, she might ask why I'm torturing my sister, and I would say, *I'm not trying to*. I just don't know what to do.

This is when Luna starts to cry. I can see her eyes just fill up, and tears slide down her cheeks. But I can't say anything else. I can't make myself go over there and hug her.

Instead, I walk to the door and slide my feet into my gold sandals. Luna's purse slouches on the floor between her shoes and a pair of James's sneakers. I wait for a moment, my hand resting on the door frame. I try to hear Luna breathing, but I can't.

"I'll go," I say. "But I'm taking your wallet."

I stand there for a second and she doesn't say anything. Then I step into the hallway and just as I'm closing the door—

"Fee," she says. "I need a little time. Maybe . . . take the long way home?"

I take a breath, and my hand hovers over the doorknob for a moment. Then I say, "Okay," but I'm closing the door, and I don't know if she hears me at all.

Outside, I sit down on the steps of the apartment next door. It's six o'clock and there are church bells ringing somewhere, their sound metallic and echoing in the day's leftover heat. I don't know what to do with myself besides go to the drugstore, and that won't take more than ten minutes.

I take out my phone and shade the screen with my hand so I can see it. I have a text from my mother, but I don't read it. And one more: this one from Tessa. It says this:

Have you seen the carousel yet?

I puzzle over the words for a minute. It's the first thing she's said to me in two months without my saying something first.

"Carousel," I say out loud, and then I see it: the dark red cover of *Catcher*. I pull out the copy in my bag.

"Oo-kay," I say, for the second time tonight, though I'm saying it this time to Tessa, who is not here, or maybe to the universe, which is sending me somewhere tonight, right when I need somewhere to go.

forty-one

THE EXPRESS 4 TRAIN STOPS where I want it to, and I come up to the street feeling victorious: Phoebe Ferris, Subway Queen. At least I got something right today. I stand on Lexington Ave. for a moment, then figure out which way is west and walk down East Sixty-Eighth Street toward the park. I want to stop somewhere and waste time, but this block is mostly residential, just narrow trees and pretty stone buildings. Air conditioners hum from windows, and when I get to the last few buildings before the park, I stop for a minute under a building's green awning that stretches all the way across the sidewalk, and look at my phone. There's Tessa's text, still, and my mother's, which I see now just says *What's new today?* followed by a smiley face. *What's new?* I imagine typing. *Oh, nothing, except your older daughter is subconsciously trying to be you in pretty much every way possible and I'm just here to clean up the mess.* I slip the phone back in my bag and keep walking.

When I enter the park, three runners pass from behind me, one with a stroller and two with little dogs moving so fast their legs are blurred. Then a cyclist flies by on my right, shining with spandex. I'm in the wake of a wave of fitness here, but I'm walking slowly, taking it all in. The park is so green it's like some setting has been adjusted on a television screen. Yellow cabs pass on the road to my left, one after another, taking a shortcut through the park, I guess. The road curves and winds gently, and it leads me right to the carousel.

When I thought of the carousel I pictured it out in the air, open to the elements, but instead it's enclosed in a many-sided building made of red-and-tan-striped brick. I already checked, so I know that the carousel runs only until six o'clock today. But it's six forty-five, and the building is still open.

To the west, softball fields stretch out under the lowering, golden sun. There's a game at the farthest one, and tiny people in purple uniforms run around its big square. I wouldn't mind walking over there to sit in the grass and watch the game for while. It would be nice to pretend that I'm not on a mission, that I don't have somewhere to be.

Instead, I turn back to the carousel, then lift my phone and take a photo. In the sun I can hardly see my screen, but I know it's not right. The photo just looks like a brick building with open spaces filled with shadows. You can hardly tell that there's a carousel inside. I know this isn't what Tessa has been picturing, and it certainly isn't what Holden and Phoebe saw in *Catcher*.

We read the book with Ms. Stanton last year and some of the

girls didn't really get it. Even Willa: every day when we'd start to talk about it, she'd raise her hand and say, "Big surprise: Holden's pissed about something again." Tessa loved the book, so she'd spend half the class defending Holden for being crabby. "His little brother *died*," she'd say. In one way, though, Willa was right. The whole book is one long series of complaints: the people he thinks are phonies, the kids his age who aren't as smart as he wants them to be. He drops in the stuff about his little brother dying of leukemia so gently that if you were skimming the book, you might not even notice it, but that's where his anger comes from. And that's what I liked best about the book—not that his brother died, but the way Holden would keep circling around to it as he told us about wandering around the city. He didn't make a big deal about it, but it kept coming up, over and over. You could tell it was the thing that broke his heart and kept breaking it.

That's what I wrote in my essay, anyway, the same essay for which Tessa wrote about the symbolism of the carousel. I argued that Salinger is using Holden to show that we all have something—one thing, usually—that weighs on us. One thing that keeps cracking us open no matter how we try to glue ourselves back together.

The last time the four members of my family were in a room at the same time was when Luna turned fifteen. It was December, and my father was in Buffalo for a visit. Three days. He was supposed to leave early on the morning of Luna's birthday—he had a show somewhere—but a snowstorm hit in the middle of the night and all the flights were canceled. I remember waking up to find the whole world wrapped in white, and more snow falling from the sky like powdered sugar, half an inch per hour. When I looked out my window I could see that the lights in our garage apartment were on, and I knew my father was still there.

Pilar and Tessa both walked over from their houses at lunchtime—Tessa wore her mother's ancient snowshoes, even though it wasn't really necessary because the plows had come through, and she only had to cross the street. She just liked how they looked. Pilar showed up with her hair glittering, encrusted with snow, even though she had been wearing a hat. She had to wrap it in a towel.

Luna stood in the kitchen, her shoulders angled toward the garage and our father.

"What do we do about Dad?" she asked.

My mother was digging through the junk drawer looking for birthday candles, and she didn't look up.

"Go tell him to come over," she said.

He did. He ate enchiladas in our dining room and sang "Happy Birthday" with the rest of us while Luna sat in the glow of fifteen tiny candles, an unconvincing half smile frozen on her face. Now that I think about it, that's the only time I can remember hearing my parents sing together outside of their records.

My parents talked a little, but I don't remember what they said. He helped her shovel the driveway for an hour after lunch, wearing his not-warm-enough canvas jacket and one of my old wool hats. We were supposed to be watching a movie—*Sixteen Candles*, even though Luna was fifteen—but Luna and I were mostly watching our parents out in the snow. They talked the whole time, but I couldn't figure out what they were saying. I wished, not for the last time, that I could read lips. My father smiled a lot, which was pretty normal, as far as I knew, and my mother smiled from time to time. They looked like two people who had known each other for a long time. Which they were. Two people who, after all of this, didn't *exactly* hate each other.

But then he got the call that his flight had been rescheduled for six o'clock, and an hour later, Luna and I were standing on the porch in our boots, waving to him as the taxi pulled away. I remember being happy about the way the day—the extra day—had gone, but I was only thirteen. After he left, Luna barely talked to my mom or me for three days. Anger came off her like static electricity. Eventually it seemed to fade, and things went back to normal. Nothing changed. He didn't call any more than he had before that. And then, about a year or so later, he stopped calling at all.

Now, I walk closer and lean against the metal fence in one of the large openings in the carousel building's walls. Across from me, standing still, is a black horse with a white mane and tail, adorned with a complicated array of blankets and banners, saddle and halter. Its neck is a perfect curve, its head arcing down toward the floor. I snap the picture and there in the shadows I can see it on the screen: this is the horse that Tessa would ride, if she were here and the carousel were running. This is the one she'd choose. And if we got to the carousel too late to ride, like I did today, we could sit on the bench outside it like Holden did, and maybe we could finally talk.

I don't want to send the photograph alone, but I don't know what to type. I want to tell her I saw my father. I want to tell her about Luna, and where I have to go next. I want to say *Wish you were here* or *Next time we'll come together*, but nothing seems right.

I sit for a minute on that bench facing the carousel and I watch the clouds float over it as if they have somewhere to be. Then I click my phone on again and type, *This is the best I could do*, and then, *xo*. I hit send and the photograph wings away to the satellites, then to Tessa, wherever she is right now. Maybe in her bedroom across from my empty one; maybe on the honeysuckle trellis, making her escape; maybe sitting on the swings at the park down the street. I imagine her hearing her phone chime in her pocket, taking it out to see what I've sent. I imagine her missing me, whatever that would look like.

When I leave the park I walk from Fifth Avenue into the East Sixties, heading north in the direction of the 6 train. Just across from the station entrance I see a small bookstore with a narrow, glass-paned wooden door. USED AND RARE BOOKS, it says on a wide sign over the doorway. I stand on the sidewalk for a minute, reading the sign, and then I go in.

It's cooler inside the store but still a little stuffy, as if the air-conditioning isn't working well enough. It's darker in there, lit by incandescent lights in glass globes, and I have to wait for my eyes to adjust.

"Hello," says a voice from the back. I look up and see the silhouette of a woman on the second level, a few steps up from the floor. "What can I help you find?"

"I'm not sure," I say. I reach out and touch a row of leather-bound dictionaries. "Poetry, I think."

"That's up here," she says. I can see now that she's in her fifties, probably, pretty, with long red-brown hair pulled back into a knot. She has an armful of books and she sets them down on a table as I climb the stairs. She motions to a bookshelf on the other side of the landing, and then walks over to meet me there.

"Anyone in particular?"

I scan the shelves, but there are so many names—Frost, Dickinson, Glück, O'Hara—I don't know where to start. "I don't know that much about poetry," I say. "Just what I've read in English class. I like it, though." I'm hoping this does not sound totally lame.

She nods, a small smile on her lips. "You need a place to start," she says. She pulls a book from the shelf. "How about this?"

It's a navy blue book with sharp silver lettering: *American Women Poets*, it says, and then in smaller letters: *Twentieth Century*.

I like the way the book feels in my hands, and I like that it's full of poems I haven't read yet. The pages are a little yellowed, but there's no writing inside.

"Okay," I say. I follow the woman to the cash register. I pay her with a twenty and she gives me back a ten and some change.

When I sling my bag over my shoulder, I can feel the good weight of my new book inside.

After that, I ride down to Astor Place and then get out and walk toward Washington Square. I don't know where I'm going—retracing my steps from the other night?—but on a street where the buildings are hung with NYU flags, I see a bunch of girls walking together. They must be summer students or something, because they have backpacks. I don't know what makes me notice them. Maybe it's the way they're walking, leaning toward each other and laughing, that reminds me of my friends. The friends I don't really have anymore. Without thinking, I follow them, a little aimlessly, and when they go into a coffeehouse half a block away, I go in too.

I'm a whole state away from Queen City Coffee, but the sounds inside this place are exactly the same: clinking dishes, a low hum of conversation, the whirr of milk steaming. Orders being called out from the counter. I don't really drink coffee—I see way too many coffee junkies when I work to want to get involved—but I love the smell of it, and the scent of this place lowers my blood pressure almost immediately. The girls ahead of me order a bunch of iced coffee drinks, and then it's my turn. The cashier has short blond hair and a tiny silver stud in her nose. She smiles.

"What can I get for you?"

"Two percent vanilla latte, please," I say. "Medium." She nods and puts the order into the register. I hand her one of Luna's twenties. When she gives me my change I put two dollars in the tip jar.

"Thanks," she says.

"I have the same job as you," I say. "Back home."

There's no one behind me in line, so I lean against the counter and wait for my drink.

"Where's home?" the girl behind the counter asks.

When I open my mouth to answer, I've already decided that I want to be someone else today.

"DC," I say.

"Even hotter than here, right?" she says. The girls I followed in get their drinks in to-go cups and leave through the glass door.

Aunt Kit lives there, so I've spent plenty of summer weeks wandering from air-conditioned museum to museum. I nod. "This seems like nothing."

"You go to NYU?" she asks.

I pause for a second and then I nod.

"Me too. For photography." She wipes the counter with a white cloth. "What's your major?"

I know my answer without thinking about it. This is getting easier.

"English," I say.

"Have you had Professor Kirk yet?"

I shake my head.

"She's awesome. Take her class soon." She puts her hand over the counter. "I'm Emily, by the way."

"Phoebe," I say, shaking it. Who knows why, but my alternate identity doesn't seem to need a pseudonym.

"Vanilla latte," the barista calls, and I take the porcelain cup and saucer from him.

"Hey," Emily says. "We're looking for another cashier. If you need a job, I mean."

"Thanks," I say. "I've been thinking about it."

I sit down at a table by the window, take out my new book and open it in the middle. I read a poem by Rita Dove, then one by Anne Sexton. I read one by Elizabeth Bishop called "One Art," which is about losing: things, places, people. The end of the poem seems so true and vivid and perfect that it makes me want to cry, especially with all the losing and finding I've done lately. I whisper-read it here at the table because I want to say the words out loud. "'It's evident the art of losing's not hard to master, though it may look like (*Write* it!) like disaster.'"

Exactly. I want to figure out how to do this: tell the truth like I'm telling a secret. Say what I've always known in a way that seems totally new.

On the train to Brooklyn, I lean back in the plastic seat and close my eyes. Archer still hasn't texted, and soon I'll be forced to consider the fact that I leave tomorrow and I might not see him before I do. This leaves a hollow feeling in my belly, as if someone took something from me and forgot to give it back. I could text him, I know, but I don't know what to say. I can't speak lyrics right now. I'd rather talk to him in real life.

But even though that feels shitty—it just does—I'm here, and I'm getting something done. I'm helping Luna. I saw my father. I did what I came here to do. I know I won't leave New York regretting any of it.

When she was a senior, Luna had a friend named Leah who got pregnant the fall before they graduated. She was quiet and thoughtful and really smart, and Sister Rosamond seemed especially brokenhearted when Leah's bump first started to show. For a while no one was sure if she'd be allowed to go to graduation, but the nuns came through and she walked across the stage in a long white gown like the rest of the girls, her face glowing over a dozen red roses and her beautiful belly. Luna threw her a baby shower a few weeks later, and she got up super early to bake three dozen cookies in the shape of teddy bears.

Now, on the train, I wonder what a pregnant Luna would be like. Would she crave chocolate-covered pretzels or bright red watermelon, leaving the crescent-shaped rinds all over the kitchen table? Would she find perfect slim jersey dresses that would fit close to the curve of her belly, and walk around with her hands on either side of it as if she were covering the baby's ears? Would she move back home? Maybe she'd have to give everything up. But maybe not: my mother didn't, at least not right away. A scene flashes in my head: me touring with the Moons like Aunt Kit did with Shelter, Luna's baby in soundproof earmuffs, asleep in my arms. Sure, my mother would kill me, but I'd get to go somewhere, to be with Luna and Archer and my nameless niece or nephew.

Of course, I don't know whether Luna would have the baby at all.

Somewhere in Lower Manhattan I notice that there's a girl in the seat across from me, a big white sketch pad open across her lap. Her hair is wound into a hundred tiny black braids over her shoulders. I'm trying not to look at her but after I while I realize that she's looking at me. I catch her eye.

"You're drawing me," I say, a statement, not a question. The wall of the train tunnel lights up with sparks from the track.

The girl smiles and bites her lip. "Yes." She holds her pencil in the air over the paper. "Is that okay?"

"I guess," I say, but I'm smiling too. There are only a few people on this train car, but still it really feels like she's chosen me.

"I'm an art student," she says. "Sometimes I ride the train around for a few hours and sketch." She flips through her pad and I see the portraits she's drawn, shaded in pencil and full of quick jagged lines. "Usually the people don't notice."

We pull away from Bowling Green and start that long, lurching ride under the river, the train screeching on the tracks.

"I guess I don't have anything else to do but notice," I say. I glance out the window as if there's something to see, but it's just dark walls and graffiti in the tunnels. "I should tell you that I'm getting off at Borough Hall."

"Then I guess I'd better finish," she says. "You can see it if you want."

I shrug. Part of me does want to see it, but more than that I want to believe that she sees me the way no one else does, that she has found a way through her pencil to see the me I haven't even figured out yet.

When the train stops at Borough Hall I smile at the girl and she looks up and smiles back. She puts her pencil flat against the page and starts to angle the sketch pad toward me. But before I can see it I hop up and stand near the doors before they open.

"Thanks," I say, but I shake my head. I'm looking out the windows, waiting for the platform to appear in front of me. I'm almost afraid to look—I'd rather just imagine she got it right. "I'm sure it's great," I say, and when the train's doors slide open, I step out and don't look back.

forty-two

MEG
AUGUST 1993

OUT THE HOTEL WINDOW, I could see a few buildings on Fifth Avenue rise above the trees across the park, dark against the sun-washed sky. I squinted into the brightness and then turned back to the room. In front of me, the bed looked like a cloud, except instead of water vapor and mist there were thousand-thread-count sheets and a silk duvet. And Kieran, on the left side of the mattress, looking at me.

"I feel like we're John and Yoko," he said. "Let's have a bed-in." He reached toward me and I crawled across the bed and settled in his arms.

"I think we need a cause," I said, my head against his chest. "Peace, maybe. In homage to the ones who came before."

"Peace is great," Kieran said, "but the *cause* is that we're at the Ritz and we need to take advantage of it." He tipped one of the open champagne bottles on the bedside table over a glass flute, but it was empty. Only a few pale golden drops fell out. "Hmm," he said, half to himself. "We're going to have to get more."

It felt magical, being there. It was like heaven, everything white and glowing and half-blurred. But the truth was that everything was magical, lately. Like the week before, when Paul Westerberg came to our show in Minneapolis. I had thought Kieran was going to fall apart on the floor right then, just disintegrate into pieces right there on the stage. But he didn't. And Paul came backstage afterward and drank beers with us, still wearing his sunglasses, and after a while he seemed like just a guy and not someone who used to be the singer for the Replacements, a band Kieran has idolized since he was twelve years old. Things changed like that, lately. They transformed.

"If you could eat anything right now," Kieran said, "what would you order?"

I thought about it. "Hot fudge sundae, samosas, and . . . coconut soup from the Thai place we went to in December, on Fifty-Seventh. That's only a few blocks away."

Kieran gestured to the phone. "Make it happen, babe." He rolled onto his side. "Make that guy say, *It's my pleasurrrre.*"

"The concierge," I said. "That's what he's called."

"Whatever," Kieran said, smiling. "He'll get whatever we want, Rick said."

"Okay," I said.

I picked up the receiver and the voice was already answering before I got it to my ear.

"Would you like the sundae while we're getting the rest?" he asked. "We have that on hand."

"Of course," I said. It seemed like the right answer, and I did want that sundae right then. I'd never been able to snap my fingers and produce fancy ice cream before. It was like having a magical power.

"We'll send it right up," he said.

I remembered my manners. "Thank you," I said.

"You're very welcome."

When I hung up the phone, I stood up on the bed, my feet sinking into the duvet like I was walking on a cloud. I did a little Charleston-like dance move, while Kieran watched.

"Did you think we'd get here?" he asked. "In the beginning, I mean."

"I don't know," I said.

"I think I always did." He pushes his hair out of his eyes. "I knew as soon as I saw you."

I took a step toward him, then leaned down and kissed him on the nose. I pulled him up to standing.

"Did you know," I said, "that we'd one day jump on a really big bed at the Ritz?" I started jumping and he followed, the two of us in rhythm.

"Yes!" Kieran shouted, and somehow, over our jumping, I heard a knock at the door. I fell to the mattress, bouncing, and hopped off onto the floor. Kieran was still jumping when I opened the door.

And there, in a silver dish on a white-cloth-covered cart in the hallway, was the most beautiful hot fudge sundae I had ever seen. With two spoons.

forty-three

Out on Court Street, it's after eight o'clock and the sky is darkening, streaked with pink and gray cirrus clouds. I'm standing on a sidewalk speckled with gum in Jackson Pollock patterns. Above me, the Duane Reade sign glows neon scarlet and strangely, I find it comforting. But I don't want to go inside.

Because if I go inside, there's an ending to this story. Maybe Luna is pregnant and maybe she's not, but either way, we have to pick a way forward. Here, right now, it's Schrödinger's uterus. She seemed so heartbroken when I left—I'm afraid everything will be different for both of us either way.

My phone rings in my backpack then, and I step closer to the building and pull it out. It's Aunt Kit, so I answer.

"Darling niece," she says, instead of hello.

"Darling aunt," I say.

"I hear you're visiting our old haunts. Where are you now?"

I look up at the drugstore sign. "Um, near Luna's. Just stopping at the store."

"Look, rosebud, I'm on a mission here. Will you please call your mother back?" She waits one beat. "I know she's a pain sometimes, but she loves you."

"I know that," I say. "I just need a little space."

"*Totally* understandable," Kit says, drawing out the words. "But as you have your space, just know that I'm losing mine. She keeps calling me . . . and *calling me*." She pauses. "Listen, I know she wants you to talk to Luna. Have you done it yet?"

I take a breath. The door to Duane Reade slides open, and I can hear the song that's playing inside: Madonna's "Like a Prayer." Indeed.

"I've talked to her, sure," I say, "in that I have spoken words in her presence." Kit exhales a laugh, and I smile too. "But I haven't told her I think she should go back to school."

"Why not?" Kit says this in a voice that isn't at all accusing, just curious.

"Because I don't know if she should." As I say it for the first time, I realize that it's true.

"It's okay not to know," Kit says. A car honks on the street in front of me and I strain to hear her. "And I can understand wanting to let her make her own decisions. But I can also understand your mom's worry."

I probably could too, if I knew where the worry came from. "Aunt Kit?"

"What, marigold?" She's used flower nicknames for Luna and me for as long as I can remember. In this moment, I wish I could pull her through the phone to help me with all of this. To tell me what to do. But instead I just ask her a question.

"What was it like? When Shelter was together?" I take a breath. "I know you were there."

Kit doesn't say anything for a moment. "Sometimes it was incredible," she says. "And sometimes it was really hard for your mom." She pauses. "I'll tell you about it sometime. But you should ask your mom about it."

"She won't tell us. She's never told us anything."

"Try again." Kit says this gently. "But in the meantime, call her, okay?"

"Okay."

"And be careful in the big city. *Adios*, dandelion."

"Bye," I say. When I hang up, I feel a rush of sadness run through me like a sudden rainstorm.

An old woman wrapped in a purple shawl leaves the store and the doors whoosh open. Air-conditioning envelops me like a cloud. So I walk forward, and when I step in I can almost *see* the coolness of the air, glowing blue and luminescent. The fluorescent lights hum over my head.

I've never bought a pregnancy test before. I've never had a reason to buy a pregnancy test. I don't know what aisle they're in, or how to pick one, but I do know I don't want the test to be the only thing in my basket.

I wind a labyrinthine path through the aisles, figuring I'll come upon the tests eventually. I pick out the kind of strawberry lip gloss Luna used to wear when she was little, one with a bright red sparkly label and cartoon berries on the cap. I get the kind I used to like best too: orange creamsicle. We got them every year in our Christmas stockings when we were kids, and now I'm trying to remember when that stopped. Even without opening this tube, I can still remember the plastic sweetness on my lips, always half-melted from being carried in my pocket.

In the candy aisle I get M&M's for Luna, and a Milky Way for me. I pick up six different kinds of gum and read the ingredients as if I know what any of the words mean. Probably I should just find the tests. Probably they're in the aisle with the condoms? Buy one before, or the other after. Probably I'm starting to look like a suspicious person and the security guard will soon start to follow me around the aisles.

Finally I find the tests. They range in price from seven dollars to twenty-eight, and I'm not certain what could possibly be worth paying twenty-one dollars more. It tells you if your baby is a boy or a girl? If she'll get into Harvard? It gives you a negative result if you want one, time-traveling back to make a pregnancy untrue? That would be worth it, I guess.

I choose three tests on the lower end of the price range, figuring that I'm making up in quantity what might be missing in quality.

My mother must have done this, twenty years ago. She must have stood in a store with a basket, or no basket, if she was brave enough to buy it alone. She has a sister, of course, but my mother was on tour then, and I don't think Aunt Kit went out with them much until Luna was born. Just now, I would give anything to know what it was like for my mother, but you couldn't pay me enough to call her up and ask. Because she'd want to know why, and because I would have to tell her. And because she'd know from my voice.

The last time we were in New York together, my mother and Luna and I, was when we came to look at colleges in the summer before Luna's senior year. We stayed where we always do, with my mom's friend Iris from art school (a fantastically wacky painter with a pit bull named Jack and hair bleached so blond it's practically white) in her crazy loft on Prince Street. She bought it a million years ago, when artists could afford to live in that neighborhood, and though I know my mother wouldn't trade our house on Ashland, she loves Iris's apartment. Her favorite thing is the tiny terrace off the living room. I won't even go out there—it seems too rickety, and I can imagine crashing six floors down when the wrought iron finally disintegrates after a hundred years of hanging on up there. But every time I'd wake up in the morning, she'd be out there, sitting in an aluminum-framed lawn chair, drinking matcha tea. I wonder now if she was listening to the traffic on the street below and imagining some other version of her life, one where Luna and I hadn't come along when we did and she might have stayed in New York, stayed in Shelter. I wonder if she missed that.

The cashier is a girl, thank god, maybe Luna's age or a little older, with a purple streak painted down the center of her blond hair. She doesn't say anything about the pregnancy tests as she rings them up, but she does smile at me.

"I used to love that lip gloss," she says, holding the package up in front of her.

"I still love it," I say. "At least I think I do." My voice comes out shaky and strange-sounding, and I wonder if she can smell the whiskey on my breath, the whiskey I drank two hours ago in Luna and James's kitchen. I want to tell her that I'm not the least bit drunk, that the world seems blurry but the problem is with the world and not with me. I want to tell her that my sister might be pregnant and that stories repeat sometimes but everything gets jumbled in the second telling. I want to tell her that this could break my mother's heart.

But I don't tell her any of this. We just smile without looking at each other and I pay with two twenties from Luna's wallet. And then I take my change and the bag and I just walk right out of the store, out in the street, out toward Luna.

forty-four

I'D LEFT THE DOOR UNLOCKED when I went out and it's still open when I get back. In fact, Luna hasn't moved at all. She's not asleep, just lying with her head on the armrest again, staring at the ceiling.

I shut the door with my hip and walk over to the couch, then dump the bag out on the table. Luna ignores the tests and picks up the strawberry lip gloss first. She uses her silver-painted fingernail to peel the plastic away from the cardboard, and then she breaks the seal on the tube.

I flop down on the couch.

"You can have that," I say, "but the candy's mine. Except the M&M's. Those are yours. But I think you should remember that the lip products and the candy are not the important purchases here."

She sits back down on the couch and opens the lip gloss anyway, running the tube over her lips. Then she turns and tips backward again, lying flat. I look around, but there's no sign of James in the apartment.

"I'll take them in a minute," Luna says.

"I think you should take them now."

She closes her eyes. "Just let me lie here a second."

"You have been lying there for hours." I take a breath. "I got three of them," I say, leaning forward to line them up on the table. My mother's robot flower looks down on them. "All different brands. I figured that way we'd make sure the results were accurate." Since this is apparently a science experiment we're running here.

Luna smiles in a lopsided way, but she gets up. She takes the three boxes, stacked one on top of the other, and goes into the bathroom. When she closes the door I can hear the rustling of cellophane and the tearing of cardboard. I'm listening so hard I swear I can hear her unfold the directions and lay them on the sink. Then her voice, echoing off the ceramic tiles.

"Oh, give me a home," she starts to sing, "where the buffalo roam, where the deer and the antelope play."

For a split second, I smile without meaning to, as if this is any old day and Luna is the silly version of herself that I like best. But then I feel anger bubble up like spilled soda, and my lungs tighten so much it's hard to breathe.

"Enough with the songs," I say.

"I don't want you to hear me pee," she says, her voice coming through the door muffled.

"That's good," I say, "because I don't want to hear you pee either."

I free my own lip gloss from its packaging and run the tube over my lips. It's the exact taste of being ten years old, and for a split second, this almost makes me cry.

Luna opens the door, and I try to read her face before she says anything. She looks flushed, not pale, and her eyes are wide.

"The first one is negative," she says. "Should I take the others?"

I don't have to think about it. I bought them, didn't I?

"Yes," I say.

A few minutes later she comes back with all three sticks. She fans them out between her fingers, holding them up high, and I can see that each has a single pink line.

"All negative," she says, and the relief makes the anaconda-tight feeling around my heart go away. But then in its place is just exhaustion, and I sink down on the couch.

"I don't need the visual aids," I say. "Keep the pee sticks in the bathroom, please."

"Or I could frame them," she says. She's flushed and smiling but her eyes are still sad, shiny like my mother's when she knows something is shitty but she doesn't want to admit it. She takes the sticks and the boxes and puts them back into the Duane Reade bag. Then she goes into the kitchen and throws it into the garbage under the sink, pushing it down deep in the can. She washes her hands and then comes back into the living room.

"Do you want me to pick up some food?" I ask. "I could go to the Thai place again. Red curry and spring rolls, maybe. Coconut soup?" I just got back a half hour ago and I already feel claustropho-bic, though I'd like to chalk it up to a New York/small apartment thing. "Or Indian. Garlic naan and malai kofta."

"I'm not hungry," Luna says. She leans back to lie down on the couch again. She puts her bare feet high up on the back of the couch and holds the package of M&M's by its edge, crinkling the paper package.

"There was this one time," she says, "in June, outside Madison. Somewhere in Wisconsin, anyway. It was late and we couldn't find the motel, so we decided just to sleep in the van. But I couldn't fall asleep." She shakes her head. "It was too stuffy; I felt like I couldn't breathe. So I went outside. I climbed out the window without opening the door so I wouldn't wake anyone, and I lay down right there in the grass by the edge of the parking lot." She stops, remembering. "I couldn't sleep out there either but at least I could breathe. I counted the stars for two hours. James freaked when he woke up and I wasn't in the passenger seat." I can hear her smiling.

"That's what I felt like, before," she says. "And now I feel like I can see the stars."

Outside on the street, a car honks three times, sharp and quick. I hear its door slam, and the engine rev as whoever it is drives away.

"How long have you known?" I say. "I mean, how long have you been worrying?"

"Two weeks." Luna pushes her hair away from her face. "Maybe. My periods have never really been regular, but I forgot to take my pill a couple of times." She looks at me. "I know it was stupid. Please don't ever be that stupid."

I think about my going-nowhere almost-relationship with Ben, or the fact that Archer walked out of the practice space hours ago and still hasn't called.

"I'm not really there yet," I say.

"That's fine," she says. "That's good." She tears open the package and pours a few M&M's into her palm. "I wouldn't have had it," she says without looking at me. I know she means the baby.

"Okay," I say.

"I'm not Mom," she says, for the second time this week. This time she sounds less sure, her voice wavering and small.

I nod, but she still isn't looking at me anyway.

"I wonder what it was like for her," I say.

"What?"

"When Mom found out she was pregnant with you. I mean, it must have been just after they'd done the cover of *SPIN*, *Sea of Tranquility* was selling so well, and then . . ." I trail off.

Luna sits up. "And then she took a pregnancy test in a hotel room in Seattle and I entered stage left. Or womb left, I guess." She flutters her fingers in the air. "Vagina left."

"I get it," I say, holding up a stop-sign hand. "You were born. But how do you know where she was when she found out?"

Luna pulls her feet under her. "She told me once. She played the show that night anyway, even though she was throwing up in the back ten minutes before they went onstage." She makes a face. "She told me she was happy when she found out. But I don't know if I believe her. How could she have been?"

"I don't know," I say. "She gave everything up so easily. I don't think Mom ever really cared if she was famous or not. Maybe she was ready to let it go."

Luna sits still, considering this. "Maybe," she says.

"Anyway, I was the biggest mistake, right?"

"What?" Luna turns her head and looks at me, the first time she has looked directly at me since she sat down.

"That's what you told me when I was a kid. You said you were an accident, but I was a mistake."

Luna's eyes widen. "What? Shit, Fee, I'm sorry about that." She sighs. "I didn't mean it. I don't even remember saying it."

"It's okay," I say, even though maybe it isn't.

"But you know, Phoebe, I thought if anyone was going to understand about Dad," Luna says, "it would be you." She looks at me, narrowing her eyes. "You know how it feels."

"I do understand," I say. "But it doesn't mean that I'm not curious about him." I bend down to open my purse. The magazine is still in the inside pocket, waiting. It feels like the right time to show her. I hold it out in my hand.

"Look."

She does. She looks. She holds the magazine in both hands and studies it as if the headlines were written in some other language, one she knew a long time ago but has forgotten in the time since.

"I've never seen this," she says. "Not in real life, anyway. Where did you get it?"

"On eBay," I say. "I know it's dumb. I just thought if I could hold it, it would help me figure everything out. But it didn't really help anything." I place my fingers flat on each of my cheeks. They feel hot.

Luna touches the *First Girl on the Moon* headline with her pointer finger. "It helps me," she says.

"How?"

"I don't know. It's just comforting." With her left hand, she starts to smooth the creases in the cover, the same way I always do. "Seeing them like that. It makes me think everything will be okay."

"But that doesn't make sense. Things weren't okay for them."

She lifts it closer and squints at the photograph of our parents. "Well," she says, "they didn't stay together, but we're here, and we're okay. Right?"

"Sure," I say. I almost mean it.

She looks up at me then, her brow furrowed. "You couldn't have just told me that you went to see him?" She doesn't sound accusing, exactly, just curious, and for once, I don't feel as if I have to defend myself. I just try to explain.

"I thought about it. But I didn't think you wanted to know," I say. "And anyway, it wasn't like it was some big deal. I was curious, that was all."

"You talked to him?" Luna asks.

"A little. Mostly he just showed Archer around. He was recording this girl with pink streaks in her hair. She was nice, though."

"How old was she?"

"Older than you. Twenty-eight, maybe? Her name was Prue, I think." I close my eyes for a second and think of the smell of my father's studio, records and amps and the rubbery, burnt scent of cables and cords. "Anyway, *you* never told me before this week that he came to your show."

"I know," Luna says, her voice soft. "I'm sorry."

"*You* said you hadn't seen him since you came to New York."

Luna shakes her head. "I said I hadn't talked to him. I didn't. After our set, I stayed in the back until he left." She opens the magazine and starts paging through. "Prue played that show with us."

"Page seventy-seven," I say, and it reminds me of being on the airplane days ago, pretending to Jessica that I was someone I'm not. But this is who I am: the daughter of two people who could make a band work for a while, but couldn't make their family work for more than a few years. I am secretive. I am devoted. I am focused and confused. I am lost and found and a little bit spiteful. I am a lot . . . a *lot* patient. I'm figuring it out, what I am. And that's enough for now.

"Prue is nice enough," Luna says. "Though she came up to me after he left and told me how great it must be to have a dad like him." She scoffs. "This was after she talked to him for fifteen minutes, maybe. I guess he told her he liked her set. I thought maybe he was just hitting on her, but I guess he was serious, if they've been working together." Luna stops, and I wonder if she's thinking about what it would be like to work with my father on the Moons' next record. I wonder if she's even considering it.

Luna slides down to lie on the couch again. "What was his show like?" she asks.

"It was nice, I guess. Packed. It was strange seeing him play for all these people who obviously adore him." I can feel my lips begin to tremble, and I press them together. "He's my father and I don't even know him."

"But he wants to know you."

"I think so." I shrug. "You too."

"I don't want to," she says, and I don't say anything. We sit there, not talking, until a few minutes later, when a motorcycle roars down the street so fast the windows rattle. In the quiet space left after the sound of it fades away, I take a breath. Just then, I remember what James said earlier. It floats up like a bubble in my memory.

"What did James mean, Luna?" I ask. "When he said you should tell the truth?"

"I have no idea." She brings one hand up to cover her eyes and rubs her temples with her fingers and thumb. "I don't have any idea at all."

I sit there and look at the record sitting still on the turntable, and think about what to say next. But then Luna's breathing becomes softer, as regular as the recording of ocean waves my mother uses sometimes, and I know she's asleep. And since she's sleeping where I'm supposed to sleep, since I'm tired but jittery, I decide to leave.

forty-five

MY FATHER CAME TO SCHOOL with me once. I was in third grade
and it was show-and-tell, which, when I was eight, sometimes
involved bringing a person, not just a seashell from a beach vacation or a favorite stuffed rabbit. One of my classmates had brought
his uncle who was a policeman and he passed his badge around the
room so we could all hold the heavy piece of metal in our hands.
That was the moment I decided I wanted to bring my father, but
I'm not sure why. Maybe because he was around so rarely it seemed
like something special, something worthy of show-and-tell. I didn't
understand that for most of the other kids, having a father wasn't a
big deal.

He followed me into the classroom and then sat down in my
teacher's chair. He played a song on his guitar, the title track from
Slight Chance, I think, and the sound of his chords was both familiar

and strange there in the room with our desks and lunch bags and boxes of crayons. I can still see it in my mind, the letters of the alphabet strung on a garland over his head, the green chalkboard behind him smudgy with dust. Teachers I didn't even know clustered in the doorway and watched him play, nodding along, and Abby, who I couldn't stand, mouthed the words along with him. Later Abby told me that her mother was a big fan of my father, as if that made Abby special, not me.

By the time he was finished with his third and last song, I knew that I had done the wrong thing, because now I had to share my father, who I hardly ever saw. Here in the classroom, he didn't belong only to me.

And really, I guess, he never did.

The street is quiet when I get outside of Luna's building, the last bit of silvery light fading from the sky. I head up to Court Street, past the Barnes & Noble on the corner, still open, cross the street and keep going. Farther down Court, the Indian place where Luna and I ate on my first night is lit up and golden, the saffron-yellow silk curtains in the window shining like fire. I think about going in for naan bread and cucumber raita, maybe some chai tea in their small, cream-colored cups. I haven't eaten since lunch, unless you count that candy bar. But I don't head that way. I keep walking.

I haven't yet used the Hoyt-Schermerhorn station, but thanks to the map on my phone (and the fact that it's technically on the same street where Luna lives, if much farther down), I'm reasonably certain I'll be okay. I know where I'm going now, and I like it, that I'm starting to own the city, or at least some small part of it.

Half my family lives here, and I was born here, so I guess it belongs to me already. Or maybe I belong to it. Without even trying I'm walking in that New York way, like I know where I'm going and I'm confident that my feet and the sidewalks (plus the subway, I guess) will take me there.

In the train station, my footsteps echo against the tiled walls. It's so bright down here it feels like daytime again. Water drips from the ceiling onto the tracks, pooling in slick puddles laced with garbage. It isn't pretty, except where it is: the bright squeal of the train as it slides to a stop, the decades-old letters spelling out *Hoyt-Schermerhorn*.

I have to take the G train to get to my father's apartment, and when it arrives at the Broadway station, I get out. It's a different Brooklyn up on the street, grittier and uglier, with fewer trees and no brownstones as far as I can see. Graffiti tags in bubbly letters cover the roll-down grates of a dry cleaner and a falafel place, and I see a few vaguely hipsterish guys maybe five years older than me coming out of a grocery on the corner. It seems like they've been sent by central casting, or by Luna, in order to prove her thesis about Williamsburg and my dad.

I memorized the number on the train, but I still take the paper out of my pocket. My father's handwriting is slanted to the right as if it were in a hurry, one half of his letters trying to get somewhere before the other half.

When I find it, three blocks away, it's a two-story, sand-colored building with black painted doors, two at a time, and big windows looking out onto the street. The door to his apartment opens out on the street, it seems, because there is only one buzzer and only one name. *K. Ferris*, it says, in the same green label-maker tape I've seen before.

I stand on the doorstep for a moment, like I did at my father's studio with Luna last year, and again with Archer just a few days ago. But this time, when I get the courage to let my finger press the bell, it doesn't surprise me one bit.

forty-six

MEG
APRIL 1993

My first thought was that it was the biggest table I'd ever seen, and my second was that I wanted to tap-dance on it. Kit and I had taken lessons when we were kids, and though I hadn't really thought about tapping in years, something about that long, smooth expanse of wood made me want to do it.

We were here in the Capitol Records offices to sign our contract, the boys dressed in suits and me in a knockoff Chanel jacket and skirt. Kit had found them in a vintage shop in the East Village and insisted I wear them today. The seam was ripped under one arm, but as long as I didn't take the jacket off, no one could tell. And I couldn't imagine why I'd have to take the jacket off. Unless I got really enthusiastic with the tap dancing, or the air-conditioning broke. The windows were all sealed up there.

Our manager, Leif, was here, his blond hair more carefully

messed than normal. We were all sitting silently, looking at each other. There was no clock in here: it was a Land Without Time.

The door opened then and there was Rick, the exec we'd been dealing with since the A&R guy handed us over. Today, he had a Cheshire cat smile. The boys stood up, so I did too. It felt a little awkward.

"Are you guys ready to become part of the Capitol family?" he asked. A secretary followed him into the room with a stack of papers.

"Yes, sir," said Kieran.

"Sure," I said.

"She's our star," Leif said. He tried to put his arm around my shoulder, but I dipped away before he could. "She's got the voice, the brains, and the look."

Dan started to sing Roxette's "She's Got the Look," but quietly enough that Rick didn't seem to notice. Leif didn't tell him to stop, but you could tell that was what he was thinking.

The week before, we'd all gone out to see Bikini Kill at Wetlands and Leif had come along, even though it was decidedly not his scene.

He'd put his hand on my lower back during "Rebel Girl" and then slid it even lower.

"You're special," he said, his lips next to my ear. His voice slurred and softened until I could pretend I didn't even know what he was talking about. I looked at Kathleen Hanna onstage and thought about how she'd probably kick Leif in the balls and be done with it. Something was stopping me from doing that, but Kathleen saved me anyway.

"Girls to the front!" she yelled from the stage. I looked at Leif and shrugged, then left all four of the guys to push my way closer to her.

I didn't tell Kieran about it. It was true that Kit hadn't liked Leif from the beginning. She called him Maple Leaf or Blade, as in Blade of Grass, and sometimes Pine Needle. She thought he was an ass, and she was probably right. But he was just one in a series of skeezy guys I'd had to deal with: bouncers, bookers, bartenders, soundmen, you-name-the-instrument players. At least this skeezy guy was going to make us some money.

Now Rick called Carter's name.

"You're going to need a nicer suit," Rick said, and Carter's face fell. He looked down at his own jacket. Rick burst into laughter, clapping his hand to Carter's shoulder.

"I'm just messing with you," he said. "Though, honestly, I can give you the name of my tailor. He does great work." His face turned serious. "I'll have my secretary give you his card." He said this though the secretary was right there in the room with us, and he could have easily used her name. Unless he was talking about some other secretary. Maybe he had two.

I wondered then if I'd get a secretary.

"All right," Rick said. "Let's do this." He motioned for us to sit down and we did.

Leif put the contract on the table in front of me.

"Let's have Meg sign first," he said, like he was giving me a gift. He put a pen down next to the contract. I expected it to be special, somehow, but it was just a normal plastic Bic.

Across the table, Kieran was smiling at me, his dimple

showing. I smiled back at him, that boy who'd started this whole thing in the first place. Who'd found me, and helped me make the band.

I picked up the pen.

forty-seven

My father smiles when he sees me, when he pulls the door wide enough to see.

"We meet again," he says. He's standing in a small hallway and I'm still on the front stoop. My hand is on the railing, the black metal cool under my hand. I consider pivoting neatly around and leaping off the porch. But instead I make myself smile.

"Sorry," I say. "I know I should have called."

"It's fine." He takes a step back and motions me in. "That's why I gave you the address. I hoped you'd stop by."

I peek over his shoulder, looking for what, I don't know. Prue, that pretty singer with the pink streaks in her hair? A cat, maybe, curled up on the edge of his couch? But the apartment is empty, as far as I can tell. It's still and quiet, no music playing on the stereo.

Neither of us knows what to do, so we just stand for a moment in the entryway under a lamp made of amber glass. I wish I had a coat to give him, or maybe a scarf, so he could busy himself hanging it up. It would be weird to hand him my purse, I think.

"Come on in," he says finally, and gestures toward the living room.

I follow him, trying to notice everything. It's different today, in his apartment, without the stands full of guitars and the sound-boards of the studio. He's not wearing headphones and there's not as much to look at. There are a few abstract paintings on the walls of the living room, blurry with rain-soaked, cool shades of blue. There's only one honey-colored acoustic guitar lying flat across a low glass coffee table, as if he had been playing to his empty apart-ment when I rang the bell. I hadn't heard anything out on the street.

"So this is your natural habitat," I say. I seem to have lost my ability to carry on a conversation like a normal person. But it's true that I can't pretend I'm just watching a guy work, like I did in the studio. This is more than that.

"The studio's probably more natural for me," he says. "I'm still not sure about this place."

"I like it," I say, and I do. The windows are huge and have the vaguely watery look of old glass. I can see the streetlights dis-tort prettily through the panes. Leaded glass windows in geometric shapes splinter the light in jagged patterns on the ceiling, and the walls are the perfect shade of pale gray.

"I'm glad," he says.

We stand there for another moment, and I'm almost glad to see that my father is as awkward as I am. He seems to have forgot-ten that it's customary to ask visitors to sit down. So I walk over to the farthest wall, where he has hung a Shelter tour poster I've never seen, framed in thick black wood. The letters are deep blue screen printed on a pearl-gray background, and though the show was played on May twenty-ninth in Austin, there's no year. I can't get a sense of what they would have been like just then. Was it at the beginning, when they still thought everything was going to turn out all right for them?

My father supplies the answer without my having to ask.

"That was our first tour," he says. "Right before *Houses* came out."

I look at the letters, the rough, spindly sketch of a boxlike house at the bottom, its yellow windows burning with light. I don't know what else to say other than "Oh," so I keep that brilliance to myself. I wait for him to keep talking, to tell me something else.

He stands next to me.

"That was my favorite tour, I think." I'm surprised to hear him say this. He takes a breath, lets it out slowly. His voice sounds almost shy. "Looking back, anyway. It was easier before everything got started. No one knew us, and no one expected us to know what we were doing."

His phone rings then from his pocket, a long bell like an old-fashioned rotary phone, and he takes it out to look at the screen.

"Do you mind if I take this, Phoebe?" he asks. "I'm recording this band tomorrow, and they're really particular about their setup."

"Go ahead," I say. Honestly, I'm glad he's walking away for a minute. I want to keep looking around without feeling as if I'm getting a guided tour of the Museum of Kieran Ferris.

Across the room is a wide metal bookshelf lined with books.

It's possible that some of these were my mother's, if their books got mixed up when they lived together. I want to find something of hers in this apartment, or something that shows he thinks about Luna and me. I want proof that he didn't forget about all of us until I showed up on his doorstep a few days ago.

On the edge of the top shelf is a stark white hardcover copy of David Byrne's *How Music Works*. I think of Archer, and all the doorsteps I've stood on lately.

I can hear my father talking on the phone, not what he's saying, really, just the cadence of his words, his calm tones. I want him to talk to me like this. There's a tight feeling in my chest again, and I'm not sure if it's my lungs or my heart or just my ribs squeezing everything somehow. I take a deep breath and it catches when I let it out.

There are a couple of rocks on the middle shelf—little more than pebbles, really—gray and worn smooth by a lake or a river. I touch one of them, hold it between my finger and my thumb, and then slip it into my pocket.

As soon as I do it I feel better, fastened more strongly to the floor, the earth. I feel as if this was the right thing to do, to come here.

My father walks back into the room.

"I'm sorry about that," he says. "Bassists can be so neurotic about their sound. I'm sure you know that."

I don't say anything and then he says, "Archer. Your friend. He plays bass, right?"

"Oh, yeah. He's not really like that." I clasp my necklace between my fingers. "At least I don't think so."

My father shakes his head. "They're all like that," he says, smiling.

I turn back toward the bookshelf. Maybe he's right, and maybe I'll never know either way.

"Look at this," my father says. Around the corner in the dining room is a huge record cabinet with four tiers and sliding doors on each made of gray glass. I walk closer and look at some of the titles through the glass. He has a section of Dylan albums and a few sections of sixties soul. He has Nirvana and Weezer and Belly and the Replacements.

"I made it," he says, "and now I might have to stay here forever, because I don't think it'll fit out the door." He rubs a smudge on one of the glass doors with his thumb. "Or I guess if the new owner didn't want it, I'd have to—saw it up or something." He's almost talking to himself now.

"I'm sure the new owner would want it," I say.

"You'd be surprised. Most people don't have so many records."

"I know," I say, even though the people in my life, they do. My mother, my sister, James, and Archer, all of them weighted down with vinyl. "So you'll just have to stay here, then." I like that idea, somehow, that he'll stay in this place I know, where I can picture him and his guitar and record cabinet. Even if I don't talk to him for another three years, or longer.

He nods, smiling. "I think I will." He leans against the doorway. "Do you want something to eat?"

"Okay," I say. A flicker of panic crosses his face. So I say, "Do you have anything?"

He glances toward the kitchen. "Probably not."

I'm a little reluctant to leave since I'm just starting to feel comfortable, but my stomach growls at the thought of food.

"We could go out," I say.

"Sure," he says, relieved. "What do you feel like eating?"

A silly thought crosses my mind: this is the father I've always wanted. The kind who would ask what I wanted to eat and then just make it happen. So I think about it.

"Pancakes," I say.

He smiles. "Let's do it," he says.

Walking out through the same narrow hallway, my eyes rest on the wooden bookshelf there, which looks like it came from an old high school library, or that it spent decades pushed against the back wall of a classroom before ending up in my father's living room. Tucked in the corner of the third shelf from the top is a small metal sculpture, a twisting figure made of thick silver wire. It looks like a bird, wings unfolded and neck stretched out. I stop and touch it, and then I turn around to him.

"Did Mom make this?"

He nods, looking at it. "A long time ago. She used to make them in the van sometimes when we were touring. Birds and trees. She'd bring spools of wire and pliers and she'd make one every hour on the long trips." I look at his face to watch him remember, and he keeps looking at the sculpture and not at me. "She gave them all away," he says. He picks the bird up and sets it in the palm of his other hand, looking at it for a minute. Then he puts it back. "It's a little bent, I think," he says. "I've moved with it a couple of times. It always finds its way back on the shelf." He looks at me. "Are you going to tell her I still have it?"

I tilt my head a little. "Do you want me to?"

"Let me get back to you on that," he says.

As we walk out the front door, I put my hand in my pocket and touch the stone I stole from my father's other bookshelf. It's smooth and cool, and I know then that I'll put it in my bag later, with the copy of *SPIN* and the copy of *Catcher* and my poetry book. I'll feel its weight in there, just like my father must feel the weight of my mother's bird every time he moves to a different apartment, or maybe even every time he walks by in the hallway and it catches the lamplight on its outstretched wings. Sometimes the heaviest things are the ones that don't weigh much at all.

forty-eight

DOWN THE STREET FROM MY father's building is a diner with wide glass windows and a pink neon sign. It's mostly empty when we get there, so we sit in a black vinyl booth big enough for six people, pressed up against the windows facing the street. Past the cars parked by the curb I can see the signs for the G train where I got off a while ago, and a Laundromat filled with gleaming white washing machines.

My father leans back in his seat and opens the menu. The waitress—late twenties, blond hair, and a tiny, sparkly nose ring—smiles like she knows him. She lights a tiny candle in a jam jar and sets in the middle of the table. It flickers, then settles and burns strongly.

"I'll be back when you're ready," the waitress says. Her smile is a little wide, but sincere, and I like her for it.

"I know what I want," I say, without opening the menu. "Blueberry pancakes."

"And you?" She looks at my father.

He closes his. "Eggs, home fries, and toast, please."

"Sounds good. Drinks?"

I consider ordering a beer just to see what my father will do, but I'm not brave enough.

"Water's fine," I say. My father nods, and the waitress heads back toward the kitchen.

I try to look across the street so I don't have to look at my father, but since it's getting dark out, I mostly just see our own reflections. Past that, I can make out a woman with blond braids and a black dress, carrying two pillowcases stuffed with clothes and struggling to open the door to the Laundromat. An older guy walking a small brown mutt hurries to help her. I'm planning to keep watching the scene, or what I can see of it, anyway, but my father decides to speak.

"Is everything okay with Luna?" he asks.

"It's fine." I look at him, and then at the saltshaker. "She was tired tonight, and I wasn't."

He runs his hand along the edge of the table. "But she doesn't know you're here." I can tell that he's still looking at me, so I lift my eyes again. I don't see any reason to lie about this.

"No," I say. "She's mad that I came to see you last time." I smile. "So I did the logical thing and came again."

He smiles too, and turns his head to look toward the restaurant's counter. The waitress is coming with our waters. For just a moment, in profile like that, he looks like the tiny photo on the back of *Promise*, only bigger.

"For what it's worth," he says, "I'm glad you did."

My mother hates that phrase, *for what it's worth*. "So what you're telling me," she always says, "is that you're already figuring what you have to say isn't worth much. Then just don't say it!"

She's probably right, but I'm willing to let him off the hook tonight. Plus, it *is* worth something, him telling me that he's glad I came. I take the copy of *SPIN* out of my bag and push it across the table to him.

"Wow," he says, reaching out. "I haven't seen this in a long time." He angles it up toward him, and I can't see the cover for a second, and then he sets it back down. "Look how pretty your mom was." He looks up at me. "You look so much like her."

"Me?" I touch my face then, without meaning to, like Jessica on the plane, touching her face because she thought it had changed somehow. "I think it's Luna who does," I say.

He nods. "Oh, she does too, but more than anything Luna *sounds* like her."

I pick up a packet of sugar and crinkle it between my fingers. What I really want to do is rip it open and pour it on the table, then draw patterns in the crystals. I don't know why.

"Mom says Luna's better," I say.

He thinks about it for a moment, tilting his head. "Maybe. But sometimes I think there's no one better than your mom." He glances toward the window and in the reflection, it looks as if he's checking his hair. "If she put out an album now, people would go nuts for it."

I laugh, or maybe it's more of a scoff. A scoff-laugh.

"She wouldn't," I say. "She doesn't sing much anymore."

"I can't imagine that," he says. He's smiling, and I can see in his cheek the dimple that mirrors mine. "Or maybe it's that I don't believe it. I bet she sings when no one else is around."

"Our house isn't that big," I say. He shrugs, and I don't know if he means that he doesn't think that matters or that he doesn't really remember how big our house is.

The waitress comes back then, and sets my father's eggs and toast in front of him, then my pancakes in front of me. Steam rises from the food, and suddenly I'm so hungry I feel weak. I take a bite.

My father picks up his fork, but he doesn't start to eat.

"I heard her voice before I ever met her, you know," he says.

I'm chewing, and the pancakes are heaven. "Really?" I say, my mouth still full.

"She was in another band. Cassiopeia. Did you know that?"

I shake my head. So not only does my mother refuse to talk about Shelter, it seems that there are entire other bands—maybe whole other *constellations* of bands, from the sound of it—that she's also hid from us.

"With Carter and Dan," he says. "Just the three of them." He picks up a piece of toast and puts some scrambled egg on it, but he doesn't take a bite. He just holds it. "I walked into a bar in Buffalo and I heard this voice that was like water. It filled everything. I wanted to listen to it forever." He shifts his eyes away from mine while he says this, and for some reason, I feel as if I shouldn't be looking at his face right now. It looks too open, too honest, and I look away too, toward the candle's flame burning steady and gold. "I asked everyone there if they knew who she was."

"Did they?"

"Of course. She grew up there. I had just come for college, and then I dropped out anyway. I didn't know what I was doing. I was in a band, but it wasn't going anywhere. But then I saw her." Something changes in his face when he says this.

"Did you talk to her?" I ask.

"I waited at the end of the bar while she put her guitar away, and when she came down there I offered to buy her a drink." I can hear him start to smile, and I look at him. "She told me her drinks were free already, but she'd sit next to me while she drank. One drink." He raises his pointer finger. "I asked her that night, but it took me a month to convince her to start Shelter with me." He smiles. "She wouldn't leave Carter and Dan, so I guess I was basically asking to join their band."

"So then what happened?" I ask. My voice is quiet. I'm not talking about what happened next. I'm time-traveling. I'm asking about what happened *after* all that.

"What do you mean?"

I raise my voice just a little. "Between you. Why did you break up?"

He doesn't look surprised at the question, but he's not in a hurry to answer, either. He takes a bite of his toast and egg and then chews and swallows. I wait.

"It's not a math problem," he says. "You can't find the one and only answer." He exhales slowly. "There were a lot of reasons."

His voice softens a little when he says this, and it makes me think about when I was younger and he'd call from Berlin or Edinburgh when he was on tour. His voice on the phone would sound tinny and watery at the same time, and while he talked about the shows and the food and this one hotel where the rooms were so small he had to sleep with his guitar in the bed, I'd imagine the telephone wires strung underneath the oceans, running next to the coral, over the sand. When he fell silent I'd think about some lonely sea turtle out off the coast of Ireland, say, chewing on the wires and chewing on his words. There always seemed to be holes in our conversations. It was better to have a reason besides the obvious: most of the time, my father didn't know what to say to me.

"I don't mean to turn this into a whole thing," I say, "but I've always wanted to ask you . . . why you left." I'm looking right at him, now, and he doesn't look away.

"I was really young," he says.

"You were twenty-six," I say. I've done the math. It doesn't sound that young to me.

"Yes," he says.

"I turned seventeen three weeks ago," I say, "and I don't think I'd leave."

He glances at the ceiling and then back down. "You wouldn't," he says. "Your mother wouldn't. She didn't, I mean." He smiles then, a smile so big and wide I think for a second that he's lost his mind. "She was so freaking tough. I mean, beautiful, you know, with that voice that could just knock people on the floor. More than that, she was fierce." He's in some kind of reverie, remembering.

"There was this band called Salt Sky that we played with a few times, right in the beginning." He shakes his head. "The singer had a crush on her. I think he actually would have tried to poach her if he thought she was willing." My father puts his fork down. "He drove her nuts. Anyway, he got really drunk one night and tried to kiss her. It was late, after the show. We were loading our gear out the back door." My father stops for a second, runs his hand through his hair. "I didn't see what he did, but I saw what happened afterward. She socked him right in the mouth."

I smile. I can see my mother doing that.

"He landed on his back in the alley," my father says. "I was frozen, just standing there watching her. I didn't know what I was supposed to do." He laughs a little. "We'd only been dating for three months. I would have done anything to protect her. It just . . . didn't seem like she needed help." He smiles, but it doesn't quite reach his eyes.

I'm riveted, leaning forward, my hands on the edge of the table in front of me.

"Anyway, she let him lie there a second, and then she put out her hand and helped him up. He stood there, wide-eyed, rubbing his mouth, and she just said one thing to him. *No.*" My father seems sort of amazed. "Then she took my hand and we just got in the van. I think I knew I was going to marry her, right there in that alley."

This may be the most I've ever heard my father talk at one time. He looks almost embarrassed, and glances out the window. I look out there too, but it's so dark now that I can't see much more than the Laundromat sign glowing white. Besides that, I only see us: my father and me.

He takes a breath. "She was always strong. So it makes sense that she would make such a nice life for you and Luna. I admired her for that."

I feel a sudden fury spread like a flame in my belly. It's great that he admired her while she was working her ass off raising two girls by herself. "Did you ever tell her that?"

He shakes his head. "I'm sure I didn't," he says. "I'm kind of an ass. I'm sure your mom has told you."

He's wrong there. Even when Luna would go on her tirades about our father in the last couple of years, my mother would say very little.

"She actually . . . She doesn't say much about you at all." As I say it I wonder if that's better or worse.

My father is looking at his plate, studying his eggs as if he's trying to memorize them, their lacy edges, their yellow-and-white swirl.

"Luna thinks you're an ass, though." I offer this detail as if it's a consolation.

My father's exhale comes out as a soft laugh, nervous around its edges.

"I don't blame her," he says. "I wasn't any good at it."

"At what?"

"At being a dad." He puts his hand on his cheek. "There were too many other things I wanted to do."

I pour syrup on the last few bites of my pancakes, then set the pitcher down a little too hard. The candle and the sugar jar rattle.

"You could have still done them," I say.

He nods. "You're probably right. I just couldn't figure out how." He lowers his voice and leans toward me. "Meg found out she was pregnant and she just wanted to stop. I guess I didn't. I convinced her, and we went out for a few more tours. Your aunt Kit came with us."

I know this, of course, but I don't tell him that I've seen some of the pictures. In one in particular, I remember Aunt Kit with her pixie cut, looking like a tinier, more birdlike version of my mother, smiling wide, wearing six-month-old Luna in a front carrier and clamping her hands over Luna's ears. Did they really take Luna and me to the shows? Or was this just a practice? I've always wondered, but I don't want to get distracted now.

"Why did you stop calling us?" I ask.

He looks at me as if he's trying to figure something out. As if I'm one of those 3-D pictures that you have to stare at for a long time, trying to unfocus your eyes, until the picture appears.

So I keep talking. "I mean, you say you wanted us in your life. But you've been gone. Totally gone. Until this week, I hadn't seen you in almost three years." I'm speaking faster now, my words tripping over one another.

My father puts his two hands on the edge of the table, then looks up at me. "I thought you didn't want to see me," he says.

I blink. "Why would you think that?"

"I'm beginning to see that I might have been wrong," he says. "Phoebe, Luna told me not to call."

My heart drops out then, and that feeling gives me a flash of a memory from when we were small: Luna and I dropping Barbie dolls two stories down our grandmother's laundry chute. I feel anger bubble up again.

"What?" I say. "When?"

"A few summers ago." He looks down, twists a silver ring on his right middle finger. "She said that you were almost in high school and things were going to be different. She said it was okay when you were younger, the fact that I wasn't around very much, but now you two had decided that it would be easier if I weren't around at all."

The waitress appears then and sets our check down on the table. Under the total she's drawn a smiley face and written *Thanks!* in blue-inked, loopy scrawl. I want to crumple it in my hand. I want to tear it into tiny pieces.

I take a breath without looking at my father. I'm waiting for him to say something else, but he doesn't, and I don't even know what his face looks like now, whether he feels embarrassed or just sad. But what I do know, right away, is that when Luna told my father not to call three years ago, she wasn't talking about things changing for me, not really. Or not *only* me, anyway. She was talking about herself. And looking back on her anger these past few years, she didn't want him to believe her at all. But he did. He didn't fight for us. He didn't argue, so I lost out on having a dad.

I look at my father. "It wasn't Luna's choice to make," I say. "It was mine." I try to keep my voice steady. "And I can't believe you fell for it. She wanted you to choose to be our dad. She *wanted* you to call."

He sighs. He picks up a sugar packet from the bowl at the center of the table and crinkles it between his fingers. "I think you're right," he says. "I know that now. But I didn't know it then. Teenage girls . . ." He says this as if it's an explanation. "I thought I'd give her a little time and she'd come around."

"Why didn't you just talk to Mom?" I asked. "That would be the normal, parental thing to do."

I say this though obviously he's never been a normal parent.

I wait, and he stays quiet. Across the restaurant, our waitress nearly drops her tray and bursts out laughing. I look at my father and he looks at me. Finally he starts to talk again.

"I did. She told me that I should listen to Luna." He looks to the side and I can see his jaw clench. "She said to give her time. And I figured Meg had the right to say that. But then the months passed, and the years, even, and I couldn't figure out how to do it. How to fix it, I mean. I waited too long, and then it seemed like it was out of my hands." He tosses his hands up as he says this, then rests them on the table in front of him.

I slide my plate toward the end of the table. "It wasn't."

He drops the sugar packet back into the bowl and looks straight at me. "This is why I'm so happy you came to see me. Honestly, Phoebe, seeing you at the door of my studio, after the show, even tonight . . ." He shakes his head. "It's the greatest thing."

I want to shake my own head, or scream, or get up and walk out of here, but I don't. I finger the silver bangle bracelet my mother gave me before I left. I breathe in and out. I try to calm down, but it doesn't really work.

"Do you come here a lot?" I ask. I'm biting the inside of my cheek.

"Sometimes," he says.

"'The light will trap you, the light will catch you, but summer's not long. Summerlong.'" I actually sing the song, and as I hear the words come out of my mouth, I have a thought: I'm a better lyricist than my father.

He looks at me. "I haven't heard that song in a while."

"I heard it at the grocery store last month," I say. "I think that's the standard place it's played now."

"Ouch," he says, pretending to flinch. The ends of his mouth curve up into a small smile.

"They play it on the radio, too. 92.9 FM Hot Mixx Radio," I say.

"Christ," my father says, shaking his head, and I realize he must not listen to the radio much.

I shrug. "It's okay. Your new record is actually pretty great."

"Thanks."

"But what the hell does that song mean?"

"You know," he says, "I really can't remember."

He puts a twenty down over the check and then adjusts it, lining it up so the edges are even. I've imagined this before: What would it be like if eating pancakes with my father were completely normal? It could be just a thing I did sometimes, if I didn't have to go all the way to Brooklyn to do it. I look at him now and realize that I'm trying to memorize him because, really, who knows when I'll see him again? It is crazy to think that he'll be back in our lives now. Right? I'm not sure what that would even mean.

I can picture my father on the sofa in my parents' old apartment in the West Village, his guitar in his lap. I don't know if it's a real memory or one my mind has created, cobbled together from photographs I've seen over the years. I know the sofa was green and the walls were blue, but I was only two years old when they'd moved out, so is it possible I really remember?

My father looks up. "I'm glad you stopped by," he says. "Don't be mad at Luna. She was trying to protect you."

"She was trying to protect herself," I say. "Luna thinks about Luna first."

"Okay." He looks at me. "She's like me, maybe. So I have to forgive her."

I gather my purse and stand up, and he follows me, out of the booth and out of the restaurant and onto the sidewalk. As I walk with him behind me I try to think of the things I've learned about my father so far. He reads. He sings Beatles songs to pretty girls if the opportunity presents itself. He makes furniture too big to fit out the door. He screws up, but eventually admits it. *That's* not like Luna at all. Maybe it's like me.

"I'm just going to get on the train here," I said, pointing to the stop on the next corner.

"Are you sure?" my father asks, but he seems a little relieved.

"I'm sure." I want to be able to walk away from this, and now. I need to figure out what to do next.

"Well, come back again," he says. "Bring Luna."

"Sure," I say. I don't tell him that I'm leaving tomorrow, and that I know that if Luna didn't ring his doorbell the last time we were there, she might never do it.

"Go see her again," I say. "They play in Red Hook before they leave for the tour. Next week." I try to smile but it only goes halfway. "Maybe she'll talk to you this time."

My father nods. He puts his hand in his pocket then, and I can hear change rattling around. He pulls out a yellow MetroCard.

"I have a MetroCard," I say. "A weekly pass."

"This one has twenty dollars on it, I think." He hands it to me. "You can use it when yours runs out." I take it, even though I don't have any use for it, because I know my father just wants to give me something. I don't tell him that I already have his rock in my pocket, not to mention his dimple in my cheek.

"See you soon," he says, and stands there looking like he's not sure what to do. So I let him off the hook again. I step forward, and I hug him, or maybe it's that I let him hug me. And then I step back and smile and turn around.

When I get to the subway entrance, I know he's still watching. He's standing there, his back to the diner windows, waiting for me to look at him. But I don't look. I just walk down the subway stairs, trailing my right hand lightly on the railing, avoiding the sticky spots of stuck-on gum. I don't turn around to see him watch me leave.

forty-nine

MEG
MARCH 1993

I'M THE LAST ONE OFFSTAGE, and I feel so light-blind that I can barely see anything when I step into the hallway. I reach out and somehow Kieran's hand is there, pulling me forward, toward him. He folds me into his arms.

"Amazing," he says. "You were amazing." Some kind of energy crackles like electricity in the air. I can almost see it over Kieran's shoulder, blue as sparks at night. It's a spectacular feeling, beautiful and a little scary, and I can't tell if the sound I hear is the crowd or my blood rushing in my ears.

In front of us, Carter turns around. There's a huge smile on his face.

"What the hell was that?" he says.

"That was 'Sea of Tranquility,'" Kieran says.

"Yeah," Dan says to me. "You killed it out there. We killed it."

I'm smiling, but I feel dizzy. I lean hard on Kieran.

"Are you okay?" he asks.

"Yeah," I say. "I'm just"—I take a breath—"overwhelmed." I've always liked being onstage, but this was something else. This was fervor. The crowd was crazy for us. It was a little scary, honestly.

Kieran must see the look on my face, so he reaches out to touch my cheek.

"This is what we've been waiting for," he says. "And it was for you, babe. They went nuts over your lyrics. And that fucking beautiful voice." He kisses me then, leans me backward for a long moment and pulls me back up.

I can still hear the crowd screaming and clapping, hoping we'll come back for a second encore, I think.

"Should we?" I say. I take a deep breath, trying to steady my pulse. My blood feels carbonated.

I look at Kieran. He smiles and takes my hand.

"Let's do it," he says.

Fifty

WHEN I FINALLY GET BACK to Luna's street, I sit down on the scratchy sandstone steps of the building next door, propping my bag against my feet. From this spot, if I lean against the railing I can just see Luna's living room window up near the roof. It's dark, so I think she must be sleeping, either still on the couch or in her own bed. Either way, I don't want to go inside and I don't want to talk to her. I take my phone out of my bag and scroll through my music.

I'm looking for "Sea of Tranquility," the title track from Shelter's biggest record. The one that came out before my mom got pregnant with Luna. The one about an empty sea on the moon. I have listened to this song approximately five thousand times in my life, partly because this one is a duet. My parents sing it together.

I find it. I press play.

The guitar lines at the beginning are both my mother's and

my father's, but her voice comes in first. In fact, it takes kind of a while for him to start singing too, but once he comes in he's there for the rest of the song. Right now, I'm trying to figure out if they sound younger here, twenty years ago, but to me, they just sound like themselves.

In the video for this song, the band plays in a field at night under a smudgy, glowing moon. This footage is cut with scenes of them playing on a stage in an empty auditorium, its red velvet curtains open, but no one's home. In both places, my mother wears laced-up Doc Martens, black tights, and a supershort skirt. Her skin glows and her hair is loose. My father is in jeans and a T-shirt, as usual. They're either happy or good at pretending.

Who needs water? my parents sing, together, on my phone right now and also somewhere in the past. *We can still pretend it's an ocean.* Because so much of life is about pretending, right? Pretending that you know what you're doing, pretending you're happy, pretending things are okay. But that's not the way I want to write.

The song ends and I take my earbuds out. I've had enough musical therapy for tonight. There's also the fact that I have four texts from my mother, increasing in freak-out level. I click to the last one.

Girlie, the text says, *answer me or I'm driving down there.*

So I type out a reply, finally. The last thing I need is her showing up right now, when I'd have to talk to her about all of this face-to-face. I don't know what to say in a text, even, and I'm still so pissed at her. She knew what Luna said to my father, and she said nothing. I'm sure she wanted to try to insulate Luna from his fame, from that whole world my mother decided to leave, but honestly? That's not a good enough reason. And now she expects me to keep Luna from taking the same path she took, and it's not my freaking job.

Sorry, I say. *We're so busy. Trying to fit a whole summer into a few days. Having fun. Will call tomorrow.* I turn off my phone and put it into my bag before she can reply.

Let's take an inventory here, just for fun. Just a quick list of the Things Wrong with Phoebe Ferris's Life. 1. My sister has been lying to me for three years. 2. My mother has been lying to me for just as long. 3. My father is just living his sort-of-rock-star life in Williamsburg, for god's sake, pretending it's fine that he hasn't talked to me in three years because, oh look, I've just showed up on his doorstep. 4. Neither the sweet, adorable bassist nor the sweet, adorable lacrosse player will ever call me again.

I turn toward the street and see a figure walking toward me down the sidewalk, moving between the circles of lamplight. When he gets closer, I see that it's James. He doesn't look upset anymore, only a little surprised to find me out here.

"Phoebe," he says, when he gets close enough, "were you out?" As usual, his perfect British accent makes him sound like a character in a movie, not a person in my life. Yet here he is. He sits down next to me on the stairs.

I nod. "I was with my dad."

"Really," he says. He looks at me and waits to see what I'll say.

"Yeah," I say, shaking my head a little. "Don't tell Luna. It's no big deal. I was just bored."

James nods, as if this is perfectly understandable. "And Luna?" he says. He points upstairs. He's asking for something like a weather report.

I don't know even how to begin to explain how Luna is.

"She's fine," I say. "She fell asleep pretty early."

"She tires herself out," he says. He reaches out and touches the leaf of a potted petunia next to the stairs. In the lamplight, the white petals glow as if they're lit from inside.

"She's like my mom," I say. "Though Luna gets much more furious." I give him a sideways glance and a halfway smile. "You sure you're up for that?"

He smiles too. "Yeah," he says, shrugging. "I'm sure. But you're different, aren't you?"

"I'm different from all of them," I say. "I came from the aliens." I think about what Luna said about wishing for some different father. "Or maybe from Paul Westerberg. If I'm lucky."

James looks out toward the street. There's a small cat—I hope it's a cat—sniffing in the shadows next to some bushes. "It was a shit thing for me to do," he says. "Walking out like that."

"In my experience," I say, "everybody does shit things once in a while."

I wonder if Luna will tell him about the pregnancy tests, or if they will stay hidden at the bottom of the kitchen trash can until James tosses the bag into the garbage can outside. And if Luna will always remember tonight, when things could have gone either way. When she let one of her secrets go and kept the other one. Because that's the thing. She could have been honest with me, up there on the couch. And she decided not to.

"When you said Luna should tell the truth," I begin. It's not quite a question. "You were talking about my dad."

James looks at me. "Yes," he says.

"She told him not to call us," I say. "Three years ago." I feel that same anger again, pulsing through me like heat. James nods. "When did she tell you about it?"

"A few months ago."

He looks down at the petunia pot and I look at my hands. I peel the leftover gold nail polish off my thumbnail and then look up at him. "Why?"

"I don't know." He shakes his head. "I don't think it was any one thing. I think she wanted him to start being there more."

"So she told him not to be there at all?"

"I think even Luna would admit that it wasn't the best method." His voice is soft.

He's quiet, and we sit there without talking. The wind ruffles the branches of the spindly tree by the street. I blink hard, and I can feel that my lashes are wet. My nose starts to run.

"It's ridiculous," I say. "I'm so angry at her, and here I am, crying." I sniffle. Very glamorous. "It's like I don't even know how to be mad at her the right way." I'm about to wipe my nose with the back of my hand—yuck, I know—when James hands me a hand-kerchief from his pocket.

I take it and wipe my nose, and then I just look at him. "You carry a handkerchief?"

"I'm British," he says, shrugging.

I smile and press my hands into my eyes.

"I can't explain everything she does," James says. "She loves you, though. You should talk it through."

"I will," I say, even though I wouldn't really know how to begin. "Someday." I breathe out slowly, though my lips.

"Sometimes I think you're a little too perfect," I tell him.

"No," he says, but a smile is starting to turn up the corners of his mouth.

"You take care of her," I say.

"I try," he says. "She's pretty amazing."

"She is," I say. "But she's also a pain in the ass."

He laughs. "If you tell her I agreed with you, I'll deny it. To my deathbed."

I look up at the strip of sky I can see between the brownstones. It's nearly black and empty of stars.

"Are you sure you want all this?" I say.

James is retying his shoelace. "All what?" he says.

"Venus Moth. Bigger tours." I take a breath. "It didn't go so well for our parents."

"We're not your parents, Fee," James says. "I think we'll be able to hold it together. And if not, we'll just stop."

"You could stop?" I say. It all seems so fun, so glittery, that right now I feel that if it were me, it would be hard to walk away.

"For Luna, I would stop," James says. He stands up then and stands on the sidewalk in front of me.

His phone dings. A text coming in. "Shit," he says, the word clipped by his pretty accent. "Archer's still down at the Indian place. I told him I'd let you know that, if you were around."

My heart flutters and my blood starts to heat up. "I'm around," I say.

James nods, tapping his fingers on the stair. "So I'm letting you know."

I hesitate. James shakes his head. "Be easy on him. Most of us are helpless against the charms of a Ferris girl."

He puts up his hand then, palm out, as if he's waiting for me to give him a high five. So I do.

I practically run up Schermerhorn, and when I get to Court Street I'm breathless. Archer is standing outside with a cigarette in his hand, the smoke curling up toward the sky. It takes him a second to notice me, to angle his body my way, and before he does, I watch him.

I don't say anything at first. I just walk right up to him and kiss him there on the sidewalk. I've always hated cigarettes, but in that moment, Archer tastes like campfire, like starlit, sky-cooled summer nights. He tastes like sparks.

When our lips part, I step back far enough that I can really see him.

"Hi," I say.

He smiles. "Well, hi."

I press my palms together and bring my fingers to my lips.

"Got a minute?" I say.

Archer and I walk toward the Promenade, not back toward Luna's apartment, and we don't even discuss it. It's like the Promenade is magnetic north and we're needles loose under a compass glass, help-less against its pull. It's dark out there, of course, but the lamplights glow like candles, warm and gold. Manhattan opens up before us, across the sparkling river, lined with lit-up buildings. They are more ideas than buildings, really: just tall columns filled with square beads of light.

North of us is the Brooklyn Bridge, strung with white lights across the dusky sky. It looks like it might be magical, as if someone enormous, some giant, were having a party and has hung fairy lights over the river. Archer takes my hand and we walk toward it.

"How about I take you to the airport tomorrow?" Archer says.

"Sure," I say. "Do you have a car?"

"No." He shakes his head. "But I know a guy with a van."

I laugh. "I finally get to ride in it!"

Archer pulls me over to the railing that edges the Promenade, sliding his hand across my lower back. He hooks his fingers around my hip. "You may regret your enthusiasm," he says.

We stand there and don't say anything for a few moments. The buildings glitter and a tiny white boat slides across the river like a toy.

"Luna says you're a mess," I say.

"And what do you think?" Archer asks. His voice is cautious, soft.

"I think she's wrong."

When I turn my head toward Archer, he's looking at me. He reaches forward, puts his hand on the side of my face, and traces my lips with his thumb. I stay still for a moment, looking at him, and then I move closer. I fit myself into his arms, and my lips find his.

Behind me, all the lamps in all the buildings of Manhattan burn in their windows, placing golden squares in the sky. But I don't see it, and Archer doesn't, because we're not looking at anything at all.

fifty-one

MEG

JANUARY 1993

"LISTEN TO THIS," KIERAN SAID, coming into the room. He held the Gretsch across his body, his left hand on the frets. I was sitting in the middle of the living room, my notebook open on the floor in front of me. I sat and listened as he played a melody I'd never heard before, clear and bright in the quiet room.

"That's pretty nice, isn't it?" he asked.

"I love it," I said. My voice was scratchy, near hoarse. I had blown it out at our show the night before.

Kieran looked pleased. "Why are you sitting there?"

I pointed out the window. "This is the only spot where I can see the moon," I said. Our apartment was in a carriage house, which was a fancy way of saying it was above a garage. Cheap Buffalo rent for three bedrooms, one with a bed and another packed full of amps and guitars. The third was supposed to be my art studio, but the truth was, I hadn't painted or sculpted anything in a few months.

There were trees outside of almost all the windows, so many that the apartment felt as if it were built in a tree. Now, in winter, the branches were bare. From that spot, I could see one square of sky and the moon in the middle like a pearl button.

"I'm trying to write about it," I said.

Kieran began to hum "Moon River."

"Yeah," I said, "I know. The moon has been done before."

"No," Kieran said, squatting down next to me to look out the window. "It's a great idea. You just need a new angle." He looks back at me. "Write about the empty seas. The Sea of Tranquility."

I heard the teakettle begin to whistle. Kieran got up.

"The water's done," he said. "I'm going to bring you honey tea. We'll take care of that voice of yours."

"Yes," I said. "Bring me some tea, honey." He smiled and passed through the dining room and out of sight.

The night was so clear and the moon so bright that I could see the dark spaces on the moon's surface. It seemed crazy to call something a sea when it wasn't filled with water—when it wasn't filled with anything at all. But I supposed there was a long time when humans didn't know that. There's always so much we don't know, and we just make it up.

Who needs water? I wrote. *We can still pretend it's an ocean.*

I looked out our tree house window. The moon hadn't moved, as far as I could see. It would stay there all night. At the bottom of the paper, I wrote *Kieran Ferris*, and above it, my name—my imaginary one—*Meg Ferris.*

fifty-two

IN THE MORNING, LUNA TAKES me to a crepe place in Cobble Hill
for breakfast. We barely talk on the way there, and we sit in the
courtyard out back and eat golden crepes with honey and yogurt
and jewel-bright berries. Sunlight spills across the table and pansies
bloom in a pot next to my chair.

Across from me, Luna sits at the table smiling, as if she's
orchestrated the sun and the crepes and the flowers in their pot.
Her hair is pulled into a perfect ballerina knot at the crown of her
head and even after eating her lipstick is still flawless, the deep red
of crushed cherries. I'm planning to tell her that everything might
look lovely, but things are still messed up. A perfect breakfast isn't
going to convince me otherwise. But then Luna says something that
surprises me completely.

"James said he told you," she says.

I squint, furrowing my brow. "Told me what?"

"About Dad," she says. She presses her lips together. "That I told him not to call."

I blink. My mind spins in the direction of *WTF?* for a few moments, but then somehow I know what James was trying to do. He decided to defuse the bomb before I dropped it. He found a way to make Luna talk about it without her really noticing.

Right now, she looks straight ahead, her face and her hands perfectly still.

"I'm not sorry," she says, but her voice doesn't sound as defensive as I'd expect. It sounds calm and even. She takes a long breath. "I thought it was the best thing."

"Do you still think it was the best thing?" I ask.

She stirs her cappuccino with a tiny spoon. "I don't know."

The old anger sails in with a perfect summer breeze, and the latter pushes my napkin onto the ground. "Well, I don't think it was the best thing, Luna," I say. "And it wasn't *your* decision to make." Luna's eyes are wide. I'm still holding my fork and I know that's a little weird. I think of what she said to James yesterday afternoon: "You'll just have to be pissed." But that's not what she says to me now.

"I'm sorry," Luna says. It's so unexpected that I set my fork down on my plate with a clatter.

A few petals fall from the tree above us onto my plate. I cover my eyes with my hands for a second and take them away. And then I say, "Okay." I don't know what else to say.

A tortoiseshell cat walks across the fence. It stops in the middle and stares at me. It meows.

"Yeah, hi, cat," I say. I sit still and just breathe. This is when

I could tell Luna what my mother wants me to say: that Luna shouldn't go on tour now, that she should go back to school. But I know that it's not my job to tell her that. I'm not even sure it's the right thing for Luna to do.

I reach into my pocket and pull out the MetroCard our father gave me. It's yellow and shiny and it's worth something, but in the end it's just a piece of plastic. I hold it out to Luna.

"What's this for?" she asks.

"It still has money on it," I say. "Maybe twenty dollars." It's strange, feeling my father's words in my mouth.

"Why did you put so much money on it?" Luna asks. She puts her lecture voice on. "You know the unlimited passes are the best deal. I thought you bought one of those at the airport."

I almost tell her then, that I went to see our father again. I even open my mouth to do it. But something stops me.

"I don't know," I say. "It was an accident."

"Well," Luna says, "you should be more careful."

I feel a smile spread slowly across my lips. "Yeah," I say. "I should."

Luna looks at me carefully. "You saw Archer last night?"

"Yeah." I can't keep myself from smiling, but I don't really care.

"All right, all right," she says. "You can have the boy."

I look at her, my beautiful sister, who always gets her own way.

"Thanks, Luna," I say, "but I don't need your permission."

There's a flash of surprise in her eyes, but then she smiles the smallest bit.

"I have to pee," she says. She stands up and walks into the restaurant, leaving her purse on the table. I lift the flap and I can see the lip gloss I bought her last night tucked inside.

I look up at the fence but the cat is gone, and there's no one to talk to. So I pick up my phone, and I dial my mother.

"Phoebe Elizabeth," she says.

"Hi," I say. A small brown sparrow drops from the tree in the corner of the yard to eat crumbs on the ground.

"You are a hard girl to track down."

"I know." I take a breath. "I needed some space."

She's quiet for a moment. I can almost hear her thinking, wondering what I'm talking about.

"Well," she says, "you have a whole city."

"I know," I say. "I love it here."

She clears her throat. "Everything on schedule?"

"Yep," I say. "I land around six."

"I know that part," she says. "The itinerary has been up on the fridge since you left." I picture our kitchen: the window stuck half-open, the porcelain farmhouse sink, Dusty's water bowl on the floor. It feels so long since I've been there. "How are you getting to the airport?"

"Archer is taking me," I say.

"Who's Archer?"

"Luna's bassist," I say. She must know their names by now. It's as if she's trying not to learn them, or pretending she doesn't know. A new cat, black with white on its paws and its face, steps carefully across the fence.

My mother is quiet at first. "The one with the eyes?"

I laugh. "Yeah," I say. I pick up my water glass and the ice clinks inside it.

"It would have to be either that one or the one with the smile. Though he's the drummer, right?"

"Josh, yeah." I'm smiling, and there's no one to see it except that cat.

We don't usually talk about boys, my mother and me, and it occurs to me that maybe that's part of the reason she never talks about my father, or about Jake. I decide, in that moment, that maybe it's time to ask. One thing at a time.

"You can tell me, you know." I tip my head to the side as if she can see me, but she can't, of course.

"Tell you what?"

"That you're dating Jake." I wait. "He's your boyfriend, right?" I'll see my mother in a few hours, but somehow it's easier to say these things over the phone. I picture the satellites high above the earth, blinking away. Can it possibly be true that my voice will travel all the way up there before it reaches my mother?

She doesn't say anything for a moment. "I guess you could say that."

"So why don't you ever talk about him that way?"

"I don't know." I hear her inhale. "Maybe it's easier not to. I didn't know what you would think." She sounds, for once, like she's the teenager.

"I think it's fine," I say.

"Good," she says. "Thanks."

We're both quiet. Luna comes out the back door of the restaurant and sits down at the table. *Mom*, I mouth to her, and she nods.

The waitress appears for the first time in a long time to put our check at the edge of the table. Luna picks it up.

"Do you regret anything, Mom?"

"What do you mean?"

"I mean all the stuff with Dad, and Shelter. Do you wish you hadn't done it at all?"

Luna is watching my face, sitting so still I wonder if she's even breathing.

"Of course I don't," she says. "It gave me you. And I loved your father, even if things didn't work out."

"I want to hear about it," I say. "So does Luna. Will you tell us? Not now, but soon."

My mother is quiet for so long I'm not sure she's still there.

"Okay," she says. More petals fall from the tree above us like pale pink confetti. "How is Luna?"

"She's fine," I say. "She's good." I look at Luna while I'm saying this and she looks right back at me, smiling a little. I take it as a sign.

"Do you want to talk to her?" I ask my mother.

"Yes," she says, right away. She's completely sure.

I hold the phone out to Luna. She waits a moment, her lips pursed the way they do when she's thinking. She touches her empty cappuccino cup, closing her fingers around the white porcelain. Then she reaches out and takes the phone. She holds it up to her ear and takes a quiet breath.

"Hi, Mom," she says.

fifty-three

TWO HOURS LATER, ARCHER TURNS the key and the van shudders a little, like something alive and sleepy and reluctant to wake up. The engine starts with a hum and a purr. I must look worried.

"Betty the Van is happy you're here," he says. "Especially since Luna avoids her because she doesn't want to go all the way out to the practice space and unload in the middle of the night." He pulls away from the curb and the van makes a groaning sound.

"Come on," I say. "You're the brawny men, right? Otherwise she might as well have an all-girl band." This reminds me of my mother and the girl bands she never started, she and my sister as the sole girls onstage. I know that the guys in their bands must be good for something other than unloading.

Archer takes the first turn a little too quickly, and something large and heavy slides across the back of the van. My fingers clutch the sides of my seat.

"Are you sure you know how to drive this thing?"

He shakes his head, but he's smiling, his eyes looking toward the street. "I'm not at all sure," he says. "That's what we have Josh for."

In the sun, the street looks like a glassy black river. An old woman crosses slowly in front of us, singing as she walks to a small schnauzer by her feet.

"I talked to Luna," Archer says. "This morning."

I snap my head toward him. "You called her?"

He nods.

"About what?" I ask.

"I asked if she'd like to add a date in Buffalo." He glides into a long, slow stop at a yellow light. "So Luna's going to have our booker call."

"Really?" I say.

"She thinks we'll get one pretty easily." He turns, and a couple of CDs go skittering across the dashboard. "I guess we're a little bit famous now."

I think of what my mother said, days ago, that being a little famous is the best kind. "Looks like it to me."

"I hear Buffalo in December is just lovely," Archer says.

"Hey," I say. "All that snow and cold hype is exaggerated. It's actually pretty nice in December." I shrug. "Usually." I think about Luna's birthday snowstorm three years ago. I can still see my parents shoveling snow into the same pile in our yard.

"I'm willing to brave it."

"So why didn't Luna tell me about the show?"

"I told her I wanted to," he says. "There's this girl in Buffalo I want to see." He sneaks a glance at me at the next stoplight,
and I know what he sees: me sitting in the passenger seat, grinning.
"Plus," he says, "we'll be driving through Buffalo in October on
our way west."

Just like that, I know I'll see Archer again, and when.

Forty minutes later, we're outside the airport, standing next to
Betty the Van at the departures drop-off.

Archer pulls my suitcase out of the back and I wait. I can feel
the heat rise from the asphalt like steam over a volcano. I won't miss
the inferno feeling of this city, but I'll miss almost everything else.

"I'm not much for good-byes," Archer says. He looks down at
his feet. "Actually, I can't believe I drove you."

I laugh. "Thanks a lot."

He's shaking his head, smiling. "That's not what I mean."

"I know."

"I did bring you something. I wanted to make you a mix for
the plane, but it's hard to do it now, you know?" He's talking fast,
and sounds nervous. "I'm sure your dad made actual cassette-tape
mixes for your mom. I sort of wish I could do that. But I figured
something out." He hands me a tiny white iPod shuffle. I take it and
it feels so small, so light, that if my mom and dad time-traveled here
from 1994, I'm sure they wouldn't believe there are songs in there.

"It was Natalie's," Archer says. "She left it, along with everything else. So it's just a loan. You can give it back to me when I see
you in Buffalo."

"Okay," I say. He hands me a piece of paper then, lined and
torn from a notebook. In blue ink and perfect, tiny printing, he's

written out all the songs and artists.

"I had to write everything down because it's a shuffle, and, um, things are going to come up in random order, so it's not perfect." He takes a breath. "It's no cassette tape, that's for sure. Sometimes I think we're missing out on a lot."

"I think my mom still has her old Walkman," I say, "so next time you can make me a tape."

"Meg Ferris's Walkman," Archer says. "My thirteen-year-old self would never have believed it."

"In the meantime, I love it," I say. "Thank you." He's put "Treetop" on there, my favorite song from the Moons' last record. "Only one song from the Moons?"

"Haven't you heard enough of us this week? That one's my favorite right now."

"Mine too."

He points to the paper. "I put 'Sea of Tranquility' on there. It's such a pretty song, and it didn't seem right to leave Shelter off."

He can't possibly know that I listened to that song just last night, but it seems perfect anyway.

"You picked the right one," I say. I run my finger down the titles. Here are the Lemonheads, Pavement, and Juliana Hatfield to round out the '90s, along with Luna's pretend dad Paul Westerberg. He has Otis Redding and Elvis Costello and David Byrne, whose stoop we've stood on together. Bands I've never heard of, like Radiator Hospital and Waxahatchee. And way down at the end is the Weakerthans' "Left and Leaving," a song that could break my heart. If I didn't know I'd see him in a month and a half, that is.

I fold the paper and put it in my purse. I'm already thinking about the mix I'll make for him when I get back home.

"Well," Archer says.

"Well." I try to keep my breathing even, but my heart has started beating faster. It's amazing the way you can forget you have one at all, until it kicks up to its highest setting.

"This is not what I expected to happen this week," he says. He puts one hand, palm flat, on the van's door, and I do the same thing. The paint is hot and smooth.

"Me neither," I say.

"I'm glad it did."

"Me too."

Archer laughs. "This is really an awesome conversation."

"We're so expressive." I look around. "I hope someone's writing this down. Pure gold."

"I have an excuse." Archer leans his hip and shoulder on Betty the Van. "I'm not a word guy," he says. "But you are."

I smile. "I'm a word guy?"

"Word girl." He stands up. He actually seems a little flustered, and it's adorable.

"Oh, right." I nod. "Wait. Does that mean I have to offer some big pronouncement?" I arc my hand through the air like a game show hostess and I feel like Luna, always gesturing, always moving my hands through the air.

"No," Archer says. "Not unless you want to."

I think for a minute, and I remember Jackie's inscription in Michael's copy of *Catcher*, which I still have in my bag. I can see the blue-inked cursive when I close my eyes. "'I'm glad that some days of our lives were spent together,'" I say, quoting Jackie.

Archer looks at me, a half smile on his lips, and I try to memorize the exact way he looks right now: his sea-blue eyes, his long lashes.

"Just go with it," I say. "I'll explain sometime."

"Okay," Archer says. "Though I'm hoping for more days together. Can we have more days?"

I laugh. "Definitely."

A plane roars above us, and I look up at its silver belly slicing through the sky. Then I look at Archer.

"You need to go get on the plane." He steps forward and slips his hand into mine, pulling me closer. "But first you should probably kiss me."

"Probably," I say, shrugging, like it's no big deal. And then I do.

When I walk away from Archer, I don't turn around at first. I pull my suitcase all the way to the terminal door, and then I take out my phone. I want to send him one last text while I'm here in the city, one more before I go. So I type out the lyric that's been circling my head all day. I finally know how it goes.

Just when you've lost yourself, wherever you've been,
You'll reach the end and find yourself ready to begin.

I look at the words on the glowing screen for a second, and then I press send. I know when I turn around to take a last look, Archer will be standing next to the van, watching me, and we'll both lift our hands and wave.

ACKNOWLEDGMENTS

THE BEST THING THAT CAN happen to a writer is for everything to come together like a really good song. I'm here to tell you: this book is that song. So it's time to thank the members of the band.

Thanks to my agent, Jay Mandel, who is kind and funny and generally fantastic, and the rest of my team at William Morris Endeavor: Laura Bonner (who has taken *Girls in the Moon* international), Janine Kamouh (who gives great notes), and Lauren Shonkoff (who is just plain great).

I feel lucky to have my fierce and fabulous editor, Kristen Pettit. She was the one who first wanted to hear from Meg, and once I started writing those chapters, the book clicked together. Jenna Stempel designed the cover of my dreams. Thanks to Elizabeth Lynch, who keeps things running with a smile, and the rest of the excellent team at Harper: Alexandra Rakaczki, Gina Rizzo, Janet

Rosenberg, and Elizabeth Ward.

I'm grateful to the New York Foundation for the Arts for fellowships in 2008 and 2015. This early support and encouragement was crucial.

So many friends have helped me while I wrote this novel. Anne Marie Comaratta read along with me as I revised the first draft, chapter by chapter. Her enthusiasm never dimmed, and it helped keep mine alight. Sherry Taylor understands what I'm trying to say, even when I'm having trouble getting it on the page. Thanks to my friends who read the manuscript: Angela Hur, Kristin Jamberdino, Caitie McAneney Klimchuk, Courtney Smyton, and Missy Zgliczynski, and to Brian Castner, my writer friend. Jodi Bryon and Brett Essler are stellar humans and my home base when I'm in NYC. Jaime Herbeck is always on my side, and Kathleen Glasgow helps keep me sane. Jim Pribek gave me a whole collection of possible names for the boys' school in this novel. I chose Alfred Delp, a German Jesuit member of the resistance to the Nazis, because his bravery deserves to be honored.

Mick Cochrane, the world's best mentor and friend, always helps me find my way. My life would look very different if I hadn't ended up in his classroom years ago, and I like my life just the way it is. Thanks, Mick, for always believing in me.

I'm still learning from Eric Gansworth, fifteen years later, which is why I'm really lucky he's my friend. Plus, he's a great reader of my work, and he always makes me laugh.

Many thanks to my teachers in the MFA program at the University of Notre Dame: Valerie Sayers, Sonia Gernes, William O'Rourke, and Steve Tomasula, and to my talented cohort there.

Thanks, also, to my colleagues and students at Canisius College. I'm so happy to be a part of that community. Speaking of community: hugs to my fellow debut authors in the Sweet Sixteens. I'm grateful for their honesty and humor. Thanks, too, to the book bloggers who do so much for all writers and readers.

All of the songs I've ever loved run like a current through this book, so I should thank the musicians and songwriters who have inspired me over the years. This seems as good a time as any to mention that the Weakerthans stopped playing shows together a few years before Luna could have skipped school to go to their last concert, but if I'm creating my own universe, the Weakerthans are going to stay together as long as possible. Special thanks to John K. Samson for his kindness.

Thanks to my whole family, and especially to my parents, Mary Beth and Dennis McNally, who read me approximately a million books during my childhood, and who have supported me no matter what paths I've taken. My brother, Patrick, has always been my fan. I'm his fan, too.

To Juno, Daphne, and Luella, who made me want to write a story about sisters and mothers and daughters. And to Jesse: So much of the music I love comes from you, so I'm certain this story started with us. I couldn't do this without you.

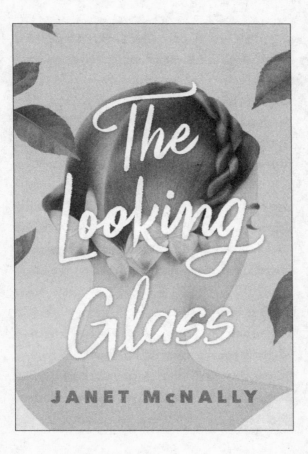

What Ballerinas Do

HERE I AM, BAREFOOT ON a stool in the wardrobe room, trying as hard as I can to stay still. There are masses of tulle around me on the floor, piled like drifts of cotton candy. I'm floating in a pastel sea. I'm a very small, very fidgety boat.

It feels like every molecule in my body is vibrating, electrons pinging around in my atoms, shaking my soul loose. This is what I've been like lately. My problem right now is this: if I don't stop wiggling, our seamstress Miriam is going to kill me.

She looks up at me now, eyes narrowed, mouth full of silver pins. She's been making costumes for forty years, so she's pretty good at talking with sharp things in her mouth, but right now she doesn't bother. She just *looks* at me and I feel like a five-year-old caught misbehaving. I understand why she's mad, though. Today is our last class, and she's trying to finish before we leave so I can dance after a dinner for donors in August. And I'm not helping.

This will be my gravestone:

Here lies Sylvie Blake, who had a pretty good run until Miriam killed her with a sewing needle.

"Sorry," I say to Miriam. "I don't know what's wrong with me."

Miriam shakes her head, but I can see a hint of a smile in her eyes, even if it hasn't quite made it to her mouth yet. I know I'm one of her favorites, so she lets me get away with things, up to a point.

"Spine straight," she says through half-closed lips, jabbing a pin into my pearl-gray tutu. "Unless you want your skirt crooked." And even though I don't really care if my skirt is crooked, I try my best to pull my spine into a straight line. My Level Three teacher Miss Inez used to tell us to pretend we were fastened to a thread hanging from the ceiling: *head, neck, backbone, tailbone*, all in a row. *Femur, patella, tibia, fibula*, each pointing straight down to our feet. I imagine it now: the string fastening me, all those bones hanging, completely still, but it doesn't work. Miriam clicks her tongue.

"You're just like your sister," she says, half to herself. "She could never stay still either."

At the sound of this word—*sister*—all the molecules in my body move just a little to the left. I stand there, my tiniest parts swirling imperceptibly. Here's what I'm thinking: I'd give almost anything lately to stop feeling like an actual galaxy.

Walt Whitman was right, I guess. *I contain multitudes.* And Julia is the one who did it to me.

Today is my birthday, and it was supposed to be different. Today I was going to figure out how to leave it all behind, be something other than a sad sack or a celestial event. But instead, I'm standing on this stool, feeling so suddenly dizzy that I press my right thumb lightly to the inside of my left wrist. There's nothing but my own skin in the spot, but this is exactly where my sister's tattoo is. I was there when she got it, holding her right hand in my own. The ink spells out three words in swooping cursive:

Twenty-six bones

With my fingers on my wrist I can feel the tiny thump of my pulse below my skin, the way it marks how hard my heart is pumping. Even broken hearts keep working most of the time.

That's still the most surprising thing.

"Sugarplum," Miriam says. That's what she always calls me, and it makes me think of *Nutcracker* songs, fake snow under stage lights, man-sized mice. The ever-present weirdo beauty of ballet.

"Are you all right?" she asks.

I glance down at her and see she's looking up at me, sharp dark eyes under her crown of silver hair. I shrug before I can stop myself. I expect Miriam to chastise me and say, *Ballerinas don't shrug*, the same way she often says, *Ballerinas don't slouch*. But she doesn't. She smiles. She gives me her hand for balance and helps me get down.

"Go have a good last class," she says. She slips the tutu down over my legs and I step out of it carefully, without letting its new pinned hem touch the floor. It's as delicate as a spiderweb, lighter than air. But that doesn't really matter. It would fall to the ground the same as anything else.

There are rules in this world, or at least there are supposed to be. To be honest, Julia always seemed exempt. She was magic. She broke the laws of physics, slipped past the reach of gravity every day. She was made of sparkle and shimmer and grit. But the truth about magic is this: it's hard to keep believing in it once it's gone.

Whipped

"WE NEED TO TALK ABOUT gravity," Tommy says. At least that's what I think he says. His voice sounds really far away.

Right now, I'm turning fouettés so fast I must be throwing sparks. I'm finally able to move the way my body wants to, and I'm making up for lost time. The room streaks around me like an Impressionist painting left out in the rain, but I'm spotting the window frame hard so I'm not dizzy. A warm honey-gold feeling rises in my belly, fueling me. It might be sorrow. It might be fossilized hope. Either way, it keeps me spinning.

Fouetté means "whipped," and that's what I'm doing to the air. Just making my own weather, my own personal cyclone. And it's all going beautifully until I hit forty-eight turns. Then the ticker-tape count in my head switches off and my ankle falls out of orbit like a faulty satellite. I stop spotting and sputter to a stop, put both feet on the floor to catch myself. The room whirls.

And there's Tommy, a dozen feet away, one hand on the barre. His posture is perfect, all vertical lines, the muscles of his arms so defined they might be cut from marble. Old Marble-Arms, we call him. Well, not really. But still, he might as well be half Greek god, half fairy-tale prince.

(It's my job to break the hard news to the princesses: he's looking for a prince of his own.)

"I saw that," Tommy says. The studio slows and tilts a little, then rights itself. Blood swirls in my veins.

"Saw what?"

His voice goes all deep and dramatic like a nature-documentary narrator. "Here we see the elusive dancer," he says, "threatened in her natural habitat." I roll my eyes, but he doesn't stop. "Much like the puffer fish and its poison sting, or the squid, which expels a cloud of ink, the young ballerina has her own method of defense."

"I don't know what the hell you're talking about," I say. Which is true, but it doesn't stop him.

Tommy gestures his hands toward one another, fingers curved like they're about to wrap around a neck.

"Someone was going to strangle me?" I say.

"No," he says, faux-exasperated. "Yuki and Rachel were coming over to hug you goodbye. You didn't see them? I assumed that's why you turned into a spinning top."

I shake my head. "No," I say. But I can't help looking across the studio toward Yuki and Rachel. My friends, or at least they used to be, when I knew how to talk to them. When they knew how to talk to me. I used to be like them at the end of each year: dripping with last-class nostalgia, standing with the rest of the class in a cluster near the doorway. It's clear more hugs are in the forecast.

There are my classmates, floating around as sweet and wispy as cotton candy, sugar spun to air. Lately I'm feeling more like a Lemonhead: tart and sharp and hard to chew.

"Ballet dancers aren't supposed to be cuddly," I say to Tommy. "We're supposed to be beautiful. Elegant." I arrange my arms into fifth position and pose.

"Bitchy," Tommy says. "I get it."

I roll my eyes. He points across the room to Emma, who, unbeknownst to her, plays the part of our nemesis when it seems fun to have one. Her cider-colored hair in a perfect bun, no strays escaping but also no sign of hair spray. *It's a conundrum*, I always used to say (a little-known Nancy Drew title: *The Mystery of the Immovable Bun*), and then Tommy would answer in a stage whisper: *Dark magic.* I'd believe it. After all, her grand jeté is pretty otherworldly, and she's just the type to sell her soul.

"You want to be like She Who Must Not Be Named?" Tommy says.

I shake my head. "Not particularly."

Tommy flips up his palms, triumphant. "Then let yourself be hugged once in a while."

"Okay," I say. "*You* can hug me whenever you want."

Tommy smiles. He tips his head to the side. "Let's talk about the fouettés," he says. He raises his eyebrows. "Forty-eight. Pretty stellar."

Because of course he was counting too. None of us can stop. It's a disease.

I shrug.

"Come on, Sylvie," Tommy says. "It's way more than you'd need for *Swan Lake*."

He's right. To dance Odette/Odile you have to be able to do thirty-two fouettés in a row. Not exactly easy, but I can do it. I mean, I better be able to do it because I've been practicing all year. In the beginning, I think part of me believed that there was some number I could hit and everything would feel okay again. That if I spun long enough, my molecules would settle back into their proper places.

And then my sister would come home.

But at this point, that's not going to happen. Julia's been gone since my fifteenth birthday and today I turn sixteen. A year is long enough, right? It's time to stop hoping and try to move on.

I cup my foot in my palm and straighten my leg above my head, toes pointing toward the ceiling. If I were anywhere else this would look like showing off, but here it's nothing special. So utterly normal it's almost boring.

"Screw *Swan Lake*," I say.

"My thoughts exactly." Tommy leans back against the barre, head tilted. James Dean in tights. "Waterfowl have absolutely no place in ballet."

"Damn straight," I say. I try not to smile.

Tommy and I have grown up together, here in the studio. We've been friends since we were seven. Tommy's mom was a ballerina herself, first in Buenos Aires, where she was born, and later in New York. She quit when Tommy was born, but as she tells us, she knew he'd be a dancer. It's in his blood, she says.

It was the same for me, I guess. I followed Julia to the Academy. When Tommy and I were younger, we'd sneak into her classes and sit cross-legged against the wall, watching the older dancers. We learned to be invisible in our sweatpants and ballet slippers, still trembling with warmth from our own class down the hall. The rooms smelled of wood and sweat and rosin, and they smell the exact same way now. It's disorienting, actually. It leaves me breathless sometimes, the way the past comes tumbling into the present, forcing me to remember.

If it would only stay where it belongs—in the past—this would all be much easier.

Now I turn and look at myself squarely in the mirror. When we were younger, Miss Inez used to warn us that we couldn't depend on mirrors to tell us if we were doing things right. Reflections are flipped around and far away, locked somewhere behind the glass. We perceive them differently. "You have to trust your own body," she'd say, in her raspy Barcelonan accent. "You can't trust a looking glass." I don't know why she called it that, if it were an accident of translation or a purposeful renaming, but it made us all remember. I still do.

I step forward, rest my fingers on the barre. It's smooth and cool and still, an object fixed in space. I swear, just the steadiness of it is enough to make me cry.

What the hell is wrong with me?

"You seem a little jittery," Tommy says, reading my mind. "Are you having an early quarter-life crisis?" He rubs his shoulder. "Sixteen is the new twelve, I assure you."

"Good to know," I say. I turn around and fold at my waist, pressing my forehead to my legs.

"I'm serious, Syl."

"I'm fine," I say to my knees. I hope they believe me, because it's unlikely that Tommy will. I'm not ready to explain things to him. I don't want his Eternal Optimism™ shining in my face. Not about this.

"Okay," Tommy says, his voice floating down from above me. I stay folded.

My pinkie toe stings, and I wonder if my blister has opened. I wiggle my toes inside my pointe shoes and feel an electric twinge of pain. I won't be surprised if my new tights are bloodstained when I take them off. *Baptized*, Julia used to say.

When I stand up straight, Tommy is still there, his brown eyes watching me.

"Let's get out of here," he says. "I think you need a break. And the faster you go to dinner with your parents, the faster you can come have cake with Sadie and me. She's been baking all day."

"All day?" I say. "For one cake?" I picture an eleven-tier wedding cake, covered in sugar flowers. Sadie in a frilly apron, her hair powdered-wig white, dusted with flour.

Tommy shrugs. "That's what she says. Let's just hope it's edible, because either way, we have to eat it." He gives me a gentle shove toward the hallway. "Go get ready. I'll meet you outside."

He walks over toward Rachel and Yuki, to be taken into their candied embrace, I'm sure. I don't wait around to see. Right now, it sounds so good to get out of here.

But my escape plan needs an escape plan, because as soon as I set foot in the hallway I hear someone call out my name. It's Miss Diana, my favorite teacher and Julia's too, the only one in this whole place besides Tommy who hasn't acted like my sister never existed at all. I know I should be comforted by seeing her, but instead— inexplicably—panic spreads through my blood like heat. And it only gets worse when I see her lift a small white package in her hand like she's on a ship, signaling to shore. Signaling to me.

I don't know what makes me do it, but I make like a squid that's run out of ink. I just hightail it out of there, leaping down the hallway before I can stop myself.

Running from what I don't want to know.